Vic Metzger, Norman Hastings, and the Dahlbergs were not the only ones to go suddenly, violently berserk that night. Beginning early Friday evening and continuing into Saturday morning more than a score of normal-seeming citizens exploded into mindless mayhem. The toll of dead and injured mounted steadily. As the reports flashed over the nation's newswires, a terrible pattern began to emerge. . . .

# THE BRAIN EATERS

## Gary Brandner

FAWCETT GOLD MEDAL • NEW YORK

# Prologue

The helicopter came in low, following an electrified fence that bordered a cracked and neglected blacktop road. Half a dozen Holsteins grazed in a pasture beyond the fence. They seemed to know exactly how close they could come to the wire without getting a jolt of electricity. The cows barely glanced up at the chopper. They were accustomed to the walloping commotion above their feeding grounds.

Two men rode inside the modified Lockheed 286E. Stuart Anderson, tall and slim, his eyes hidden behind tinted aviator glasses, was at the controls. The seat to his right had been removed for the installation of special equipment. There Lloyd Bratz, stocky and self-assured, knelt over the butt end of a gray metal canister that was sunk into a special port in the floor. An orange lever was held fast to the side of the cylinder by a twisted and sealed wire.

"Anytime you're ready," Stu Anderson said in a bored tone.

Lloyd Bratz chuckled.

"What's funny?"

"I was just wondering what people would say about the purple cows we're about to make."

"What are you talking about?"

"You know the old poem 'I never saw a purple cow, I never hope to see one. . . .' "

" 'But I can tell you anyhow,' " Anderson finished, " 'I'd rather see than be one.' "

"People have no imagination. It might be kicks."

1

"Sure. Just spray the gunk, will you?"

"Right. Purple cows coming up."

Bratz used wire cutters to break the seal holding the lever flat against the side of the upended canister. He pulled away the twisted wire and eased back on the lever.

A soft *whish* could be heard inside the copter as the pressurized solution inside the canister was released. It hissed back through a pipe running beneath the floor of the machine to an exhaust port at the rear, where the downdraft from the rotor blades would be minimal.

Anderson tilted the helicopter to the right. Bratz craned around to look behind them.

"What the fuck?" he said.

A soft white mist trailed from the exhaust port and quickly dispersed.

"What's the matter?" Anderson said.

"Isn't the stuff supposed to be purple?"

"Sure. That's the whole idea, so we can map a clear dispersal pattern down on the ground."

"Well, it ain't."

Anderson tilted the copter to give himself a view of what was happening behind them. Behind the tinted lenses his eyes widened.

"Jesus Christ, shut it off."

"What?" Lloyd Bratz was distracted, staring at the scene below.

"Shut the damn thing off!"

Bratz grasped the canister lever and returned it to the original position, flat against the cylinder. The soft hissing stopped. Behind them the cloud of mist faded into the atmosphere.

Anderson wheeled the chopper up and around, heading back in the direction from which they had come. Lloyd Bratz leaned down over the canister and ran his fingertips over the smooth gray-painted surface.

"What do you think went wrong?"

"I'm damned if I know."

"Are we in trouble, Stu?"

2

"I guess that all depends on what we squirted over the countryside."

The office was bare of any pictures or decoration. There were no ashtrays, no books, not even a calendar. The office held no clue to the personality of the man who worked there. The walls were solid institutional green with no windows. The only sound was the muted hum of a ventilating fan. The two pilots stood at semiattention, facing the man sitting behind the spartan metal desk.

"Were you not aware," said the man at the desk, "of the manner in which the canister of pressurized purple dye was identified?"

The pilots looked at each other for a moment. Then Stuart Anderson spoke. "We knew, but I guess we just assumed—"

"You assumed?" the man at the desk said, cutting him off. "You *assumed*?"

There was an uncomfortable pause.

"Are you men in the habit of making assumptions where you should be double- and triple-checking?"

"No, sir," Anderson said in a subdued tone.

"I most fervently hope not. Considering the kind of work we are doing here, a misplaced assumption could be disastrous. I only hope that in this case we will escape serious repurcussions."

"I don't know how it could have happened," Lloyd Bratz said. "Stu and me went over everything on the preflight check like we always do. I know that canister was tagged for the dye-dispersal test before we locked it in."

"What, then, is your explanation?"

Again, the pilots exchanged a look.

"The canisters might have been switched," Anderson suggested.

The man at the desk looked pained. "Are you suggesting there was a deliberate exchange?"

"It's possible."

3

"But hardly probable, considering our security measures."

"It wouldn't be the first time security has messed up," Bratz said.

"The past performance of security is no excuse for your laxity in this case."

Again, the silence in the room was prolonged until the atmosphere grew oppressive. This time Lloyd Bratz spoke.

"We caught it after only a few seconds."

"A few seconds. I see. Have you any idea what was in the canister you opened today?"

Both men shook their heads.

The man at the desk sighed heavily. "No, of course you couldn't know. I only hope that we have some incredible luck now to counteract your incredible carelessness."

"What was in the canister?" Anderson asked.

"A product that was tested and judged faulty. It was supposed to be tagged for disposal."

"There couldn't have been much harm done," Bratz said. "There was nothing below us but a few cows."

"Is there not a road in that sector?"

"The old Shawano County Road," Anderson said. "It hasn't been used since they widened Highway Seventy-five."

"Let us devoutly hope not. I will require a completed discrepancy report from each of you first thing in the morning."

The two men waited. When the man at the desk made no move to dismiss them, Anderson said, "Is it all right if we leave now?"

"No, it is not. I want you to report to the infirmary."

"You mean right away?" Bratz said.

"I mean immediately."

"But my wife's waiting for me outside with the car."

"And I have a dinner date," Anderson added.

"I will see that your wife and your dinner companion are informed of your whereabouts. The things you need will be brought to you at the infirmary this evening."

4

"Wait a minute," Anderson said. "Does that mean we're going to have to stay overnight?"

"A bit longer than that, I'm afraid."

"I can't do that," Bratz said. "I've got plans for the weekend."

"I have a full schedule, too," said Anderson.

"I don't think you men understand. This is not a matter in which you have a choice."

"To hell with that," Bratz said. "I'm not going to be locked up in any hospital room."

As he started for the door, the man at the desk touched a concealed button. The door opened, and two men in brown uniforms blocked the exit. They carried carbines at the port-arms position.

"Please escort Mr. Anderson and Mr. Bratz to the infirmary," said the man at the desk.

The uniformed men parted slightly. The helicopter pilots looked back once, then walked out, followed by the guards.

Left alone, the man at the desk spread his hands out flat before him and stared down for a long minute at the veins and knuckles. Then he unlocked a drawer and took out a compact telephone. He pressed the ball of his right thumb to a sensing plate on the phone, received an answering beep, and punched out a series of numbers.

In an office tucked away inconspicuously in one of the marble buildings of Washington, D.C., a telephone rang.

# Chapter 1

It was a quiet Friday night at Vic's Old Milwaukee Tavern. At the bar Vic Metzger was arbitrating an emotional discussion between two customers on the strategy employed the night before by the Brewers in losing to the Cleveland Indians. At the pool table two regulars from the garage down the street went through their tired routine of trying to psych each other out.

There were no video games in Vic's. There was an old-fashioned pinball machine that had not been repaired since Karl Gotch kicked a leg off it. The jukebox was stocked with country-western records and some good oldies. The television set over the bar was tuned to the all-sports cable channel. A soccer game was in progress, which none of the customers bothered to watch.

On his usual stool Hank Stransky sat staring at the half-empty glass of beer and the uneaten bratwurst in front of him. By this time he had usually put away three of four sausages and as many bottles of Miller's. Miller's was all he drank since Schlitz moved out of town. The traitors.

That night Hank was having a tough time getting anything down. It was the damn headache. Hank had suffered his share of headaches before, usually in the morning after mixing too much bourbon and beer. Those were nothing compared to this. Little hair of the dog and they'd go away.

This headache was something else. It started the night before while he was watching "Hill Street Blues." It wasn't much at first, just a little buzz of pain in back of the eyes.

Hank had swallowed some aspirin, had a bottle of Miller's, and gone to bed. The damn headache stayed with him, and he didn't sleep for shit. That morning it was worse. Breakfast didn't help. Pauline's hot cakes and sausages tasted like garbage. He yelled at her, even though it wasn't her fault.

That day on the job it got steadily worse. His crew was ripping out a section of street in South Milwaukee. The jackhammers had never bothered him before, but that day it felt as if they were digging right into his skull.

Hank tried a sip of the beer and almost retched.

"Hey, Vic," he said, "what the fuck are you pourin' here, horse piss?"

Vic eased himself out of the baseball debate and came up the bar.

"What's the problem, Hank?"

"Your fuckin' beer is the problem. It tastes like piss."

"Okay," Vic said, "but whose?"

"I ain't in the mood for any of your stale jokes," Hank said.

"Sorry." Vic cocked his head, the better to see through the smoke of the Camel that grew in the corner of his mouth. "You know, you don't look so good."

"Last week I thought I was gettin' the flu. Now this goddam headache is drivin' me up the walls."

"You want an aspirin?"

"I ate aspirin last night like they was peanuts. Didn't do fuckall. Gimme a fresh beer."

Vic cleared the bar and wiped it off with a damp towel. He opened a cold Miller's, poured it into a fresh glass with a professional half-inch head of foam, and put glass and bottle in front of Hank Stransky. Hank kept staring down at the bar with one hand clamped to the back of his head.

"Maybe you ought to see a doctor," Vic said.

"For a headache? Bullshit."

Vic shrugged and edged away to rejoin the baseball discussion. He glanced back uneasily from time to time at Hank Stransky.

Hank had never been sick a day in his fucking life. Then

last week he had that touch of flu, or whatever it was, but that sure as hell hadn't kept him off the job. Hell, even when the grader ran over his foot, he didn't lose any time. He was one tough Polack. Nothing could hurt him. He squeezed his hard, calloused hands together and stared at the scarred knuckles. He hurt, and he didn't know what the fuck to do.

Vic turned away from the baseball fans and started back up the bar toward Hank Stransky. He didn't like the kind of noises the guy was making. Vic opened his mouth to ask what was the matter, but then Hank raised his head and looked at him, and the words never got said.

There were plenty of fares out on the streets of Manhattan on Friday night, flapping their arms and whistling for cabs. DuBois Williamson would ordinarily have kept at it another couple of hours until the punks and muggers outnumbered the fares. Not that night. Not with this fucking headache. He slapped his *Out of Service* sign in the window and swung around to head for the Queensboro Bridge and home.

It hurt DuBois Williamson to pass up the forty or fifty bucks he could make by staying on the streets that night, but his head hurt him even more. He wondered if it could be a migraine. He'd never had one of them, but he heard they hurt like a son of a bitch. Could you get a migraine for the first time when you were over forty? Didn't seem fair.

At the intersection of Fifty-ninth and Lexington he had to slam on the brakes and hit the horn when some fool of a Jersey driver in a Volkswagen Rabbit stopped ahead of him to let pedestrians cross the street. Shit, didn't the fool know better than that? An instant later he was blasted from behind by the horn of some asshole in a delivery van.

Williamson leaned out of the window and glared back at the pimple-faced kid driving the van.

"Blow it out your ass, motherfucker!"

He was immediately ashamed of himself. What the hell was wrong with him? DuBois Williamson hadn't talked that kind of shit since he was in high school back in Chicago. He sure as hell didn't talk that way around Ruby. "I didn't marry no dirt-mouth nigger," she said. "I married me a grown-up man, and if you can't talk like one, I'll just start lookin' around."

In the rearview mirror DuBois saw the pimple-faced kid flip him the bone. Dumb little fuck. He probably had to count out loud to find the right finger.

The Jersey driver finally moved, and DuBois inched his cab forward with the traffic. Man, he had never had no headache like this. Not even the time the fourteen-year-old hype hit him from behind with the twelve-inch length of pipe. DuBois was doing the kid a favor. Taking him home. Now he had a bulletproof shield behind the driver's seat. Cost him four hundred bucks, but the way the world was today, you needed it.

But the shield couldn't do him any good now. He was stone hurtin'. All he wanted to do was get home to Ruby. He'd put his head down between those fine brown tits and let her say those special sweet things that always made him feel good. Man, he'd give a lot to feel good now.

Why didn't these motherfuckers move faster? DuBois's head like to explode while they crawled along Fifty-ninth.

He tried to think about something else until he could get home. Something sweet. He thought about the trip him and Ruby just took back to his old hometown. Drove all the way in their almost-new Chrysler LeBaron. Some vacation for a cabdriver. But it was good times. Oh my, yes.

Not the old Chicago neighborhood. That turned out to be full of jive-ass punks dealing dope on the streets and old people who were locked in their rooms, scared shitless. Things change. The neighborhood was tough when DuBois was growing up there. Tough but clean. Now it was plain ugly.

But the country, now, once you got away from all the people crowded together, that was something else. He drove Ruby all the way up through Wisconsin, right to where they ran into Lake Superior.

Ruby had lived all her life in Harlem and now Brooklyn, and the way her eyes got big looking at the neat little towns and the miles and miles of green pastures with cows and silos and water towers and all that country shit just made him feel fine. They didn't stop too much, because DuBois didn't want no hassle with prejudiced people, and there always were some, no matter how sweet a little town looked.

It turned out they didn't have no trouble with people or anything else, unless you counted the bee that stung him on the neck while he was trying to pick some wild strawberries.

It wasn't until they were heading back to New York that things turned sour. For a couple of days he thought he was coming down with something. Ruby wanted him to stay home and rest, but after what they'd spent on the vacation, he couldn't afford to keep the cab off the streets. In a couple of days he felt all right again; then, yesterday, the headache started. Just a little one at first, but the fucker kept getting worse, until now DuBois had all he could do to keep from screaming.

Norman Hastings of Fort Worth figured he had the hang now of getting a taxi in New York. You just stepped out into the street and waved the sucker down. You wait on the curb for one to come over to you—a man could starve to death. When the cab stopped, you pushed your way in, and never mind who else was heading for it. Already he had lost a cab in front of Radio City Music Hall to a nicely dressed lady who had knocked him aside as if she were playing tight end for the Cowboys. Norman Hastings was not going to let that happen again.

He saw the empty cab moving slowly along in the traffic and gave him a wave and a fingers-in-the-mouth whistle at the same time. Well, the coon driving the cab just pointed a thumb at the *Out of Service* sign stuck in the window and looked away.

"Out of service, my ass," Norman Hastings said under his breath. He started toward the stalled cab; then the driver turned to look at him, and he saw the expression on the broad black face. Norman Hastings forgot all about wanting a cab.

* * *

Andrea Keith sat across the table from her new husband and tried very hard to smile as the waiter poured champagne into their glasses. The smile did not come easy, because Andrea had a splitting, grinding headache. She would rather have died than admit it. What would Justin think if on their very wedding night his bride turned up with a headache? Very funny, ha-ha. No, she would tough it out before she let her wedding night become a smutty joke.

It couldn't have been the champagne. She hadn't drunk more than a sip or two. Besides, the headache had started the previous day. Tension, she had thought at the time. The excitement of getting married and all. It would go away. But it didn't go away. It got worse.

Andrea peered over Justin's shoulder and through the window at the lights of Seattle. The restaurant on top of the Space Needle was one of those revolving affairs. You couldn't actually feel it turning, but every time you looked out, there was a different view of the city. That probably didn't help the headache any.

She tried to concentrate on what Justin was saying. Something about his new job in the contracts department at Boeing. Why didn't he shut his ugly mouth?

My God, where had that thought come from? This was the man she loved. The only man she had ever been to bed with. The man she intended to live with the rest of her life. Her husband.

"Here's to my wife," he said, raising his glass to her. "My wife. It still sounds funny, but I like it."

Andrea grasped her own glass by the stem and tried very hard not to spill any.

"And how about you?" Justin said. "You've got a new name to get used to. We'll have to practice together."

Andrea made her mouth stretch into something like a smile. She touched her glass to Justin's and put it down without drinking any. She wondered if they kept any aspirin in the ladies' room.

"I think I'll go powder my nose," she said. To Andrea

her voice sounded high and a touch hysterical. Justin did not seem to notice.

"Hurry back," he said. "I'll be lonely."

She did the smile thing again, rose carefully from her chair, and walked between the small, intimate tables toward the rest rooms. It took a great effort to hold herself erect and walk in a slow, ladylike manner. She wanted to burst into a wild, screaming run.

Andrea Olson Keith's whole life had been ladylike. They had some old yearbooks at the Kappa house, and sometimes she looked at the old pictures of students back in the sixties. Straight hair, patched-together clothes, bare feet. An unwashed, hippie look. Their fists raised for one silly cause or another. She was certainly glad she hadn't gone to school in those days.

Not that there wasn't a certain amount of cutting up on campus now. Her Kappa sisters knew how to have a good time. They smoked a little grass and messed around a little, but somehow it always remained ladylike.

Andrea's parents would probably have preferred that she go on to graduate. But what would be the use? She was twenty, and she knew her own mind. She had never planned to make art her career. It was just a nice clean major. Justin had his degree; he was ambitious and would soon be making enough to support them comfortably.

Andrea could still paint when she felt like it and raise babies and do volunteer things with other well-dressed young wives. Phooey on being a liberated woman. This was exactly the kind of life Andrea wanted.

Grandma Olson had understood that. For some women, taking care of a man and a family was fulfillment enough. The poor old dear had been too crippled with arthritis to come out to the wedding, but Andrea had flown back to Wisconsin to see her.

She had spent a week there on the farm visiting with all the relatives and eating homemade biscuits and pies and heaps of mashed potatoes. She had laughingly said that her wedding dress might not fit when she got back to Seattle.

12

It had been a wonderful visit. She spent hours wandering over the pasture—the north forty—just as she had done when she was a little girl and her parents went back for vacations. She climbed the same tree, threw rocks in the same creek, and even scratched her knee the way she used to climbing through the same barbed-wire fence.

When it was time to come back, Grandpa Olson had insisted on driving her to Milwaukee to catch the plane, even though she would have willingly taken the bus. It turned out he wanted the chance to talk to her alone. He wasn't sure his son had told her all the things a bride ought to know, the old man said, and he spoke awkwardly of the intimacies of married life while Andrea nodded gravely and suppressed a smile.

Now, stumbling across the crowded restaurant with her head about to explode, Andrea wished with all her heart that she could transport herself back to the cool, comfortable farmhouse where Grandma could make the pain go away.

Justin Keith swallowed the champagne that was left in his glass and refilled it. He felt wonderful. He was a little worried about Andrea, though. She had barely touched her champagne. Justin hoped there was nothing seriously wrong. Andrea had been acting strange all day. When she returned from the visit to her grandparents, he was afraid she was coming down with the flu. That passed, and she seemed all right until the previous day. When he called that night, Andrea's mother told him she had a slight headache and was resting. The traditional nervousness of a bride, he supposed.

Well, a bridegroom could be a little nervous, too.

Justin allowed himself to wonder, just for a moment, in the secret part of his mind, if he was doing the right thing. Sure, he loved Andrea, and they were good together, and there wasn't anybody else he'd rather marry. It was just that he wondered if he should be getting married at all. He was only twenty-two, just starting out in life. Might there not be some adventures ahead that he would have to pass up as a married man?

He pushed away the disloyal thought and tried to concentrate on how warm and snuggly Andrea felt in his arms. At five feet eight, he had always felt small and kind of inadequate among other men. Andrea, a perfectly built five feet one, made him feel like King Kong.

He saw her coming toward him across the large room. She walked with the careful posture and graceful step that made her look taller than she was. Andrea was always a lady, he thought. Justin smiled as he stood up to greet her. Then he saw the look on his bride's face, and his smile froze.

# Chapter 2

The walls of the old Milwaukee *Herald* building were streaked with the soot of many decades. The bricks were crumbling at the edges. Many of the windowpanes were cracked and taped over. The roof leaked under heavy rain, and the floors always creaked. The newspaper for which the building was named was in approximately the same state of decay. Beyond hope of renovation. Moribund. The *Herald* continued to exist only as a tax shelter for the absentee owners.

The staff, editorial and production, had no illusions about their future or the future of the *Herald*. It was a distant number three in a city that could barely support two daily newspapers. The employees were a dispirited lot of has-beens and no-talents gloomily putting in their time. For most of them the *Herald* was the last stop on a downhill road. Better than the unemployment lines. But not much.

Since it was an afternoon paper, the editorial offices of the *Herald* were virtually deserted on Friday evening. The staff had long since fled to their homes or to a bar where they could dull the pain with the anesthetic of their choice.

In the gloom of the old-fashioned city room, with its silent typewriters—no fancy computer terminals for the *Herald*—sat Corey Macklin. He had a lanky six-foot-two build, close-cropped brown hair, and an eyebrow scar that gave him a slightly mocking expression. At thirty-five, he should have been more than a general-assignment reporter, but there were reasons. Unlike most of his coworkers, Corey had not written off the future. He still had hopes. Corey's problems were with his past.

He was working late that Friday night in a futile effort to make some kind of a worthwhile story out of his latest assignment—a citizen's protest over the topless bars that had sprung up around the airport. Heaven forbid that visitors coming into Mitchell Field should think Milwaukee was some kind of hellhole.

Topless bars, for Christ' sake. In San Francisco, where Corey had worked a few years back, the topless bar was considered a quaint, harmless token of the past. Like pinup girls. In Milwaukee they were just discovering the insidious power of boobs to inflame young minds.

Corey could see now that there was no way the story would play without pictures. He had talked the editor out of a photographer for half a day, but the only worthwhile shots they got would never see publication. The ship might be sinking, but management would never fall back on tits to stay afloat.

Corey Macklin had no intention of going down with this particular ship. His efforts concentrated on keeping his own head above water until he got his ticket off the *Herald* and out of Milwaukee. That ticket would be the Big Story. The story that would make him. The one every reporter dreams about but only one in a thousand finds. Corey Macklin would find it, or he would die trying.

Three years before, Corey Macklin had been a lot closer

to the Big Story than he was now. In those days he'd been considered a rising star by people in his profession. He was then an investigative reporter in San Francisco. His dedication and the quality of his work had brought him offers from the Associated Press, Time-Life, and CBS.

He was a young man who had it made. He had a good salary, a bright future, lots of friends, and a special lady who slept with him without turning it into a contest. Yes, Corey Macklin had it made. Then he broke the Story. Alas, not the Big Story, but for him it could have been the Last Story.

It concerned a popular, if controversial, member of Women for Women who was appointed special women's rights adviser to the city council. While working on a related story, Corey discovered that the popular WFW lady was actually a drag queen from New Orleans named Horace Benton.

In a rare lapse of journalistic good sense, Corey wrote the story. Worse, he played it for laughs. In any other city it might have been good for a few chuckles, but this was San Francisco. In one short column he had insulted the feminists, the homosexual community, local civic leaders, and the city government. Within a week the rising star was an out-of-work troublemaker. His friends were suddenly busy elsewhere, and his lady moved in with a local TV anchorman.

For about a month Corey stayed drunk, hoping that by the time he sobered up, the whole thing would have blown over and he could pick up his career. No way. The AP, Time-Life, and CBS were no longer interested. Neither was any other major news outlet. In vain, Corey protested that he was neither antifeminist nor antigay. Too late; the word was out. And so was Corey Macklin.

At about the time he closed out his bank account, Corey found a job at that journalistic dustbin the Milwaukee *Herald*. It was, he reminded himself, cleaner than pimping, if not nearly as well paying.

In the past two years he had labored at the derelict old newspaper with one thought sustaining him. Get the Big

Story, the one he could turn into a book, get rich, and get out. Then he would give them all the finger—the feminists, the faggots, the San Francisco city council, and the broad now sleeping with the blow-dried anchorman. All he needed was one thing. The Big Story.

Corey gave up on the tit piece and tossed it into the *Out* basket. It might make a filler for the slim Saturday edition, back among the stereo ads. The Big Story it was not.

He walked out of the musty old building, ignoring the scattered souls who were spending their Friday evening there, and stepped out onto the street.

The day had been unusually hot for June, and it had not cooled off any when the sun went down. There was a tension in the air that could mean a storm approaching off the lake. Good. He was in the mood for a storm.

Corey got into his scarred-up Cutlass and drove south toward the crummy neighborhood where he had his crummy bachelor apartment. He snapped on the radio, got static, snapped it off. He did not really want to go back to his apartment. There was no beer in the fridge, nothing there to read, and the thought of spending Friday night watching "The Best of Johnny" did not appeal. He turned off the freeway and headed for Vic's.

Corey had stumbled on Vic's Old Milwaukee Tavern one rainy Sunday afternoon when his TV had gone out right at the kickoff of a Dallas–Green Bay game. Before the quarter ended, he had found Vic's, where the patrons showed a knowledge of the game that would have shamed the *Herald* sports staff. The beer was cold, the pretzels were free, and Vic's wife made the best sausage Corey had ever tasted. Also, the Packers had won on that particular Sunday, so everybody was in a great mood. It was one of Corey's few good times since he had come to Milwaukee.

He parked up the block and started along the sidewalk toward the crackling neon sign over Vic's. Thirty yards away he pulled up. It seemed noisier than usual, even for a Friday night. Loud voices. Breaking glass. It was something more than the ordinary argument over pool or the Brewers. Some-

17

body ran out the door into the street. Corey felt the muscles tense along his shoulders. He quickened his pace. He was about to walk straight into the Big Story.

The antithesis of the crumbling brick *Herald* was the creamy white complex of low, functional buildings occupied by the Biotron Division of Global Industries, Inc. Biotron was nestled in a pastoral setting north of Milwaukee, a few miles outside Appleton.

From the highway it resembled a small private college, with its rolling green mall and stately elms. The effect of the sturdy wall that surrounded the cluster of buildings was softened by the vines and shrubbery that grew along it in artful profusion.

The employees of Biotron, too, were in marked contrast to the crew of the *Herald*. Young, dedicated, enthusiastic, their shoes were always shined, their hair in place, their ID badges pinned just so over their left breast pockets. They were the type of employees often seen smiling out of institutional ads in *Business Week*.

One of them, biochemist Dena Falkner, was the last one working that Friday in the biochem lab. Strands of her caramel-blonde hair had come loose from the straight-back style she wore to work, and a small frown drew her brows together.

Dena's reason for working late was to review the test results for a new pesticide weapon in the battle against the gypsy moth. She watched the figures march in glowing green ranks across the screen of her computer terminal, but her mind was not on gypsy moths. Her mind was on Stuart Anderson. For some three months the company helicopter pilot had been a fun companion on dates, if a little too swift in the bedroom. It had been a couple of weeks now since she had seen him, but it was the manner of his leaving that disturbed her.

Dena had been dressing for a dinner date with Stu when a call came from Dr. Kitzmiller's office. She was told that Stu had been transferred for an indefinite period to the Rio de

Janeiro office and had to leave immediately. There were a lot of questions she wanted to ask at the time, but when your company carried sensitive government contracts, as Biotron sometimes did, you kept the questions to a minimum.

It was conceivable that Stu Anderson, in the excitement of a glamorous new assignment, could forget about their date. He was not what you would call overly sensitive. Still, there was something about it that didn't feel right.

It was not that her heart was broken. The arrangement between Dena and Stu had been strictly a convenience for both of them. For Dena, her work came first. Social life was pleasant but definitely nonessential. Rather than commute from Milwaukee, or even the shorter distance from Appleton, she had taken a small house in the almost nonexistent little town of Wheeler just up the road from the plant.

Wheeler suited Dena. It was quiet, clean, close to work, and she was not expected to take any part in the community life, which consisted of monthly grange meetings and an annual Waupaca County Settlers' picnic. When she wanted to be with a man, there was always Stu. Or there had been until two weeks before.

Then, a few days earlier, Dena had noticed another strange thing. Not only was there a new man replacing Stu on the helicopter crew, but the other pilot, Lloyd Bratz, was gone, too. She had called Lloyd's home in Appleton, but the telephone seemed to be out of order.

On an impulse, Dena cut off the computer, locked her desk, and left the plant. She aimed her Datsun down the highway toward Appleton. She was relieved to see that the recent highway repair was complete and there was no need to detour.

Lloyd and Helen Bratz lived in a mobile-home park called Lakeview Terrace, which ignored the fact that Lake Winnebago was on the far end of town and well out of sight. Dena parked between painted diagonal lines in a space marked for visitors. She walked up to the neat little unit where Helen and Lloyd lived and knocked on the door.

19

The four of them had gone out to dinner together on a couple of occasions. The two men enjoyed a kind of locker-room companionship, but Dena and Helen Bratz had found little in common. Dena remembered her as a plump, quiet woman who smiled at everything anybody said. She opened the door now, keeping the night chain attached, and peered out. That night, Helen Bratz was not smiling. Her eyes had a haunted look.

"Yes?"

"Hi."

No response from the other woman, who seemed to be trying to look over Dena's shoulder.

"I'm Dena Falkner. From Biotron? Stu Anderson's date?"

Recognition came at last to Helen Bratz. "Oh, yes. Is there something . . . ?"

"I wonder if I could come in for a minute."

"Well . . . I'm kind of busy. . . ."

"I won't stay long."

Reluctantly, Helen Bratz released the chain and opened the door.

"Things are really a mess."

Dena looked around the compact living room. There were piles of clothing, stacks of dishes and cooking utensils, scattered books and papers, and a number of sturdy cardboard cartons.

"Moving?"

"Uh, yes. Lloyd was transferred, you know."

"Really? Where to?"

"Uh, out West."

Dena looked around. "Is he here now?"

"No," Helen said quickly. "He's—he's, uh, gone on ahead. To find us a place to live."

You are a really rotten liar, Dena thought. Aloud she said, "It happened rather suddenly, didn't it?"

"Yes, I guess so. That's the way it is with pilots."

"Apparently. I suppose you knew Stu was transferred, too."

"Yes, yes, I heard."

Helen Bratz kept looking at the door as though she expected someone to burst through it. Right on cue, there was a discreet knock. She ran to open it. A well-dressed man with neat gray hair and careful eyes stood outside.

"The car is here, Mrs. Bratz." His careful eyes scanned Dena.

"I'll be ready in a minute." To Dena she said, "Excuse me, but I have to go now."

Dena looked around at the cartons and the stacks of unpacked belongings.

Helen Bratz caught her questioning look. "Biotron is sending someone out in the morning to finish up the packing. What a relief. I really hate packing. Don't you?"

Helen Bratz's voice had begun to rise and threatened to slide into hysteria. The well-dressed man cleared his throat softly and glanced at the thin gold watch on his wrist.

"The car is waiting, Mrs. Bratz."

Helen looked at Dena. Her eyes immediately jumped away from contact. "I really have to go now."

"Yes, well, I'll be on my way." She felt the careful eyes of the man follow her out the door.

Dena walked to her parking place, got into the Datsun, and sat there in the dark until Helen Bratz came out with the man. Helen had a light coat thrown over her dress. She carried a small suitcase. The man helped her into the back seat of a dark blue Cadillac, then got in behind her. An unseen driver started the engine and drove away.

Dena sat in the dark for another fifteen minutes trying to fit it all together. What was haunting Helen Bratz? Why had she lied? Where *was* Stuart Anderson?

She lit a Carlton and smoked it down to the filter. She was trying to quit, but that night she deserved a smoke. At least.

# Chapter 3

Those cocksuckers were talking about him.

The hammering inside was about to break his skull apart, but Hank Stransky still knew what was going on. They were talking about him. Telling lies. Snickering behind their hands. He could tell. They kept looking over here. Thought they were fooling him.

Vic was the worst of them. A guy Hank thought was his friend. Now he saw the truth. Guy owned a shitty little tavern and thought he was better than everybody. Better than Hank Stransky, who had to work with his hands to make a living. Fucking krauthead.

For all Hank knew, it was something that krauthead put in his beer that was making the goddam headache get worse. Now he probably thought it was funny. Him and those other two assholes. In just about five seconds Hank was going to walk up there, grab one of those cocksuckers in each hand, and ask them what the hell they thought they were looking at. If only the pain would let up a little.

Now they were laughing out loud. At him. Laughing at Hank Stransky. Thought it was funny, did they? He'd show them funny. Hank tried to say something, but it didn't come out in words. Damn headache was making it hard to talk.

Down at the end of the bar Vic had shut up and was staring at him. Vic and his helpful advice.

*"Why don't you take some aspirin?"*

Dumb fuck.

*"You ought to see a doctor."*

Shove your doctor.

Vic started coming back up the bar toward him. The inside of Hank Stransky's head bubbled like the core of a volcano. He stared down at his big, smashed-up hands, trying to focus his eyes. The hands squirmed and flopped on the bar like two lumpy living things. His head was on fire. The whole world was out to get him.

Vic Metzger broke off his conversation and started back up the bar. He was really getting worried about the way Stransky was staring down at his hands and mumbling. A few paces away Vic stopped. He opened his mouth to say something, to advise Hank to go home and get some rest. Slowly, Hank raised his head and looked at him.

The words died in Vic's throat. In more than twenty years as a bartender and a pretty good drinker himself, Vic Metzger had seen men in every imaginable stage of drunkenness. He'd seen them fall, and he'd seen them puke; he watched them try to walk up walls and tunnel under the floor. He'd seen them scream and laugh and cry out loud. But never had he seen anything like what was happening to Hank Stransky.

Red blotches formed on the rough skin across Hank's cheekbones. The blotches spread across his broken nose, up to the creased forehead, and down around his mouth. They darkened and coalesced into shiny pustules as Vic watched, his stomach turning over. The pustules broke like ripe boils, discharging a gooey liquid.

Hank Stransky jumped up from the barstool and spun completely around like a man in some mad dance. He seized the Miller's bottle by the neck and chopped it against the edge of the bar. The bottle shattered, leaving Hank clenching a jagged, two-pronged dagger of glass.

From his mouth came a roar unlike anything human. A bellow of pain and rage and more. For a moment then there was silence in the tavern as the patrons froze at whatever they happened to be doing. A pool ball clicked against another. A faucet dripped in the stainless-steel sink. John Denver sang of country roads. For that terrible moment, time had stopped for Vic's Old Milwaukee Tavern and for everyone in it.

Then the place exploded in noise and movement. Half a dozen men moved toward Hank. Most of the others looked around to make sure they had an unobstructed path to the exit. They did not want to run out and look like cowards, but they weren't about to take on a crazy-acting 250-pound man armed with a broken bottle. Hank swung the jagged weapon in a face-level arc, and those who had started toward him thought better of it and backed off.

Hank spun away from them and went over the top of the bar in a ponderous roll. He got his feet under him and lumbered toward Vic. Snarling, he slashed out with the bottle. Vic managed to get his left arm up in front of his face. The sharp point of glass ripped along the meaty bottom of his forearm. Blood splashed on the bar, spattering the bottles ranged behind it and the startled drinkers on the other side.

Vic scrambled backward. Stransky, roaring like a bull, followed. Both men slipped and staggered on the blood and beer that soaked the duckboard flooring.

"Call the cops!" somebody yelled.

Vic managed to get out from behind the bar. He sidled along with his back against the wall, cradling his wounded arm.

Snorting and blowing like a maddened beast, his face a mass of running sores, Hank Stransky climbed back over the bar and rushed the people who had stood back watching. They fell away before him in a panic. One man's face was laid open from eye to chin. Another was cut across the chest, staining his Green Bay Packers T-shirt a bright crimson.

Somebody ran forward with a pool cue. He swung it from the tip end, cracking the butt solidly on the side of Stransky's head. The cue snapped in half. Hank Stransky continued to lunge and roar, giving no sign he had felt the blow.

The tavern was emptying fast as people scrambled over one another for the door. A few men stood their ground and

24

tried to subdue the raging man. He flung them away like toys, slashing blindly around him with the jagged bottle.

Somebody threw a cue ball that cracked him hard just behind the ear. Hank only shook his head, spraying about the discharge from the suppurating sores on his face. His eyes rolled wildly, focusing on nothing. He continued the full-throated bellowing, and at last even the bravest of the tavern patrons retreated, leaving only Vic Metzger crouching at the end of the bar, trying to hold together his wounded arm. Stransky advanced on him.

By the time Corey Macklin reached the tavern, the customers were ranged outside in a wide semicircle that was growing fast as others arrived to watch, attracted by the commotion.

Corey's first thought was that a bomb had gone off inside. At least two men were lying on the pavement being attended by others. There were more injured and bleeding, but with all the milling around, he could not estimate the number. In the distance a siren brayed, coming closer.

Even as the crowd yammered and surged around him, Corey began mentally composing the lead to his story.

Tragedy struck a quiet neighborhood tavern last night as [fill in later] people were injured in sudden explosive violence.

"What happened?" he asked a man with an expanse of belly hanging over his belt.

"Guy went crazy."

"Somebody inside the tavern?" Corey dug into his pocket for the wad of copy paper he always carried.

"Yeah. I was just havin' a beer, talkin' to my buddy, and this guy cracks a bottle and starts yellin'. Most god-awful noise I ever heard."

"Who was it? Did you know him?"

"I seen him here before a few times. Never knew his name."

"What did he look like?"

"Like a crazy man. Shit, if you really want to know, he's still in there."

Corey edged closer to the open door and looked inside. Barstools were upended, and pool balls and cues littered the floor, along with glasses, bottles, and other debris. The hardwood floor was wet with spilled beer and liquor and bright splashes of blood.

He recognized Vic standing against the far wall, hunched over, his arms across his chest and the front of his shirt a sopping scarlet. A thick-bodied man waving a broken beer bottle was walking unsteadily toward him.

"Hey!" Corey yelled.

The lurching man with the beer bottle paid no attention, but Corey saw Vic's eyes flick toward him, terrified, beseeching.

Corey grabbed a bottle from the floor and sent it spinning toward Vic's assailant. It struck him in the middle of the back with a hollow-sounding thump. The man grunted, stopped, and turned slowly around.

Corey's stomach lurched at what he saw. The man's eyes, shot through with blood, bulged from their sockets. His face was a mass of oozing sores. Behind one ear grew a fist-sized lump the color of eggplant. The sounds he made were something between a growl and a sob. He took a step toward Corey.

Outside, the bray of the siren died abruptly. Brakes squealed.

The man gripping the bloody beer bottle began a crazy pirouette in the center of the littered tavern floor. He clapped both hands to his leaking head, mindless of the glass shards that sliced into his face. His high-pitched, almost female scream continued as two policemen burst in behind Corey and stopped as though they had hit a wall.

"Mother of God, what is it?" said one of the policemen.

The stricken man continued to spin and scream for several seconds; then his knees buckled, and he went down. His bowels let go and added to the mess on the floor.

The policemen stood transfixed, guns drawn. The one who had spoken shifted the revolver to his left hand and crossed himself.

The body jerked and flopped for another ten seconds; then, with a final spine-cracking convulsion, it lay still.

The policemen approached warily. One of them reached down with great reluctance and put his fingers on the man's throat. After several seconds he snatched his hand back with obvious relief.

"He's dead."

"Thank God," muttered the other.

Corey moved over to where Vic Metzger still stood leaning against the wall. Vic's forearm was open in a long, jagged slash. Corey grabbed a bar towel and pressed it over the wound.

"This man needs medical help," he told the policemen.

"Ambulance coming," one of them said. Neither could immediately pull his eyes away from the dead man.

"What happened, Vic?" Corey asked. "Who was he?"

A little of the color returned to Vic's face. "Hank Stransky," he said in a hoarse whisper. "Comes in here a lot. Never caused any trouble before. He acted kind of funny tonight, but I didn't think much of it. Said he had a headache. Then things started happening to his face. . . ."

Vic broke off in a shudder that racked his whole body. Corey was busy taking notes in his personal shorthand.

"What's that about the face?" he said.

"It was like nothing I've ever seen. Big red patches came out. Then they got all lumpy."

Corey looked back at the still figure on the floor. "Are you talking about those sores on his face?"

"They weren't there when he came in. Shit, I wouldn't serve anybody looked like that. The things just broke through the skin while I was watchin'. Horrible."

Vic shuddered again. A young man in a white jacket came in carrying a medical case. Corey moved away and let him attend to Vic's arm.

The crowd outside had doubled since the arrival of the police and ambulance. Two more police cars had arrived, and uniformed officers were keeping people away from the entrance and taking names. The injured had been separated, and the situation seemed under control. No one thought to ask Corey what he was doing inside.

With no one paying him any attention, he stepped carefully through the mess on the floor back to the telephone on the wall by the men's room. He dropped in a coin and punched out the number of Jimbo Tattinger, the photographer who had worked with him on the tit story. The phone was picked up on the first ring.

"I'm on my way, sugar pie. Just hold your—"

"How about changing your plans, sweet lips?"

"What? Who is this? Macklin? What's the idea?"

"I want you and your camera at Vic's Old Milwaukee Tavern right now."

"Are you crazy? I got a date."

"Fuck your date."

"That's my plan."

"Listen, shithead, there's a story down here with picture possibilities that will get us a wire-service pickup or I'll kiss your ass."

"No use trying to sweet-talk me."

"Just get here."

"I'm on my own time."

"I'll pay you out of my own pocket, for Christ' sake."

"Overtime?"

"Oh, shit yes. Are you coming down here, or am I coming there to rip your lungs out?"

"Okay, hotshot. Where are you, exactly?"

Corey gave Jimbo the address, had him read it back, then went out to talk to the cops and the witnesses. He was actually excited about a story. It was almost like the good old days.

# Chapter 4

For the first time in the memory of the present staff, there was the crackle of excitement in the musty halls and offices of the old Milwaukee *Herald* plant. Corey Macklin's story on the bloody events at Vic's Tavern had come on a slow news day, and with Jimbo Tattinger's graphic photos, the street sales of the Saturday edition exceeded anything since the Brewers were in the World Series.

Telephones shrilled throughout the building. People moved through the halls with purposeful strides. Typewriters clacked like bursts of machine-gun fire. Even the lethargic maintenance crew went about their cleanup tasks with unaccustomed vigor.

Corey was thoroughly enjoying his spurt of fame. He had requests from three television stations—one network affiliate and two local channels—for interviews as an eyewitness. He turned them all down. This was his story, and he had no intention of sharing it. As a measure of Corey's enhanced status, city editor Porter Uhlander had, for the first time in two years, called him by his first name.

The city editor was bald except for an uneven fringe of gray above the ears. His pale jowls hung over the collar of his starched white shirt. He had the early edition of Monday's *Herald* spread out on the desk before him. Corey sat on the other side of the desk in a cracked leather chair, waiting for the editor to speak.

"You did a nice job on the Stransky story, Corey," Uhlander said. "Good follow-up today on the victims."

"Thanks, Porter." Corey tried out a mixture of brashness and humility.

"Think any of them are going to die?"

"Doesn't look like it," Corey said.

"Too bad. What have you got for tomorrow?"

"Interview with Pauline Stransky."

"The widow? Hasn't she already been on television?"

"Sure, ten seconds here, twenty seconds there. All those TV guys know is 'How do you feel, Mrs. Stransky?' Hell, how *would* she feel? I want to get a picture of the husband through her eyes." Even as he spoke, Corey knew it might be wishful thinking. Widow stories did not usually sell a lot of papers unless the widow had a forty-inch chest. Still, it was a possibility.

"If you think you can get something readable, go ahead. I'd like to keep the story running through Wednesday if we can."

"Can I have Jimbo?"

"Think you can use him?"

"He got some good stuff Friday," Corey said.

"Bloody but good," Uhlander agreed. "What can he do with the widow?"

"Character shots. Background stuff."

"A little arty for us, isn't it?"

"We can jazz it up with the right captions."

"You mean like 'From this ordinary-looking house came the ordinary man who Friday night spattered a Milwaukee neighborhood with blood'?"

"A tad lurid, but that's the general idea."

"Okay, take Jimbo."

Corey got up and started to leave.

"By the way, Corey . . ."

"Yeah?"

"I had a call from Mr. Eichorn about you."

"No kidding." Nathan Eichorn was the seldom-seen publisher of the *Herald* who did most of his business from Palm Springs or somewhere in Switzerland.

"I think he has some ideas about boosting you to a daily column."

Having his name and maybe his picture on a daily column would be a step up from city-beat reporter, but it sure as hell wouldn't make him rich. Corey's ambitions went beyond the rickety Milwaukee *Herald*. Still, he was not yet in a position to turn anything down.

He said. "Interesting. I'd like to hear more when I get back."

He found Jimbo Tattinger in the shabby photographers' lounge with a cup of coffee and a well-thumbed copy of *Hustler*. With a minimum of grumbling, Jimbo got his gear together and followed Corey out to the parking lot, where his Cutlass waited.

The neighborhood where Hank Stransky had lived was one of those west of Glendale that had sprung up in the boom following World War II. The house was a plain frame bungalo that had been enhanced with shrubbery, an add-on room, a new brick chimney, and a covered patio out in the back with a fishpond and built-in barbecue.

Pauline Stransky, wearing an outdated print dress and looking weary, answered the door. Jimbo glanced over, and Corey knew what he was thinking. No forty-inch chest.

Corey identified himself and the photographer. Mrs. Stransky led them inside with an air of resignation.

The living room—or front room, as Pauline Stransky called it—was crammed with fat, comfortable furniture, knickknack shelves, and framed photographs of people in stiff studio poses. Handwoven rag rugs were spaced strategically in spots where the carpet would get the most wear.

The widow was a tall, spare woman with a strong-looking body. She wore her graying hair pulled back and knotted. Her manner was calm as she sat on the sofa facing Corey, but red rims around her eyes showed much recent crying. The Stransky boys, ages eight and nine, sat restlessly alongside their mother. They ignored Corey, concentrating on

Jimbo Tattinger, who was putting on a show for them, hopping around and shooting up film as if he were from *People* magazine.

"You have a nice house here, Mrs. Stransky," Corey said. "Comfortable."

"Hank did a lot of the work himself."

"I can see that." Corey coughed and took out a ball-point pen. "Would you mind talking a little about your husband?"

"What do you want to know?"

"What kind of a man he was. What you liked to do together. How he was with the boys."

Pauline Stransky began to talk. Slowly at first, then with more emotion as her eyes drifted away to memories. Hank Stransky was your good, solid, salt-of-the-earth guy next door. He worked hard, always provided for the wife and kids. Maybe he drank a little too much sometimes, but didn't everybody? He never got abusive. He liked to watch sports on TV, he liked to hunt, and he liked building things. In short, Hank Stransky was the kind of a man who would put the *Herald*'s readers to sleep in a minute or send them running to the television set. As a story, he was a zero.

As soon as he decently could, Corey broke into the widow's reminiscences. "Uh, Mrs. Stransky, would it bother you to talk about last Friday?"

It took her a moment to return to the present. "I guess not," she said. "I've talked about it enough that it don't hurt so much anymore."

"I'll try and make it short," Corey said.

Mrs. Stransky turned to the two boys, who were squirming uncomfortably on the sofa. "You can go on out and play if you want to."

They bounced up eagerly and hurried out the door. Jimbo shot them leaving, then sagged into a chair.

"There ain't—isn't—much I can tell you that I haven't already told the others," she said. "Hank went out Friday night after supper. Said he was going down by Vic's. That's the last time I saw him."

"Did he often go out alone?"

"Sure. Sometimes I'd go with him, but mostly he liked to watch the sports on TV and kid around with the other guys at Vic's. I didn't mind. It gave me a chance to stay home and watch my own shows."

"Did you notice anything . . . different about him when he went out last Friday?"

"He was same as always except he didn't eat very good. Said he had some kind of headache. I guess I snoozed off watching TV, and the next thing I knew, the cops came to the door and told me Hank was dead."

Corey scribbled on the folded copy paper. "You say he had a headache."

"That's right. He didn't make much of it, but it wasn't like Hank to complain. Last week I thought he might be coming down with the grippe, but he went to work, anyway, and I guess it wasn't anything."

"He worked for the highway department, didn't he?" Corey said.

"That's right. Construction. That was his business. Hank could've had inside work, but he always said he'd go crazy with a desk job."

Her mouth twitched as the irony hit her. Corey went on quickly.

"Was there anything unusual about the job Mr. Stransky was working on at the time?"

She looked at him with a sad smile. "It sounds funny to hear you say 'Mr. Stransky.' I think he'd rather you called him Hank. Everybody did."

Corey nodded. "Hank, then."

"It was just a job like the rest. Down in South Milwaukee. Breaking up the old street, putting in a new one. At least that let him get home earlier than the week before. Then he was working up north of Appleton on the highway there. Didn't get home till after seven sometimes. Thank goodness it only lasted a week."

They talked for another fifteen minutes during which Corey's spirits sagged steadily. There appeared to be nothing

33

about Hank Stransky or his behavior prior to the violent end of his life that was in any way newsworthy. A little inside filler was all he would get out of this. Too bad Hank Stransky couldn't have been a murderous maniac. Or at least a wife beater.

Corey seized the first opportunity to say good-bye to the widow. He woke up Jimbo, who had dozed off soon after the boys went outside, and left the house.

On the drive back to the *Herald* building Jimbo said, "Tell me again how we're going to win the Pulitzer Prize with this story."

"It's not dead yet."

"The only way it runs another day is if Hank Stransky gets up out of the coffin and takes a bite out of somebody."

"You're a million laughs."

Jimbo hefted the camera, which was filled with exposed film. "What do you want me to do with these?"

"Don't feed me a straight line like that," Corey said.

"Seriously. I got a boxful of pictures of nice people in a nice house in a nice neighborhood. Make a nice family album, but you couldn't sell 'em to a Thursday throwaway."

"You've got no complaint. I got you a wire-service pickup on one of the tavern shots, didn't I?"

"True. But Tri-State News Service ain't exactly the AP."

"Jimbo, in this world you take what you can get."

The photographer made his eyes go very wide. "Words to live by. Thank you, sire."

"Stuff it," Corey said. He drove the rest of the way in silence while Jimbo grinned happily beside him.

Back at his desk Corey attacked the typewriter nonstop for twenty minutes. When he had finished, he ripped out the last sheet, scanned the story he had written on Hank Stransky's widow, and crumpled it into a ball. After a moment he smoothed out all three pages, cut it to three paragraphs, and dropped it into the *Print* basket.

Corey leaned back, making the old wooden swivel chair

creak. Good-bye, Pulitzer, he thought with a thin-lipped grin. At least he had given it his best shot. He had followed up the story of Stransky's flip-out with features on each of the eight people who had gotten cut up at the tavern. Not exactly a gold mine. They were all blue-collar types you could find at any tavern in town any night of the week. The widow and the kids added up to a yawn. Stransky's funeral might be worth a few lines; then it would be old news. The Big Story still eluded him.

On a table behind Corey's desk was a stack of dailies from across the country that had been mailed to the *Herald*. He flipped through them idly. Los Angeles had an earthquake reading four point something on the Richter scale. Cuban refugees staged a mini-riot in Miami. There was a bribery scandal in the Texas legislature. A New York cabbie drove into a crowd of pedestrians.

Just another typical day in the land of opportunity, Corey thought. Natural disasters, ethnic unrest, venality, violence.

Wait a minute.

He returned to the New York tabloid that carried the cabdriver story. DuBois Williamson, a hackie in the city for more than twenty years, considered by everybody who knew him to be a gentle, sober, peaceable man, had unaccountably slammed his cab into a crowd of pedestrians on Fifty-ninth Street, after which he had run from the cab and attacked bystanders until he fell and was run over by a truck. According to his widow, Williamson was in generally good health up to and including the day he died. That was the previous Friday.

Corey reread the story, making notes as he went along. Coincidence, probably. Sure it was. But maybe . . . just maybe . . .

He took out a fresh sheet of copy paper and drew a vertical line down the center. He headed one column *Stransky*, the other *Williamson*. Down the left margin he wrote *Age, Location, Job, Family*. Using the New York story, he filled in the information on DuBois Williamson, matching it against what he knew of Hank Stransky. Both were middle-aged: forty-five and fifty-four. Both lived in a metropolitan area: Milwaukee, Brooklyn. Both were steady blue-collar types who had been on their jobs a long time. Both were married—Stransky with two sons; Williamson, one serving in the navy.

Then he ran out of similarities and sat for a minute tapping the pen against his teeth. Finally, at the bottom of the page, he wrote FIND LINK in caps and underlined it several times.

Oscar Yates, a onetime hotshot reporter who drank himself off the Chicago *Sun-Times,* sauntered over. He carried a torn-off sheet of wire copy.

"Hey, Macklin, you the freak-out editor this week?"

Corey looked up without bothering to answer.

"You might be interested in this." Yates let the copy sheet float down on top of the papers on Corey's desk. The AP story read:

> The body of Andrea Olson Keith, 20, was returned to the Wisconsin home of her grandparents after her bizarre death in Seattle Friday. Authorities there are still speculating over what caused the bride of one day to go berserk in a restaurant atop Seattle's famed Space Needle. Four victims of the woman's knife attack were recovering. Her husband, Justin Keith, 22, was pronounced dead at the scene from stab wounds to the throat.

Corey dug through the stack of dailies for the Seattle *Post-Intelligencer.* Then he took out a fresh sheet of paper. On this one he made three vertical columns.

# Chapter 5

Dr. Frederich Kitzmiller shifted his weight from one buttock to the other in the deep leather swivel chair behind the carved mahogany desk. He tried unsuccessfully to find a comfortable position. The soft, cushiony seat was simply not made for his narrow rear end. The rest of the furnishings were equally unsuitable. The framed woman and two children smiling at him in Kodachrome were strangers to Kitzmiller, a bachelor. The prints on the wall were warm, summery landscapes. The carpet was a rich, figured burgundy.

To his left a window overlooked the rolling green mall of the Biotron complex. On the wall to his right was an antique hat rack and mirror with a polished oak frame. Kitzmiller detested the room. He spent as little time there as he could manage.

It was Dr. Kitzmiller's "friendly" office. The one where he greeted visitors to the Biotron plant when he could not get out of it. And where he held the rare briefings for the media. Kitzmiller much preferred the bare, windowless room that was part of the biochem building. Cold and austere, no distractions. He was comfortable there.

For that day's purpose, however, the "friendly" office was more suitable. The theory, with which Kitzmiller was not completely in agreement, was that the interviewee should be placed as much at his ease as possible. It was foolish, he thought, to be so ginger in the treatment of an employee, especially considering the circumstances. But the decision, alas, was not his to make.

Kitzmiller swiveled the chair to look into the oval mirror. His thin, bony face looked back at him, the ice-blue eyes bright in their deep sockets.

"I fail to see why someone else cannot handle this sort of thing," he said to the mirror. "I am a researcher, not a personnel man."

He thumbed a switch on the desk-top intercom, and a filtered voice spoke to him through the speaker. "Your name is the only one that carries enough respect, doctor. This Ed Gault is not so likely to lie to you."

"Perhaps. I am still not convinced that we are following the right path."

"It's the best possibility we have. The pilots were no help."

Kitzmiller's mouth tightened. "Speaking of the pilots, there is a difficulty."

"What's the problem? The wife was relocated, wasn't she?"

"The problem is related to the other one, Anderson. It seems he was seeing one of my people socially. Since his, ah, disappearance, she has been asking questions."

"She works for you?"

"She is in my department, yes. Quite a talented biochemist. Her name is Dena Falkner."

"Can't you transfer her? Fire her, even?"

"Not without raising still more questions."

"Stall her, then."

"That is what I have been doing. However, this woman is no fool, and her inquiries persist."

"If it gets too sticky, my people will take care of her."

Dr. Kitzmiller started to say something but changed his mind. He drummed manicured fingers on the polished desk top. His icy gaze shifted away from the mirror, toward the office door. "Do you think Mr. Gault has waited out there long enough?"

"Give him a few more minutes," said the filtered voice.

"Let him worry a little about what's going to happen to him."

Kitzmiller looked back into the mirror. "It is very disconcerting, talking to you without seeing your face."

"You know what I look like."

"That is not the point."

"I know, I know. For our purposes it's important that Gault thinks he's alone with you. It gives me a chance to watch his reactions without distracting him from the interview."

"Do you really believe he knows more than he has already told us?"

"That's what I want to find out."

"Have you followed up on the Russians?"

"You mean the agricultural mission that came through here?"

Kitzmiller made a noise in his throat. "Agriculture, bah! One of them was Anton Kuryakin. Do you know who he is?"

"Doctor, I don't think we have to—"

"He is the Soviet Union's foremost expert on biochemical warfare. And why was he here masquerading as a simple farmer? To spy on us and learn how far we have advanced; that is why."

"We know about Kuryakin," said the voice on the intercom. "The State Department is on top of the situation."

"The State Department." Kitzmiller's voice dripped contempt.

"Yes, I know. I feel the same way about them. But we can't afford to step on their toes. The Russians' toes, either, for that matter."

"Of course," said Kitzmiller. "The Russians are our friends now, are they not?"

"They are," said the voice from the speaker. "That is the official posture of the administration."

"This week," said Kitzmiller.

"Doctor, are you maybe letting your personal feelings influence your judgment here?"

"What do you know of my personal feelings?"

"You've been thoroughly backgrounded, naturally."

"Naturally."

"Your experiences in Germany were not, shall we say, pleasant."

"Let us say that."

Berlin. 1945. The Russians came down his street in the morning. Larger than life, their tunics unbuttoned, rifles slung carelessly over their shoulders. They were loud, swaggering, flushed with victory and drink.

Frederich was sixteen. He had escaped conscription into the ragtag end of the German army only because of his father's standing with the Nazi party. When the Russians came in, his father was already dead, the back of his head blown out by a bullet from his own pistol.

His mother was to live another year under the Russians after Frederich had escaped to the United States to be raised by an aunt and uncle. But of all the horrors he remembered of that time, the one that caused Frederich the continuing nightmares was the last time he saw his brother.

An infantry lieutenant, Rudy had returned home with an arm shot off at Bastogne. He had refused to flee toward the American lines when the Russians approached, choosing to stay with his mother and younger brother. They came in the afternoon and took him away. No time for good-byes. The next day everyone was ordered to the tiny neighborhood park. There Frederich, along with his mother and many of their neighbors, were forced to stand and watch. Rudy and three other young soldiers were hung by the wrists, their bodies wrapped like mummies with celluloid film and set afire. The crackle of the flames, the screams, the burned meat smell, never left Frederich Kitzmiller.

"All that was forty years ago," said the filtered voice, as though reading his thoughts. "It is a different world today. Different wars, different enemies. We all have to change with the times."

"I suppose so," said Kitzmiller, willing his mind back to the present. "I shall try."

"Let's bring in Gault," said the voice. "He ought to be sweating enough by now."

Kitzmiller nodded and touched a button on his desk.

The door opened, and Eddie Gault looked into the office. He stood uneasily at the edge of the burgundy carpet, blinking rapidly.

"Please come in, Mr. Gault. Have a seat." Dr. Kitzmiller's precise manner of speech did not achieve the intimate effect he was trying for.

Gault came forward and sat on the edge of a chair across the desk from Kitzmiller. He was a thin man with reddish hair that had retreated halfway back his head, exposing a pale, freckled scalp. His long limbs seemed to have been hung on the torso without regard for symmetry.

"Have you had a chance to do some thinking since our last discussion?" Kitzmiller said.

"It's just like I told you then," Gault said, blinking. "It was an accident. I don't know how it happened, but it did. My fault. I don't deny it."

"Eddie . . ." The first name did not roll easily off the doctor's tongue. He had a strong sense of the order of things, and it was not orderly for the chief of biochemical research to call a worker by his first name. However, he had received pointed suggestions on how to conduct the interview, and he would make an effort to follow them.

"Eddie, you have been an employee of Biotron for, what is it, three years?"

"Four. Almost five."

"Yes, just so. Your record until now has been exemplary."

"I've always tried to do my job."

"I know. You are a conscientious man. Which makes it all the more difficult to understand how you could confuse a canister clearly and unmistakably marked for disposal with one containing purple dye."

"A mistake, Dr. Kitzmiller. I'm sorry. What else can I say?"

"A most unfortunate mistake. And rather a costly one."

"Costly?"

The response, Kitzmiller thought, came too quickly. He studied the boyish, freckled face but could detect no hidden emotions. Perhaps the man behind the mirror was doing better.

"Several cows had to be destroyed."

"There was nothing in the paper."

"Fortunately, the cows were the property of our research department, and we were able to avoid publicity. Nevertheless, considering the price of dairy products today, the loss was not inconsiderable."

It was an attempt at humor that failed miserably.

"You do understand," Kitzmiller went on when there was no response, "that anything you tell me here will be confidential."

"There's nothing more I *can* tell you," Gault said. "Somehow I mixed up the labels on the canisters. It was a clumsy mistake, and I'll do whatever I can to make up for it."

Kitzmiller pressed his long, graceful hands together and touched the tips of his forefingers to his lips. "That is not for me to determine." He stole a glance at the mirror. "You will call me if you should, ah, remember any point you might have overlooked?"

"I'll do that," Gault said.

*Yes, you will*, Kitzmiller thought, *on the day pigs fly*. Aloud he said, "Thank you for coming in, Eddie. We will talk again."

Ed Gault pushed himself out of the chair and walked carefully across the carpet, his shoulders hunched as though he expected an attack from the rear. When he had gone out and the door had closed silently behind him, Dr. Kitzmiller sighed heavily. He swiveled around to the antique mirror and flipped on the intercom speaker.

"He's lying," said the disembodied voice.

"I know," said Kitzmiller wearily. "I know."

Eddie walked out of the building, across the green lawn, past the unobtrusive guard gate, and into the employees' parking lot. His spirits soared when he saw Roanne waiting for him in the van. Her straight milky hair shimmered in the afternoon sun.

Eddie could never quite believe his luck in finding a girl like Roanne Tesla. At thirty-six, he had been deeply involved with a woman only once before. That was with a fat, sullen girl he married in hopes it would keep him out of the army. He was drafted anyway, and when he finally got back from Nam, he found his slob of a wife seven months pregnant by God knows who. After that, he pretty much swore off women, until Roanne came into his life.

When that happened, Eddie could hardly believe his luck. She could have had a lot of guys, but for some reason she chose him. He decided it was part of her general rebellion against most everything, which she lumped under the Establishment, and against her father in particular. She rarely spoke of the father, but Eddie gathered he was a square, conservative Republican and would probably not have chosen Eddie Gault for his daughter. That was fine with Eddie. If Roanne's rebellion against her father put her in Eddie's bed, he hoped the two never made up.

She stepped out of the van and ran toward him, her leather sandals slapping on the blacktop of the parking lot. He gathered her in, savoring the feel of her warm young body under the granny dress. She smelled like fresh-baked bread.

"How did it go?" she said.

"Okay. They didn't fire me or anything."

"That's good. Who was there?"

"Just me and Kitzmiller."

Roanne looked disappointed. Eddie felt he had let her down. He thought hard for something else to tell her.

"He said the cows died."

"He did?"

"Yeah. Or had to be killed, or something."

"I wondered what happened to them."

"They belonged to the company is why we never heard. Took them back to the labs, I guess." Eddie felt his mood beginning to sag again. "Honey, I wonder . . ."

"What?" she prompted.

"I wonder if maybe I shouldn't tell them the truth. This whole thing might be a lot more serious than we thought."

Roanne pulled back a step and looked at him. "Eddie, do you think that what's happening to the earth, the air, the water we drink, is serious?"

"Well, sure, but—"

"What you and I have done will help make other people, millions of them, aware of what is happening to our environment and who is to blame for it. I know it isn't easy. You and I are going to have to be strong and love each other and always remember how important the work is that we're doing."

Eddie chewed on his lip as he digested Roanne's words.

"Poor darling. They're putting you through a lot, aren't they." She touched his flat stomach. Her fingers moved down over his belt buckle and found the bulge of his penis. She squeezed him gently, rhythmically. "Let's go home. I'll make you feel better."

All the anxiety and tension that had been building in Eddie throughout the afternoon drained into his crotch. He let Roanne take his hand and lead him to the van.

# Chapter 6

While Dr. Kitzmiller talked to Eddie Gault that afternoon, Dena Falkner sat impatiently in the Biotron parking lot drumming her fingers on the Datsun's steering wheel. Waiting was not a thing she did well. She had never in her life gone to a movie where there was a line waiting to get in. If her reservation in a restaurant was not instantly honored, she would walk out. Some allowances, however, had to be made for the man you worked for, so that afternoon Dena was waiting.

At least waiting out there in her car was preferable to the kitschy reception room outside Dr. Kitzmiller's "friendly" office. The office itself was a joke to Biotron people. They all knew Dr. K was about as comfortable in it as he would be wearing a cowboy hat. The reception room, presided over by sturdy Mrs. Quail, was a horrid jumble of chrome, vinyl, and glass, with paintings of crying clowns. So that visitors could pass the time while waiting, there were back issues of the biochemical industry's trade magazines.

Without thinking, Dena reached into the glove box for the pack of Carltons she kept there. As she took the pack out, she caught her own eye in the rearview mirror. Feeling absurdly guilty, she put the cigarettes back.

She looked around for something to occupy her attention, and her eye fell on the folded newspaper lying on the seat beside her. It was Saturday's edition of the Milwaukee *Herald*. She picked it up and read again the story about Hank Stransky, the construction worker who had gone berserk in a

Milwaukee tavern and slashed several people with a broken bottle before dropping dead of unknown causes. There was a photo of Stransky, apparently from his employment ID, and, on the inside pages, several graphic shots of the devastated tavern and the wounded patrons.

Why the story intrigued her, Dena could not say. The *Herald* was not even her regular newspaper. Much too sensational for her taste and much too insensitive to the human condition. She had the *Journal* delivered to the bungalow in Wheeler where she lived but on impulse had picked up the *Herald* Saturday night after driving to Appleton to see a movie. She looked once more at the square, good-natured face of Hank Stransky, then tossed the paper aside as Eddie Gault came through the gate.

She had been mildly surprised to hear that Dr. Kitzmiller's appointment was with Eddie. What business could the head of product research and development have with the foreman of the disposal crew? Kitzmiller was not the type of manager who associated with the hired hands.

Dena knew Eddie Gault only slightly. He seemed to her to be a quiet, rather awkward man who did his job efficiently and with a minimum of fuss.

She got out of the Datsun and stood beside it for a moment to watch a strikingly beautiful girl run from the van to meet Eddie. An oddly mismatched couple, Dena thought. Balding, serious Eddie with this hippie-dressed young beauty.

None of your business, she told herself sternly. She recognized the twinge she felt as envy, and it annoyed her. Everybody, it seemed, had somebody. Everybody but Dena Falkner. But that was by choice, she reminded herself. She planned to be at the top of her field by the time she was thirty-five. Possibly in a university post somewhere. That left her six more years, but there would be little time for serious romantic involvements.

Three years earlier, working for a chemical company in Chicago, she had forgotten her no-involvements rule with painful results. You would think a bright young woman with a Ph.D. from Northwestern would know better than to fall for a married man. But Phil had been so charming, so warm. . . .

The hell with that line of thinking. Dena watched Eddie Gault get into the van with his girl friend. Good for him. Good for her. May you both be very happy.

She spun away and marched through the guard gate, across the lawn, and into the main building of the Biotron complex. She turned into the east wing, and walked down the hall to the end where Dr. K's office was. Mrs. Quail was arranging the pens and papers on the reception desk into neat geometric patterns.

"Is Dr. Kitzmiller free now?" she said.

Mrs. Quail looked uncomfortable. "I'm not sure. Let me buzz him."

As she reached for the button, Dr. Kitzmiller came out of the office. When he saw Dena, he stopped, looking as though he'd like to go back in, but he sighed and closed the door behind him. He did some unconvincing business of looking at his watch.

"I'm terribly sorry, Dr. Falkner," he said, "but I'm afraid we will have to reschedule our appointment. I have to supervise an experiment in the laboratory, and already I am ten minutes late."

"I won't take much of your time, doctor. How about if I walk back to biochem with you?"

"Very well, if you wish." He locked the office door, nodded brusquely to Mrs. Quail, and headed for the rear exit of the building. Dena hurried after him.

The biochemistry building, where Dena had her own office, was at the rear of the complex, near the barn where the experimental animals were kept. Beyond the fence was the rolling green pastureland owned by Biotron. In addition to staff offices, the building housed several laboratories and Dr. Kitzmiller's spartan living quarters. He liked to live close to his work, he said. It was generally felt that to Dr. K life and work were one and the same.

Dena matched her stride to Kitzmiller's as they crossed

the campuslike grounds. The carefully tended shrubs and flowers gave the place an air of ordered serenity. For her part, Dena would have liked a bit more informality in the surroundings.

"What is on your mind, Dr. Falkner?" he asked, keeping his eyes straight ahead as they walked. "I hope it is not a problem. I have problems enough. A solution, perhaps? That would be a novelty."

"I was wondering if you'd had any word from Stuart Anderson," Dena said.

"There is no reason for us to be in contact," said Kitzmiller.

"I thought you might have heard something."

"I have heard nothing."

"This project he's working on in Brazil—" Dena began.

Kitzmiller cut her off. "I'm sorry, but there is nothing I can tell you about that."

"I called Stu's sister in California last week," Dena persisted. "She hasn't heard from him, either."

"This is really not my concern, doctor. If you consider the matter important, I suggest you go through personnel."

"I have. Personnel told me his files were closed."

"I see." Kitzmiller stopped suddenly, startling her. "May I give you a bit of advice?"

Dena faced him, disconcerted by question. "Advice?"

"Leave this matter alone. Pursuing it will not lead you anywhere you want to go. Please believe that. Now, if you will excuse me, I have to make my appointment."

Dena was left standing on the walk outside biochem wondering what Dr. Kitzmiller was trying to tell her. After a minute or so she turned and walked thoughtfully back to the parking lot.

It was early, not yet six o'clock, but Dena had worked straight through lunch and was hungry. The thought of returning to the rented bungalow and cooking something there on the gas range was not appealing. She did not feel like being alone just now. A sandwich at the Wheeler Café

48

would be plenty. Dena had never been a big eater, which was just as well, since cooking was not one of her talents. And at the café she could be in the company of other people without having to be *with* them.

The Wheeler Café on Highway 75 was the premier eatery in town since Dutch's Pizza Parlor burned down in 1979. It had six red vinyl booths and an L-shaped counter with twenty stools. On the wall above the cash register was a framed photograph of the 1968 World Champion Green Bay Packers. Owner Walt Brabender was also the cook. During busy times there were two waitresses, while Eunice Brabender ran the cash register. Most of the time Noreen Stahley worked the whole place alone.

Dena took a stool and ordered a grilled cheese sandwich from Noreen. She laid the folded copy of the *Herald* on the counter beside her, wondering why she had brought it in.

Noreen the waitress, famous for having the reddest hair in Waupaca County, leaned across the counter to look at the paper. She turned it top to bottom.

"Hey, I know this guy."

"What guy?"

"This one here with his picture in the paper." She pointed to the photograph of Hank Stransky. "What'd he do?"

"Broke up a tavern in Milwaukee. Where do you know him from?"

"Right here. 'Henry A. Stransky,' " she said, reading from the photo caption. "Yeah, Hank, that was him. Came in every day with the crew was fixing the highway couple weeks ago. Seemed like a nice guy. Kidded around a little the way guys do, but no passes or anything. Family man all the way." She read into the news story. "Jeez, I can't hardly believe he'd do something like this. I guess you never know about people."

Noreen moved off to take care of another customer. Dena turned the newspaper back around and looked again at the picture of Hank Stransky. Could she have seen him with the highway crew one of the times she drove past? She remembered the big men, their bare arms lightly oiled with sweat, wearing orange hard hats with names stenciled on them. Maybe such a fleeting memory was what made the story stick in her mind.

She took a bite of her sandwich, sipped her coffee, and tried to think of other things.

Noreen came back and leaned companionably on the counter. She said, "Terrible thing about Andrea Olson, isn't it."

"What's that, Noreen?" A little local gossip might be just what she needed.

"You know the Olsons, man and wife own the farm up past the Saltzman place?"

"No."

"Both of 'em getting on in years now. Used to come into Wheeler a lot. He still does. She's crippled up and can't hardly leave the house."

"Too bad."

"Anyway, their granddaughter, Andrea—nice, quiet girl, everybody said, just married some fella out West—went completely crazy. On her wedding day, no less. She stabbed her brand-new husband to death, slashed a few other people, then got killed herself trying to jump through a plate-glass window. She was just back here, Andrea, not two weeks ago. I didn't see her myself, but—"

"You say she was here?"

"That's right," Noreen said. "She came to visit the old folks before she got married. The old man drove her back to Milwaukee not two weeks ago."

Dena took a moment to sort out her thoughts before speaking. "That would be about the time the construction crew was working on the highway."

Noreen inserted a careful forefinger through her coiffure and scratched her scalp. "Yeah, I guess it was, come to think about it."

Another customer came in, and Noreen moved off to take his order. Dena sat for a moment thinking about the bride who had stabbed her young husband to death out West.

Then she returned to the newspaper and read again the article about Hank Stransky. The reporter had a by-line at the top of the story. Dena took out a pen and underlined the name. Corey Macklin. Then she finished her sandwich and left the café.

The bizarre death of Andrea Olson Keith was also noted in the tenth-floor suite of a San Francisco hotel. The story was being discussed by an attractive Oriental woman on a local television channel. Anton Kuryakin sat in a chair pulled close to the set and listened carefully. He was a broad-faced man with thick peasant features. His brow was creased in concentration.

So intent was Kuryakin on the screen that he did not hear Viktor Raslov enter the room. Raslov was a small, intense man with steel-rimmed spectacles that kept slipping down the narrow bridge of his nose. He stood for a minute watching the other man before he spoke.

"Enjoying the American toy, are you, comrade?" The tone was meant to be sportive, but behind the lenses of his spectacles Raslov's eyes were cold.

Kuryakin did not turn around. He said, "Have you heard this news report, Viktor? A girl murdered her bridegroom with a knife, then rushed about the restaurant stabbing people at random. She died as she flung herself through a window."

"This is a violent country."

"Yes, I know, but I feel this incident should have special meaning for us."

Raslov became interested. "How is that?"

"In the newspaper account it was mentioned that the young woman had but recently returned from a visit to her grandparents in the state of Wisconsin."

Now Raslov was leaning forward. "Did the grandparents by chance live near the Biotron factory?"

Kuryakin turned to face the older man. "Only a few miles away."

"Aha. Then our suspicions were correct."

"Of course. I had no doubt what they were doing there."

Raslov's eyes flicked about the room. He tapped his ear with one finger and pointed to the walls. "Perhaps we should discuss it another time."

Kuryakin missed the cautionary signal. "This is the second such report."

"Second?" Raslov forgot momentarily his warning about listening devices.

"The first was a small item in the newspaper. A worker went berserk in a public tavern in Milwaukee. He wounded a number of bystanders before dying himself."

"And the connection?"

"This man was working on the highway near the Biotron factory."

Raslov regarded Kuryakin thoughtfully. "Then it is quite possible—" Abruptly, he remembered his surroundings and cut off the sentence. He lay a finger across his lips.

This time Kuryakin nodded his understanding. He ran thick fingers through his wiry gray-black hair. "Should we not take some action before . . . ?" He left the sentence unfinished.

"I have an appointment this afternoon with our embassy. I will discuss the matter with our people there." Raslov started for the door.

On the television screen a young black man began talking about baseball. Kuryakin snapped off the set. "I will get my coat."

With his hand on the doorknob, Raslov turned. "There is no need for you to be at the meeting. Stay and enjoy the American television. Perhaps your Chinese woman will return."

Kuryakin started to protest, but Raslov had turned away and opened the door into the hall. He spoke briefly to the two men who stood outside—thick-shouldered, short-haired men wearing suits that did not fit. They straightened their posture when Raslov spoke, glanced into the room at Kuryakin, and nodded. The door closed, and Kuryakin was left alone.

# Chapter 7

It was rumored around the offices of the Milwaukee *Herald* that Doc Ingersoll had once actually attended medical school. There was a variety of colorful stories about why he dropped out. Or was kicked out. Or maybe even graduated to medical practice and lost his license. Doc never discussed his past, and nobody ever asked him about it. The *Herald* was sort of a foreign legion among newspapers. What a man did before was his own business.

Ingersoll was a gaunt man with an unhealthy gray complexion and a cigarette seemingly growing from the corner of his mouth. He wore suits that looked like the 1940s and was the only man on the staff who wore a hat when the sun shone. Doc's clothes, his desk, even the floor wherever he happened to be standing, were continually powdered with cigarette ash.

Doc's title at the *Herald* was science editor. His job consisted largely of taking wire-service copy that could be lumped under science and medicine and chopping it to fit whatever holes were left in the page dummies. He also wrote and rewrote periodically an article warning of the dangers of drugs and alcohol. The *Herald* ran it whenever some authority questioned their commitment to community service. It was a subject with which Doc Ingersoll was familiar.

Corey Macklin found him Tuesday morning amid the scattered ashes, scissoring a sheet of UPI copy.

"Got a minute, Doc?" Corey said.

"If it's important. I'm on a hot lead here, all about the

wife of a farmer outside Indianapolis who claims to have been fucked by a creature from outer space.''

''No kidding.''

''Imagine that farmer's consternation when the offspring resembles the hired hand.''

''Didn't the *Enquirer* have that one last month?''

Doc crumpled the copy sheet into a ball and bounced it off the rim of a metal wastebasket. ''Damn, scooped again.'' He creaked around in the wooden swivel chair to face Corey, dribbling ashes into his lap. ''What's on your mind?''

''Something here I want you to take a look at.'' Corey brushed ashes aside to make a clean space on the desk and spread out the stories on Hank Stransky in Milwaukee, Du-Bois Williamson in New York, and Andrea Keith in Seattle. Next to them he placed the sheet he had prepared with three columns, each headed by the name of one of the victims.

Ingersoll coughed around his cigarette and read rapidly and expertly through the news stories. He scanned Corey's handwritten notes and looked up. ''So?''

''What do you think?''

''I think three seemingly normal people turned inexplicably violent last Friday. Apparently you are trying to find some correlation among the three.''

''Opinion?''

Ingersoll ticked off the notations on Corey's sheet with a yellow-stained finger. ''The two men here, Stransky and Williamson, would seem to have several traits in common. Age, economic level, et cetera. The big variance is in race and geographic location. The woman doesn't fit the pattern at all. She's only twenty, different sex, different social environment, and still a different location. The only points common to all three are the date of their seizures, the bizarre nature of their actions, and their own violent deaths.''

''Conclusion?''

''Coincidence.''

''Maybe, but that leaves me with no story.''

"It has been my observation over the years that real life often has disappointing story values."

"What about the way they died, Doc? Does that suggest anything to you?"

Ingersoll glanced again at the three stories. "Let's see, you got Williamson run over by a truck, Keith impaled on a shard of plate glass, and your man Stransky dead of cranial hemorrhage, apparently the result of being hit by a pool ball. No direct relation to whatever made them flip out. Why don't you put it down to 'these troubled times' and forget it."

Corey gathered his material. "Thanks anyway, Doc, but I still think there's something here."

Doc lit a fresh cigarette from the butt of his old one. "Have you considered death rays from outer space?"

He started a laugh, which turned into a coughing fit. Corey left him there and returned to his desk. He shoved the three stories and his notes into a manila folder and dropped it into a drawer. He stopped at the bulletin board to scribble his name on the sign-out sheet. He entered his destination as *downtown* and left the building.

Vic's Old Milwaukee Tavern was more or less back to normal. The debris from Friday night's excitement had been swept up, broken pool cues replaced, bloodstains washed away. When Corey Macklin entered, there were only four morning drinkers seated at the bar. Unlike the evening crowd, they were quiet, self-contained, each avoiding the eyes of the others. Vic Metzger, wearing a bandage from elbow to wrist on his left arm, came over as Corey took a stool.

"How's it going, Vic?"

"Slow. It cost me a bundle when I had to close the place up Saturday. After your story I could have charged admission. Sunday was okay, and last night, but Saturday would have been a bonanza. Everybody wanted to see blood on the floor." He nodded toward the four silent drinkers. "Now it's Monday, and nobody cares about Friday's news."

"*Sic transit gloria*, Vic. How's the arm?"

Vic worked the fingers of his left hand. "No problem. They kept me in the hospital Saturday when it swelled up and they thought maybe there was an infection. It was okay by the next morning, though, so I came down and opened up for the sightseers."

"Glad to hear it."

"Could've been a lot worse if you hadn't jumped in. Likely you saved my life. From now on your tab belongs to the house."

"Well, thanks. In that case, you can give me a beer. Draft."

"You got it."

Vic poured an icy glass of beer and set it on the bar in front of Corey. He turned away and sneezed.

"Coming down with a cold?" Corey asked.

"Nah. Had a kind of forty-eight-hour flu, I guess. Aches in the joints, little fever. Got over it, though. Aftereffects, probably. Nerves."

"I couldn't blame you after Friday night."

Vic nodded in silent agreement.

"What do you suppose made Hank Stransky flip out like that?"

"Beats the shit out of me. He was always easygoing in here. Never saw him come close to a fight with anybody. Damned strange."

"Yeah."

"The ones I feel sorry for are his wife and kids. I don't think Hank left them with a whole lot. Usually, something like that happens to a regular, we'd get up a collection. But considering the circumstances . . ." Vic let a shrug finish the thought.

"I see what you mean."

"The funeral's tomorrow morning. I plan to close the place up so I can go. There probably won't be a lot of friends there to comfort the widow. What happened ain't her fault."

"I may stop by, too," Corey said. "Where's it going to be?"

"At the Lujack Brothers, over by Harley Street. They do a nice job. It'll take some real work to fix up Hank, the way he looked."

"I guess it will." Corey finished his beer, told Vic to take care of the arm, and left the tavern.

The Lujack Brothers Mortuary was a modest brick building with a white-pillared façade that was supposed to make it look like an antebellum mansion. The effect was largely negated by the bricked-up warehouse next door and the wholesale plumbing supplier across the street.

Corey parked out in front and entered the anteroom through heavy glass doors. He crossed the thick carpet, which was bordered by plastic palmettos, and stopped where an overweight girl sat behind a sliding panel.

"Yes, sir?" The girl gave him a sympathetic smile.

Corey showed his press card, and the smile faded. "I'd like to see Mr. Lujack."

"Which Mr. Lujack did you have in mind? There are four brothers."

"Give me whichever one is in charge."

"That would be Mr. Caspar Lujack. The others are all out of town."

"Let's have him."

The girl picked up a telephone, punched one of the Lucite buttons, and said something Corey could not hear. She apparently received an affirmative answer and pointed to a heavy crimson hanging at the far end of the room. "There's a hallway behind the drapes. First door on your right."

Corey followed her directions and walked into a comfortable office furnished in walnut and leather. Caspar Lujack sat behind a carved, deeply polished desk.

The mortician was a small-boned, precise man who wore his hair slicked down with a part that was geometrically straight from forehead to crown. His silk tie was tastefully subdued, and his gray sharkskin suit looked expensive.

"How can I be of service, Mr. Macklin?"

"I'm interested in the Stransky funeral that's scheduled for tomorrow."

"You're a friend of the family?"

"Not exactly."

"Wait a minute . . . Macklin. You're the one who wrote the eyewitness story in the *Herald*. You were in the tavern when it happened."

"Yeah."

"What in the world do you think made him go wild like that?"

"I have no idea," Corey said shortly. "I wonder if I could see the body."

"Sorry, but that's impossible."

"I don't understand."

"He was cremated yesterday."

"Cremated? How come?"

"As a matter of fact, I was surprised myself when the widow called back. Not that I blame her. The condition of the body made lying in state questionable. We can hide a lot of damage with clothing, but people expect the face to be recognizable. Still, I was ready to go along with her wishes until—"

"Wait a minute," Corey broke in. "Are you saying Mrs. Stransky changed her mind about disposal of the body?"

Lujack frowned. "That's what I was in the process of explaining. In my opinion, it was the right decision. It certainly made more sense than trying to pretty up—"

"And you've already gone ahead and cremated him?"

"Yesterday afternoon. There was no reason to wait. I had the furnace going for another client. That left me today to sift the ashes and pick out a suitable urn for the funeral."

"Did you do any kind of examination of the body before shoving it in the oven?"

"Examination?"

"Like an autopsy."

"That's not my job. All I had done was drain the fluids preparatory to embalming. The cosmetic work hadn't been

58

started when Mrs. Stransky called to say she'd changed her mind.''

"Did *anybody* examine the body?''

"Not that I know about. I wasn't authorized to do any postmortem, and I'm not about to do it on my own.''

"Did you take any pictures?''

"Of the body? Certainly not. What kind of an operation do you think this is?''

"No offense, Mr. Lujack,'' Corey said. "It just seems to me somebody was in an awful hurry to dispose of Hank Stransky's remains.''

"You'll have to take that up with the widow,'' Lujack said.

"Yeah. I think I'll do that.''

Corey drove directly to the street where Hank Stransky and his family had lived. He had the old tense feeling in the pit of his stomach, the feeling he used to get when he was closing in on a meaty story. It had been a long time.

He pulled up across from the house and for a moment sat staring at the moving van that was parked out in front. A two-man crew was transferring the Stransky furniture from the house to the van. Corey got out of the car and walked across the street.

He climbed up on the porch and looked in through the open front door. The house looked bare and somehow sad. There was no sign of Pauline Stransky or the boys. Corey stopped one of the moving men on his way in.

"Any of the family around?''

"Nope. The lady left a key for us this morning. The papers were all signed and proper.''

"Where are you taking the stuff?''

The man eyed him suspiciously. "Who wants to know?''

"Corey Macklin. I'm with the *Herald*.'' He took out his press card with photo and showed it to the mover. "Have you got some ID?''

The man produced an authentic-looking identification

card from a reputable moving company. Corey made a note of his name.

"Where you taking the stuff?" he asked again.

"It goes into storage."

"That's funny."

"Not to me. I couldn't care less where the stuff goes. I just put it in the truck at one end, take it out at the other. I got to get back to work now, okay?"

Corey watched for several minutes as the two men carried the accumulated possessions of a lifetime out of Stransky's house and packed them efficiently into the van. He walked to the house next door and rang the bell.

A heavy woman in a quilted robe and floppy slippers opened the door and peered at him suspiciously. When Corey identified himself, she relaxed a little.

"I'd like to talk to Mrs. Stransky," he said. "Do you know where I can reach her?"

"Beats me. She left Sunday with the boys without so much as a good-bye—after all the years we been neighbors. You'd think she could at least've said something."

"You say she left Sunday. Was she driving?"

"No, Pauline never drove nowhere if she could help it. Couple of men, banker types, came for her in a car. Big Caddy, it was. Her and the boys, suitcases and all, got in, and off they went. Not even a good-bye."

"Banker types, you say."

"You know—suits, ties, all like that."

"You haven't any idea where they went?"

"Nope. I went over there Saturday night after things were quieted down. Took a lemon meringue pie for her and the boys. Pauline never said anything about going away. She was taking it pretty well, all things considered. Making plans for the funeral."

"Did she say anything about having Mr. Stransky cremated?"

"Not a chance. Hank didn't believe in it, and Pauline wouldn't go against Hank, living or dead, if you know what I mean."

"I see. Well, thanks for your time." Corey turned away and started down the porch steps.

"Don't you need my name for the newspaper?" the woman called after him.

"Not this time. Maybe later."

"It's Lubin. Mrs. Dorothy Lubin."

Corey took out a sheet of copy paper and scribbled on it. He gave Mrs. Lubin a wave and jogged back across the street to his car.

Back at the *Herald* building, he picked up the telephone and got the number listed for DuBois Williamson in Brooklyn, New York. He dialed the number and tapped a pencil impatiently against the receiver as he listened to a series of electronic buzzes and clicks. Finally, something like a human voice came through the earpiece.

"I'm sorry. The number you have dialed is out of service. Please check your directory to make sure you dialed correctly. Thank you." Click.

"Shit." Grinding his teeth, Corey checked his number and dialed again.

"I'm sorry. The number you have dialed is—"

He banged down the receiver, scooped up the manila folder containing his notes, and marched into Porter Uhlander's office.

The paunchy city editor belched into his fist when he saw Corey coming and edged his chair back as though he were expecting a physical attack. Corey opened the folder and spread the contents on the desk before Uhlander.

"Remember this?"

"Yesterday's news, Corey," he said.

"Read it, Porter. Three strange, violent deaths, three different cities, all on the same day, all with strong similarities."

"So do it as a feature and see if you can talk Marianne into running it in the Tuesday magazine."

"It's not a feature, damn it. It's news. For the first time in years the *Herald* stands to break a really big story. Believe me, if the *Sun-Times* and the *Tribune* get on to this, we're going to look damn foolish. Are you going to be the one to spike it?''

Porter Uhlander began a sigh that turned into a belch. ''What do you need?''

''A fast trip to New York.''

''No.''

''Come on, Porter. Are you going to let a few dollars stand in the way of fame and fortune?''

''Whose fame and fortune are we talking about?''

''Yours. Mine. The *Herald*'s. Who cares? Listen, if nothing comes of this, you can take the damn air fare out of my salary.''

''You're serious about this, aren't you.''

Corey held up his right hand in oath-taking position.

''Tourist class on the red-eye?''

''Hell, yes. I'll go air freight. Just get me there.''

Uhlander shook a handful of Tums from a plastic bottle on his desk and spilled them into his mouth. He chewed solemnly while he dug through his desk for the blank pad of trip authorizations.

''Remember—no story, and this comes out of your salary.''

''You got a deal,'' Corey said.

# Chapter 8

I like New York in June.
I'll take Manhattan.
A helluva town.

Snatches of song lyrics danced through Corey Macklin's head during the bus ride from JFK through Queens, across the Triborough Bridge to Manhattan and the West Side Terminal. Maybe Los Angeles had the sunshine, San Francisco the culture, New Orleans the food, Chicago the broad shoulders—but New York was the place to be; no doubt about it. The air was brisk and charged with excitement. Everybody seemed to be on his way to some vital appointment. Never mind the junkies and the whores and the muggers and the pimps. New York was It. The Big Apple. The place to be if you were anybody.

The red-eye flight in a cramped coach seat had left Corey with aching joints and a foul taste in his mouth, but the electric atmosphere of New York had quickly revived him. He belonged there. If things worked out, he would soon be there for good.

Corey's mood took a nosedive when, after a wait of forty-five minutes, he was allowed into the cramped office of an assistant to the medical examiner named Fado. The man had a mouth with the corners permanently turned down. He looked at Corey as though he needed a bath.

"You say you're from Minneapolis?" he said.

"Milwaukee," Corey told him. "The Milwaukee *Herald.*"

"Good for you. And you wanted what?"

"I'd like to see the body of DuBois Williamson."

"Have you got any idea the number of bodies we process through here?"

"No."

"I didn't think so. Well, I'm up to my ass in dead bodies, and you expect me to dig through them and find some coked-up jigaboo who was brought in here when?"

"Last Friday."

"Last Friday. Sure. Wonderful. Our busiest day."

"Look, it shouldn't be all that tough."

"Not in Minneapolis, maybe, but you're in the Apple now, pal."

"Would you mind checking?"

63

Fado gave him a long-suffering sigh and walked to a bank of battered file cabinets along one wall. After a five-minute search he pulled out a folder, shuffled through the sheaf of onionskin forms inside, pulled out one, and scanned the information. He took care to prevent Corey from reading over his shoulder.

"Williamson, DuBois Harrington," he read.

"That'll be him," Corey said.

"Gone."

"What do you mean, gone?"

"I mean Williamson, Dubois Harrington, has checked out. The body was signed for and removed yesterday."

"Who removed it?"

"That's confidential."

"Come on, mister. I'm with the press."

"In this town your Minneapolis *Trombone,* or whatever your sheet is, don't carry a lot of weight, pal."

"All right, what about the cause of death? Is that confidential, too?"

"Don't you read the papers?"

"I'm from out of town. Humor me."

Fado let a breath hiss out through his teeth. He read from the sheet in a rapid monotone. "Multiple fractures of the spine, pelvis, and ribs; massive damage to internal organs, including liver, spleen, kidneys, and heart. All injuries attributable to the deceased being run over by a panel truck loaded with heavy machine parts." He looked up at Corey. "Okay?"

"Does it say anything about the condition of his face?"

"What difference does it make? The guy was squashed like a busted balloon." Fado jammed the folder back into the file cabinet and slammed the drawer shut.

Corey ground his teeth but said nothing more. No use getting on the wrong side of the authorities, no matter how pigheaded they were.

He had a Danish and coffee in a hole-in-the-wall deli and was calmed down somewhat by the time he found a cab for the ride to Brooklyn. He rechecked his notes as the taxi crossed Newton Creek into Greenpoint, and some of his excitement returned. There were answers waiting for him in the house where DuBois Williamson had lived. He could feel it.

After several wrong turns and rereadings of a crumpled map, the Puerto Rican driver pulled up in front of one of a row of identical, narrow three-story houses. The street was freshly swept and had budding trees spaced along the curb in iron cages.

Corey paid the fare and under-tipped the driver, ignoring the long, hard look he got from the man. He crossed the sidewalk and climbed the stoop to the front door. The doorbell was the old-fashioned kind you turned with a key. He cranked it and waited. The possibility of failure chilled him for a moment. What if nobody was there and the place had been cleaned out like Stransky's in Milwaukee? He would have to go back empty, and it would be a cold day before he talked Porter Uhlander out of another plane ticket. Then the door opened, and his doubts vanished.

A short, very dark woman with generous breasts and hips stood there looking up at him. Her modified natural hairstyle was shot through, not unattractively, with gray. She wore a nylon dress of dark blue with a flower figure in a lighter shade.

"Mrs. Williamson?" Corey said. Looking over the woman's head, he could see two suitcases standing in the hallway.

"That's right. You from the agency?"

"Uh, no. My name is Corey Macklin. I'm a reporter. Can I talk to you?"

Ruby Williamson looked doubtful. "I'm expecting somebody."

"I won't take much of your time."

"Who is it, Momma?" a strong young voice called from inside the house.

"Reporter," she said, turning from the doorway but keeping her eyes on Corey.

A young black man with cropped hair and a neat moustache appeared behind Ruby Williamson. He frowned at Corey.

"Reporter, you say?"

"That's right."

"What paper you with?"

Corey dug for his press card. "The Milwaukee *Herald*. I—"

"Milwaukee?" The young man pronounced the name of the city as though it were in some distant galaxy. "What you doing out here?"

"This my son, Anthony," said Mrs. Williamson.

"Glad to meet you," Corey said. He stuck out a hand. The young man ignored it. Corey flashed his press card. "I'm working on a story in Milwaukee that may have some connection to what happened to Mr. Williamson. I'd really appreciate a few minutes of your time."

"You want to talk to him, Momma?" Anthony said.

"Don't make no difference to me," said the woman. "Might as well."

"Come on in, then," Anthony said without warmth. "Can't talk but a few minutes. We're about to leave."

"So I see," Corey said, glancing at the suitcases. He waited for some explanation, but when none was forthcoming, he followed mother and son into the neat little living room.

The furniture seemed oddly delicate for the sturdy old house. An exception was a well-worn recliner that was positioned to face the television set. When Ruby and Anthony Williamson pointedly avoided sitting in it, Corey carefully did the same.

"First let me say I'm sorry about what happened to Mr. Williamson."

"Are you?" said the young man. "Why?"

"Don't be dispolite, Anthony," Mrs. Williamson scolded. Then she said to Corey, "Anthony's in the navy," as though that fact would explain the lapse in manners.

"Home on leave?" Corey said, trying to make it friendly.

"Emergency leave." Anthony's deep maroon eyes held steady on Corey's face. "Death in the family."

Corey nodded, feeling a little foolish. He said, "I wonder, Mrs. Williamson, if you could just tell me about your husband. How he was before the . . . accident. Was there anything different about his behavior? Anything strange?"

Ruby Williamson put a hand to one plump cheek and let her eyes rove off to a corner of the ceiling. "Nothing so strange as to cause any notice. He was a little bit sick the first part of the week when we come back from our vacation, but he got over that."

"Sick," Corey repeated, making rapid notes. "Like a cold or the flu?"

"Kind of, except it only lasted about two days. We thought maybe he was allergic to the bee sting. Some people are."

"Bee sting?" Corey looked up at her.

"Mm-hmm. We was drivin' along the road there, and Dubois, he stop the car to go pick some strawberries. They grow right by the road out there. Well, a big ol' bee stung him on the neck, and it swole up kinda ugly till we put some ice on it next day. We thought maybe that was the cause of him bein' sick."

"Where did this happen, Mrs. Williamson?"

"Now that's a funny thing. It was out there where you live. We was just on our way into Milwaukee, Wisconsin."

Corey tried to keep the excitement out of his voice as he went on. "Was there anything different about the way your husband acted on that last morning?"

"Different?"

"Did he do anything or say anything that seemed strange to you?"

"He didn't finish his breakfast is one thing. DuBois was a man liked his bacon and eggs, sunny side up, each and every day of the year. Hardly ate a mouthful that morning. Said he had a headache."

"Headache," Corey repeated.

"He wasn't no crazy man, if that's what you're thinking," Anthony put in.

"Lord, no," said his mother. "DuBois was the most even-tempered, easygoing man you'd ever want to meet. Wouldn't step on a bug if he could walk around it." For the first time there was a tremor in her voice. "That's why it just don't make no sense, what happened. No sense at all."

"He didn't do any dope, either, if that's what you're thinking," Anthony added.

Corey ran over in his mind the best way to phrase his next request. "I wonder, Mrs. Williamson, have you made arrangements for the funeral?"

"That's all been took care of."

"What do you mean?" He spoke more sharply than he intended to.

"She means it ain't any of your business," Anthony said.

"I'm not trying to pry into your personal affairs," Corey said, "but this could be important."

"It's been took care of," Ruby Williamson said again. "The men said—"

"Momma, it ain't any of this man's business," Anthony said.

Before Corey could respond, they were startled by the doorbell. Anthony glanced at Corey and his mother, then walked out into the hallway. The front door opened. The sound of muffled voices came to the living room. Corey strained but could not make out what was being said.

After a moment Anthony returned, followed by two men in business suits. The men were in their middle thirties, both neat, clean-shaven, and expressionless. They might have been twins, had not one of them been blond, the other dark. Their eyes flicked over Corey, missing nothing.

"Ready to go, Mrs. Williamson?" one of them said.

"Yes, I—I suppose so."

Corey stood up. "Excuse me," he began, "I'm with the Milwaukee *Herald*—"

"I'm sorry, sir. We're on a very tight schedule," said the blond man.

"You're taking Mrs. Williamson somewhere?"

"Excuse me, sir." The dark man moved past Corey and took the widow's arm, assisting her gently to her feet.

"Do you mind telling me where you're going?"

The blond man stepped in front of Corey, blocking him, while his partner led Ruby Williamson toward the hall.

"May I have your name, sir?"

"Macklin. Corey Macklin."

"Please excuse us, Mr. Macklin. We really are in a hurry. Ready, Anthony?"

"Yeah, I guess." Anthony Williamson looked for a moment as though he might say something more, then turned and walked out of the house.

Corey accompanied them as far as the sidewalk. The two men hustled Ruby and her son into a Cadillac. The side windows were tinted dark enough to obscure the inside of the car. As Corey stood watching, the two men got into the front seat, and the Cadillac drove off.

"Banker types," Corey said to himself, remembering the description given by Hank Stransky's neighbor. The peculiar similarities between the two stories were beginning to add up. There was another missing body. Another caddy whisking away the survivors. Something was going on. Corey hiked two blocks to a busier street. There he hailed a cab and asked to be taken to Bellevue Hospital.


He found Norman Hastings sitting up in bed apathetically watching a television soap opera. There were bandages covering his left shoulder, hip, and leg.

"Mr. Hastings?"

"It is unless they slipped somebody else into my bed during the night."

Corey introduced himself. Hastings switched off the tinny speaker that lay next to his pillow and gestured Corey into a chair.

"I thought you guys were all through with me," he said. "Couldn't find word one in the paper today. Not even the *Post*. But hell, what's a few more violent deaths in this shithole of a city, right? You got newer and bloodier stuff to write about, I'm sure."

"I'm working on a different angle," Corey told him.

"I hope you're not one of those bleeding-heart liberals going to blame the whole thing on society, the cabdriver being black and all."

"No, Mr. Hastings, I'm not one of those."

"In that case, call me Norm. What can I do for you, Corey?"

"I'd like you to go over one more time exactly what happened on the street Friday."

Hastings shrugged, wincing as he did so and lightly touching his bandaged shoulder. "Hell, why not. I've damn near got it memorized.

"I was out in the street waving down this cab. The guy had an *Out of Service* sign in the window, but that doesn't mean anything in New York. Anyway, I finally get the cabbie's attention, and he steers over in my direction. I'm getting set to get in when I see the look on that black face. I'll never forget that look. His lips were pulled back like this, showing all his teeth. I'm talking *ugly*, Corey. His eyes were rolling around like marbles in two cups. And it got worse."

Hastings paused for a moment and seemed to be watching the silent soap opera on the television screen as he gathered his thoughts.

"What do you mean 'worse'?" Corey prompted.

"The skin on the guy's face started to push out in little bumps and pimples. They swelled up and popped right while I was looking at him. Must have all happened in a matter of seconds. I was sort of frozen there in the street, and I tell myself, 'Hey, that crazy black s.o.b. is trying to run over you.' Well, I took a headfirst dive for the curb, but he caught me a glancing blow with one headlight. Sent me sliding along the concrete, leaving about a square yard of my hide behind, not to mention most of a three-hundred-dollar suit." He gestured at the bandages that covered the left side of his body.

"At that, I guess I was lucky. Laying there in the street, I could hear *thumpy-bump* and the screams when he plowed into the people on the sidewalk. Killed four of them, hurt a dozen more. Then the son of a bitch jumped out of the cab and went after anybody he could reach with his hands. If he hadn't slipped down and been run over by that panel truck, there's no telling how many people he would have killed. Naturally, there wasn't a cop in sight. Never is when you need 'em." Hastings shook his head. "I tell you, this town is the pits. The absolute pits."

"Did you hear the driver say anything?" Corey asked.

"Say anything? Hell, no. He was completely flipped out. High on something, sure as you're born. Most of them are, you know."

Corey put away the folded sheet of copy paper with his notes on it. "Well, thanks, Norm. I'm glad you came out of it as well as you did."

"You and me both, pardner. It's a wonder I didn't get some kind of disease laying in that grubby New York street all scraped raw the way I was. Got off with just a little infection. Couple of days of fever. Come Friday, I'm flying my ass back to Dallas, and no way, nohow, is Norman Hastings ever coming back to this rotten town."

"I don't blame you," Corey said. "Good luck."

I like New York in June.
I'll take Manhattan.
A helluva town.
The songs were back in Corey's head as he caught a taxi to the Westside Terminal and a bus from there to JFK. Yes, something was definitely going on, and he, Corey Macklin, was sitting right on top of it. He grinned broadly out the window of the bus, ignoring the suspicious stares he got back from people on the streets of New York.

# Chapter 9

Eddie Gault lay back naked on the double bed, his arms spread, one hand clutching each of the bedposts. It was his favorite position, one Roanne had taught him. There were a number of things she could do to him in that position, all of which were terrific. Most times he had to concentrate like crazy to keep from coming in a few seconds once she started on him. That evening, though, it just wasn't working out. Eddie's thoughts kept straying back to his day at the plant.

Roanne could tell, of course. If a man's mind wasn't on it, there was no way he could fake it. Not like a woman. She gently pulled her head back, letting his half-erect penis slide out of her mouth. She held him for a moment, then eased herself up over his body, the long pale hair giving him a silky caress all the way up.

"Tired, baby?"

That was one of the beautiful things about Roanne. She never asked "What's wrong?" in that accusing tone women use. Nothing could make a man go limp faster than the good old "What's wrong?"

Eddie shook his head, gazing up into the crystalline blue eyes. "A little worried, I guess."

"What about?"

"You know. The canister business."

"Has anything happened? Have they said anything more to you?"

"No, but they're watching me. I think I'm being followed."

"Bastards." The word seemed especially harsh coming from the pink lips of the lovely girl. "It's not enough that they poison our atmosphere and pollute the earth; they have to persecute a man who tries to do the right thing." Then she said more softly, "Don't worry about it, baby. They lost a few cows. They'll get over it."

"Maybe it's more than the cows."

Roanne eased herself to a sitting position beside him on the bed. She let her hand remain flat on his naked stomach. Her face was grave, but Eddie was not looking beyond the round little breasts.

"What do you mean?" she asked.

"I don't know. It's rumors. Just rumors." He reached up and took hold of a breast, stroking it gently like a captive bird. Roanne did not try to take it away.

"Tell me about the rumors," she said softly.

"It's the pilots. The two who flew that day with the wrong canister."

Eddie's eyes drifted away. Roanne pressed his hand more firmly against her breast to regain his attention. "What about the pilots, baby?"

"They're gone. Two new guys are taking their place."

"Gone where?"

"Nobody knows."

"What are people saying?" Roanne's eyes had a hungry glitter.

"Nothing, actually. Just wondering how come the other guys left so sudden with no word to anybody."

"Does anyone think it has something to do with their spraying the wrong canister?"

"Not that I know of," Eddie said.

"It would serve them right if they were both poisoned."

Eddie searched her face. "Why is this such a big thing with you, Roanne? I mean, I know about the environment and all that, and sure it's important, but with you it's like . . . life or death."

"That's exactly what it is," Roanne said. Her eyes

ranged off to a corner of the ceiling as though looking into the past. "I never told you how my mother died."

"No."

"It was cancer. Cancer of the liver. It was a long, painful death."

"I'm sorry," Eddie said.

"Sorry doesn't get it. My mother was murdered."

"I don't understand."

"She was working in a plant in Atlanta that made synthetic fabrics. They used chemicals that they didn't tell the workers about. A lot of people got sick. My mother died. They poisoned her, but nobody ever paid for it. They're still operating today. Still killing the workers. Somebody has to do something about it. That's you and me, Eddie."

"But those pilots—they didn't do anything. They thought they were spraying purple dye."

Roanne stiffened. "Just doing their duty. That's the all-purpose excuse for poisoning the earth and making war. It sounds like my father. He was a pilot, too, dropping napalm and God knows what else on women and children in Vietnam. The bastard never came back."

"He was killed?"

"Better if he had been. He just disappeared after the war. Let my mother die with a rotting liver and never even wrote a letter."

"I wish you'd told me all this before," Eddie said. "It helps me understand you better." He started to rise. "But it doesn't make this business any easier for me."

Roanne gently pushed him back down on the bed. "Don't worry about it, baby. It will be all right."

She leaned forward, bringing the pink nipple of one breast to his lips. He took it eagerly into his mouth and began to suck.

In the small bedroom of her bungalow, Dena Falkner stared sleeplessly at the ceiling. There had been a tension in the air at Biotron that week like static electricity before a summer storm. The uneasiness lingered, keeping her awake.

She had not spoken to Dr. Kitzmiller since the unsatisfactory conversation on Monday, but she had the feeling he was watching her. Someone was sure as hell watching her. She could feel eyes on the back of her neck, but when she turned around, there were only innocent people engaged in innocent pursuits. Much too innocent.

She was not at all satisfied with the story of Stuart Anderson's assignment to Brazil. Three times the day before she had tried to call his sister in California. There had been no answer. It was possible, of course, that Stu's sister had simply been out at the time of the calls. Sure it was possible, but Dena did not believe it.

She sighed and snapped on the lamp on her bedside table. She picked up the book that lay there. *The Last Days of Pompeii*. A few pages of Bulwer-Lytton always had a soporific effect on her. She opened it to the place she had marked and began to read. Before she had finished a page, she heard the noise.

It was a soft bump from somewhere at the back of the house.

Another.

Dena killed the light and sat up in bed, staring into the dark. The absence of artificial lights to pollute the night had seemed a part of the charm of living in the country. Now she would have given much for the glow of a streetlight outside her window.

A scraping sound from the kitchen. It took a moment for Dena to recognize it. Someone was raising the window.

A burglar?

Not in Wheeler, Wisconsin. Everybody in town knew everybody else, and it was not a promising location for an out-of-town burglar to pick.

Rape?

The ugly word to describe the ugly act was always in the back of a woman's mind when she heard strange night sounds. Some drunken fool on his way home from a road-house?

Ridiculous, she told herself. But her throat constricted at the thought of her body being invaded.

*Scrape.*

She started to reach again for the lamp but held back. No, a light in there would just signal her presence to whoever was creeping into her house. She had no weapon, of course. Wouldn't know how to use a gun if she had one. Didn't believe in them. For a terrible moment, though, she wished for the reassuring feel of a pistol butt in her hand.

*Scrape. Thump.*

The window was all the way open now.

The metallic clatter of a spoon as it fell from the drainboard into the sink. He was coming in. He *was* in.

She would not be found lying there helpless, Dena decided. By the faint glow of the stars outside, she slipped noiselessly from the bed. From memory she found her robe where she had folded it over the back of her dressing-table chair. She pulled it on and knotted the satin belt at her waist.

A floorboard creaked.

He was coming for her.

Her hand fumbled along the top of the dressing table, searching instinctively for something, anything, that might be used for defense.

Hairbrush. Deodorant. Aspirin bottle. Electric tooth-brush.

The floor creaked again.

Dena's mind teetered on the edge of hysteria. She fought down the image of herself confronting the rapist with an electric toothbrush.

A soft scratching on the panel of the bedroom door.

Fingernails.

Dena froze, her back pressed against the wall. She did not breathe.

Her eyes were now more accustomed to the near-total darkness. She stared with painful intensity at the dim gray rectangle of the door. A strip of black appeared at the edge. It widened to an inch. Two inches.

Dena drew in her breath and opened her mouth to scream. It was purely instinctive. There was no one near enough to hear.

"Dena?"

The hoarse whisper coming from the cracked doorway jolted her like an electric shock.

"Dena, are you there? It's Lloyd. Lloyd Bratz."

The breath whistled out of her, and Dena felt for a moment as though her bones had dissolved.

"Jesus H. Christ, Lloyd, what the hell are you trying to do?"

"I'm sorry. Listen, I'm really sorry, but they're following me."

Dena found the small lamp on the table beside her bed. She snapped it on. Lloyd Bratz darted to the window and snatched the curtain across it. He turned and gave her a worried grin. He scrubbed fingers through his bristly hair.

"What's going on, Lloyd? Who's following you? What are you doing here, anyway?"

"I went to my place first, but somebody was already there watching it."

"Then you weren't transferred out West."

"What are you talking about?"

"I went to see Helen. She said you'd been transferred. She left with someone while I was there."

"Left with who?"

"I don't know. Some man, looked very official."

Bratz ground his teeth. "Son of a bitch, if they've harmed her—"

"I need a cigarette." Dena went to the closet and reached up on the high shelf for the carton of Carltons she had put there so they would be hard to reach. She tore open a fresh pack, shook one out, and lit it. She drew in the smoke gratefully and blew it out in a long streamer. "Now then," she said, "I'm ready to listen. Where did you come from?"

Lloyd glanced around quickly. "They were holding me in

the infirmary. I coldcocked a guard tonight, stole a car, and got away, but they're not far behind me."

"Slow down," Dena said. "Holding you in the infirmary for what? Are you sick? And what's this 'guard' business? Start at the beginning."

"I may not have much time, so I'll talk fast. A week ago last Friday Stu and I were flying over the old county road at the edge of the company's land to do a dispersal test. Spraying purple dye to see what the pattern is from a particular altitude with known wind conditions."

"Is Stu involved in this?" Dena broke in. "Do you know where he is?"

"I know," Lloyd said. "Let me get to it."

Dena sat on the edge of the bed and dragged on her cigarette.

"As soon as we opened the canister, we could see something was wrong. The stuff was clear, not purple. We went back and reported it and got hustled into Dr. Kitzmiller's office. He chewed us out, which I guess we had coming, but then he called in a couple of security goons, and they marched us off to the infirmary. Nobody would tell us a damn thing.

"They put us in a room by ourselves and treated us like we had the plague or something. As far as I could see, there was nothing wrong with us, except Stu got a little infection in a razor nick on his chin. He was running a little fever, too; said he felt achy, like the flu or something. I thought, Oh, shit, maybe we are sick. He seemed to get better after a couple of days, but then the headache started."

Dena barely caught a long ash that fell from the end of her cigarette. She spilled it into an ashtray and stared at the chunky pilot. He walked over to peek past the edge of the curtain, then came back.

"When was this?" she asked. "The headaches?"

"On Thursday. Stu didn't say anything at first but got kind of quiet and distracted-like. Finally, he asked for some aspirin. All of a sudden he's got the whole medical staff

78

around him. Me, I felt fine. I think that kind of disappointed them.

"Finally, Stu got fed up. He told them he felt okay, and they left him alone. He didn't feel okay, though. That headache was really starting to get to him. During the night I heard him swallowing aspirins like peanuts. When I tried to talk to him, he brushed me off. He got kind of mean. Not like Stu at all."

"Is he still there?" Dena said.

"I'm getting to it," Lloyd said. "You were pretty close to him, weren't you?"

"We liked each other. Just tell it, Lloyd."

"Friday was bad. Stu hardly said a word. People kept coming and going, examining him, giving him tests, and all the time this headache of his was getting worse. You could see it on his face. They pretty much forgot about me.

"Then, about the time they came in with our dinner, he flipped completely."

"What do you mean flipped?"

"Are you sure you want to hear the details? It's not pretty."

"Goddam it, Bratz, who do you think you're talking to, some grade-school virgin? Just tell me what happened."

"Okay. Like I said, Stu was getting pretty bad. Holding his head, groaning. Wouldn't talk except to cuss me out. I left him alone. Then, when the two guys came in with our dinners, he let out a howl and went for them."

"What do you mean?"

"I mean he went after those guys, punching, kicking, clawing, biting. He was trying to kill them. I was so stunned it took me a minute to get up and start toward him. Before I got there, three more security goons rushed in, and they all grabbed Stu and fought him down to the floor. It took all of them to do it." Lloyd Bratz hesitated, chewing his lower lip as he remembered.

"What happened next is worse than anything I've seen in my life. I was in Nam, and I've seen some bad things."

Dena reached out and touched his hand. He looked at her gratefully.

"Stu never quit fighting them," he said. "He heaved and twisted and humped his body, throwing those five guys around the room like they was stuffed with straw. All the time he was screeching in this terrible unearthly voice. The skin on his face and his arms got all blotchy red and started to break open like blisters. I heard something crack like a rifle shot. It took me a minute to realize that Stu just broke his own leg. The five guys tried harder to hold him still, but the more they tried, the more Stu thrashed around. I could hear his bones cracking and snapping, and he never quit. He gave one last heave, and blood and gunk came pouring out of his mouth. That was the end of it. Stu was dead. He literally tore himself apart."

Dena looked down at the cigarette that had burned to the filter and gone out. She dropped it into the ashtray. The shaved patches under her arms were damp with sweat. She shivered.

"I'm sorry," Lloyd said. "You wanted to hear the story, and there's no way I could have prettied it up."

"I know." Dena was a little surprised that her voice sounded so calm. "What are you going to do now?"

"I don't know. Try to get help somewhere. Find Helen."

"What can I do?" Dena said.

"Get the word out, that's all."

"What word, Lloyd? What the hell is happening here?"

A blaze of light flashed across the bedroom curtain. Bratz peeled back the edge and looked out.

"They're here," he said. "Have you got a back door?"

Dena nodded. "This way."

She led him out to the kitchen. A cool draft of night air blew in through the window where he had entered. Someone knocked in the front.

Dena slid back the bolt and opened the door that led to the small backyard. Two men, big men, stood outside. Lloyd Bratz tensed for a moment as though he might charge; then his

80

body sagged. The men stepped forward. Each of them took one of his arms.

"Who are you?" Dena said. "Where are you taking him?"

"Plant security, ma'am," said one of the men. "Mr. Bratz is under quarantine."

"Wait just a minute—" Dena began.

She broke off at the sound of a footfall behind her and spun around. Another man in a Biotron security uniform stood in the doorway leading to the front of the house. Behind him was Dr. Frederich Kitzmiller.

"I am very sorry for this intrusion, Dr. Falkner," he said. "Have you been harmed?"

"Of course not," Dena said. "What's going on here?"

Kitzmiller nodded a signal to the men behind her, and Lloyd Bratz was taken out through the back door. He did not resist.

"It is a rather involved story," Kitzmiller said.

"Yes, I'm sure it is," Dena said. As the shock wore off, she was starting to get mad.

"Please make no judgments until you have heard my explanation," he said. "If you will come to my office in the morning, we will discuss the whole matter."

"Your *real* office?" Dena said.

Kitzmiller permitted himself a chilly smile. "My so-called friendly office. I am told that people feel more comfortable there."

"I'll be there," Dena told him.

"Thank you. Good night."

Dr. Kitzmiller and the men from security went away, and the night was again silent and dark. Dena lay in bed with the lamp on, smoking and thinking. It was not until an hour before dawn that she slept.

# Chapter 10

Dr. Kitzmiller was waiting when Dena walked into the office at nine on Thursday morning. He wore one of his standard gray suits and a muted tie. The smile he put on to greet her looked as though it hurt his face.

"Thank you for coming, Dena," he said. "Please sit down."

This is going to be serious, she thought. When Dr. Kitzmiller used your first name, he meant business. She eased into the chair facing him.

"I trust you slept well."

"No one else broke into my house after you left, if that's what you mean." She was not going to make it easy for him.

"I am sorry about that," Kitzmiller said. "A most unfortunate occurrence."

"You said you were going to explain some things to me," Dena reminded him.

"Just so." He arranged the single sheet of paper before him so the edges were perfectly squared with the desk. "I assume you and Mr. Bratz discussed some of these matters last night."

"We talked."

"May I ask what he told you?"

"Lloyd said there was an accident of some kind during a spraying test from the helicopter. He said you had him and Stu Anderson locked up in the infirmary and kept them there under guard."

Dena waited for some kind of reaction from Kitzmiller. When there was none, she went on.

"He told me Stu apparently contracted some kind of an illness that affected his mind. It finally killed him. Lloyd escaped from the infirmary, he said, but he was afraid the guards were close behind him. It turned out he was right."

Kitzmiller compressed his lips into a thin line. He shifted uncomfortably in the padded swivel chair. "And do you accept Mr. Bratz's version of what happened?"

"I have no reason to doubt him."

"No. Quite right."

"Is it true, doctor?"

"In essence, yes."

Dena stared at him. She realized that what she wanted to hear was a denial. "And what about Stu?"

"I am coming to that."

"He is not in Brazil."

"No."

"Where is he? What happened to him?"

"Please allow me to explain in an orderly manner. There are important details that Mr. Bratz omitted, or of which he is unaware."

"I'd like to hear them."

"There was, as he said, an unfortunate accident that occurred during a routine aerial dispersal test. The canister of purple dye, such as is normally used for these tests, was somehow exchanged for one containing an experimental pesticide that had been rejected and marked for disposal."

"Pesticide, you say."

"That is correct. Our products at Biotron include both experimental fertilizers and pesticides."

"I am aware of that, Dr. Kitzmiller."

"Yes, of course you are. As I say, there was an accidental switch of the canisters. Most regrettable."

"Criminally careless, I'd call it."

"Perhaps. But please remember we cannot afford to be emotional over such incidents. There is an ongoing investigation, and procedures will be adjusted to ensure that it does not happen again."

"Just how dangerous was this pesticide?" Dena asked.

"We don't know. I can tell you it was considered unsuitable for the use for which it was intended."

"And this was the stuff Lloyd Bratz and Stuart sprayed over the countryside?"

"Only a small amount was actually released," Kitzmiller said quickly. "And it was limited to our test area adjacent to an old county road that is no longer used."

"That road may have been somewhat more used than you think. The highway was under repair that week. The county road was used for a time as a detour."

"I am aware of that," Kitzmiller said. "The authorities are taking proper steps to forestall any problems."

"What authorities?"

Kitzmiller's shoulders rose and fell in a minimal shrug. "Whoever has the jurisdiction. I am not concerned with these matters."

Dena was determined not to let him off the hook. "You were going to tell me what happened to Stuart Anderson."

He glanced over toward the antique hat rack with the mirror, then turned back to face Dena. "A most unfortunate accident. Mr. Anderson succumbed."

"Succumbed? Then he *is* dead."

"I am afraid so."

Dena stared at him until the chilly blue eyes flicked away from her gaze. "Then Lloyd Bratz was telling the truth. He said Stu died violently. Tore himself apart was the way he put it."

"Your friend's perceptions may have been somewhat, ah, distorted by the effects of the pesticide. It is true that Stuart Anderson is dead, but Mr. Bratz's description of the violence might be exaggerated."

"Or it might not," Dena said.

"Since I was not present at the time of Mr. Anderson's death, I cannot say."

"Why did you give me that story about Stu being transferred to Rio?"

"I apologize for the deception. Because of the delicate nature of our work, we thought it best to withhold the facts of this unfortunate business until we are sure of them."

"Where have you taken Lloyd Bratz?"

"We are keeping him under observation."

"That sounds ominous."

"It is as much in his own interest as Biotron's," Kitzmiller said.

"Oh, sure." Dena's mouth twisted in a mirthless grin. "And his wife, Helen, is she under observation, too?"

"Of course not. The company recognizes its obligation to the families of its employees. Mrs. Bratz has been relocated until such time as she can join her husband."

"That's a lot of bureaucratic gobbledygook, doctor. I expected better from you."

Kitzmiller sighed heavily. "You're right. I am not comfortable with evasions. I wish I could take you completely into my confidence, but there are compelling reasons that prevent me from doing so. I hope you will accept that."

"I suppose I'll have to."

"I would like your promise that you will keep our discussion here confidential."

"I'm not sure I can give that promise," Dena said.

He leaned toward her across the desk. The ice-blue eyes glittered. "Dr. Falkner, there is more involved here than the lives of those two pilots. More than the welfare of Biotron. Much, much more. It is essential that what I have told you is not repeated to the wrong people."

Dena regarded him levelly. He was a cold, secret man, but she had a deep respect for him. She said, "I won't say anything, doctor. Not right away. And not unless something else happens."

"I will accept that," he said. "When the facts are known, I am sure you will agree that silence now is in the best interests of all concerned."

"Maybe," Dena said.

Kitzmiller leaned back in the chair and spread his hands flat on the desk, a signal that the interview was over. Dena rose and walked out without looking back.

When he was alone, Kitzmiller turned his frosty gaze on the mirror. He thumbed the switch of the intercom, and the filtered man's voice spoke.

"She will have to be watched."

Kitzmiller nodded and turned away. With no one to see, his face relaxed into a look of inexpressible sadness.

Corey Macklin caught himself whistling as he rode the creaky elevator up to the editorial offices on the third floor of the *Herald* building. He grinned. He could not remember whistling since he was a boy. It simply was not his style. That morning, however, was different. That morning was going to open a new chapter in his life.

He got out of the elevator and strode through the city room with a broad smile on his face. People who knew him turned and looked a second time. It was not like Corey to be drunk at that time of morning, but they could think of no other reason for the happy expression. He merely smiled all the brighter and waved at them.

There was a note waiting for him at his desk. *See Uhlander.* Well, fine. That was exactly what he planned to do. He hadn't expected the editor to be in that early, but since he was, so much the better. Corey gathered and sorted his notes on Stransky-Williamson. He was ready with a strong pitch for a trip to Seattle to get the Andrea Keith story. That would make the third leg of the triangle. There was no doubt in his mind that Porter Uhlander would go for it. How could he refuse?

The editor was seated with his hands folded over his paunch when Corey walked in. A powdering of Tums flecked the corners of his mouth. Corey started to pull the cracked leather chair over when he saw the small, dapper man seated back against the wall. The man had black, close-together eyes and a shrewd mouth.

Uhlander said, "Corey, this is Mr. Eichorn."

Corey straightened up. "How do you do?" It was the first time since he had worked at the *Herald* that the publisher had put in an appearance.

Nathan Eichorn stood up and came over to shake Corey's hand. The smaller man's grip was cool and moist and quickly released.

"Please sit down," Eichorn said. Corey lowered himself into the chair, and Eichorn pulled his own closer to the editor's desk. "I've been talking to Porter here about you. I don't know if he's mentioned it."

"He did say something about a column," Corey said carefully. He did not want to sound eager about accepting some two-bit promotion.

"That was in my mind a while back, but I've got something bigger in mind for you, Corey. Much bigger."

Uhlander belched audibly. Nathan Eichorn shot him an irritated look. Corey waited.

"Does the name *Scope* mean anything to you?" Eichorn asked.

"Wasn't that the name of a proposed weekly news magazine that was being kicked around a year ago?"

"That's right." The publisher bobbed his head up and down. "Only now it's well beyond the proposal stage. I hope to get the first issue on the stands by the first of the year."

"That's pretty ambitious," Corey said. He wondered where the conversation was leading.

"Yes, it is," Eichorn agreed, "but with the right people in the right positions, I know it can be done. I have most of the staff picked out, with one major exception." He paused dramatically. "I need a managing editor."

Corey felt a tightening around his diaphragm. "That's major, all right," he said.

"I want you to take the job."

Corey looked at Porter Uhlander for some hint of what was going on. The editor's expression told him nothing. He turned back to face Nathan Eichorn. "This is . . . kind of a surprise."

"I don't doubt it. But I've been watching your work, Corey, and I like what I've seen. I've also talked to people about you, naturally including Porter here. I've had some very good reports. Very good."

"I'm glad to hear that," Corey said. "It hasn't always been that way."

"I know all about your trouble in San Francisco," Eichorn said. "Ancient history. I have faith in what you can do now, and that's all that counts with me."

"Thank you." Corey wondered at the vehemence of the man. Was he overdoing it?

"Naturally, there are a lot of details you'll want to hear," Eichorn went on. "There will be time for that later. Right now I can tell you that you'll find the salary and benefits damn generous. And if there's anything that you want and you don't see, just ask for it. Heh-heh." The publisher's laugh was unconvincing.

"It certainly sounds like an interesting opportunity." A worm of doubt was beginning to gnaw at Corey.

"I'll tell you how interesting it is," Eichorn said, leaning forward. "It's an opportunity that a lot of men in our business would kill for. I understand you have no personal ties in Milwaukee. No family or anything."

"No family," Corey said.

"Good, good. Because I want you to get started on this right away. If we're going to put the book on the stands in January, we'll have to burn a lot of midnight oil. Can you be ready to leave for Houston in the next couple of days?"

"Houston?"

"That's where our headquarters are going to be. New York real estate has priced itself right out of sight. Publishers are leaving there as fast as their leases are up. Houston is a booming young city. Vigorous. Cosmopolitan. Ideal for starting a new book like ours. So how about it? Can I pencil you in at the top of the masthead?"

Corey took several seconds to formulate his answer. "It

certainly sounds like a challenging job, Mr. Eichorn. I have to admit I'm a little stunned at the suddenness of it all.''

"That's the way I do things, Corey. Quietly study the facts, come to a decision, and bang, make my move. I didn't get to be where I am by shilly-shallying.''

"Well, I certainly appreciate it," Corey said. "There's just one thing. I'm working on what I think is a very important story right now, and I'd like to wrap it up before moving on to anything else.''

"A story?" Eichorn snapped. "No story is important enough to delay putting *Scope* together. I'm sure Porter here can assign someone else.''

Uhlander came to life at the mention of his name. "Absolutely," he said. "No problem.''

"See, Corey, how quickly these things can be solved.''

"I don't know if Porter told you," Corey said, "but this story may have wide implications. I got onto it when a Milwaukee man named Stransky—''

"I know about the story," Eichorn said. Some of the camaraderie went out of his voice. "I read my newspapers.''

"But you don't know what I learned yesterday in New York. There was a cabdriver there who—''

"The story is *not* important." The publisher's tone left no room for discussion. "Forget it. I want to hear your decision on the *Scope* job.''

"Mr. Eichorn, this isn't something I can decide in a minute. Can I think it over?''

The atmosphere grew tense in the office as no one breathed for a long moment. Then Nathan Eichorn flashed a smile on and off. "Of course. Think it over, Corey. I'll be back in town Monday. We can have dinner then, and you can tell me which way you've decided to take your career. Acceptable?''

"Acceptable," Corey agreed.

Eichorn sprang to his feet, gave Corey another quick, cool handshake, and started out of the office. In the doorway he turned.

"One thing. Whatever you decide, we're not going any further with the Stransky story."

"I don't understand."

"I've told Porter here to dump it. It's not news, and I'm tired of reading about it. So don't let that influence your decision."

The publisher was gone before Corey could assimilate what he had just said. He looked questioningly at Uhlander.

The editor's stomach rumbled. He said, "You heard the word, Corey. If you've got the brains I think you have, you'll grab the magazine job."

"But the Stransky story. You haven't seen my New York notes."

"I don't care about your New York notes. The story is dead. And so are you if you make trouble for Mr. Eichorn. Think about it."

"I will," Corey said. He got up and jammed the folder of notes under his arm. "I'll think about it."

# Chapter 11

A full week had gone by since Hank Stransky came to his spectacular end in Vic's Old Milwaukee Tavern. In those seven days the world continued much as it always had, with events great and small fitting into the ever-changing pattern. Yet another threat of war had surfaced in the Middle East. A Cleveland left-hander just up from the minors had pitched a no-hitter against the Brewers. A popular singing star had died on stage in Melbourne of a drug overdose. And two members of Vic's bowling team had missed the Thursday night match with Eagle Auto Parts, claiming illness.

With all those possible subjects of conversation, topic one at the tavern remained Hank Stransky's Friday night freak-out. To judge by the number of people who now claimed to be eyewitnesses, Vic's Tavern would have to hold about the same-size crowd as County Stadium. Oddly, had anyone been taking a count, many of the regulars who had actually been on the scene would have been found missing on that Friday a week later.

Vic Metzger sat on a tall stool, uncharacteristically silent, behind the bar. He had felt crummy most of the week. After the slash he got from Stransky's beer bottle, there had been the two-day flu, or whatever it was. Now there was this headache.

He scowled out at the roistering drinkers. Who the fuck were they? He didn't know but a few of them. And why were they so goddam loud tonight? The argument at the pool table was more piercing than usual. And the jukebox boomed like summer thunder. He should never have gotten the damn thing fixed after Karl Gotch kicked it to pieces. He would have the fucker taken out the next day.

And the women. Females had never been barred from Vic's, but they weren't exactly encouraged, either. A few years back, the only women to come around would be some wife looking for a missing husband or a hooker who had gotten out of her territory. They were no problem. You just told the wives that the husbands hadn't been in all day, and you told the hookers to get lost. The good old days.

Now more and more of them were coming in, giggling and squealing in their shrill little voices and acting for all the world like they belonged there. It was the damned women's lib; that's what it was. This last week had been the worst. It seemed that ever since Hank Stransky did his death dance, the broads had been swarming into Vic's place. Bunch of ghouls. Ruined a good tavern is what they did.

"Come on, Vic, cheer up," somebody said. "You look like you lost your last friend."

Vic glared at him. Some fresh kid he didn't even know. College punk, most likely. Who the hell did he think he was?

"You want something to drink?" Vic said.

"Well, sure, gimme a beer. Jeez, you don't need to be so touchy."

"If you don't like it, go drink somewhere else."

Jesus, he hated these punks. Drink beer until they puke and think they're men. Between the punks and the women and the strangers, this place was going to hell fast.

"Hey, can we get some service over here?"

Vic looked down the bar at the jerk in the Heileman's T-shirt and the fat-faced woman with him.

"I think you had enough."

"What are you talkin' about? We just got here."

"Then you had it somewhere else. I don't serve drunks."

Vic let his hand drop below the bar. He touched the knurled butt of the revolver he had stashed there after the business with Stransky. It was a .357 Magnum and would put a real effective hole in anybody who tried to make trouble in there. This guy looked like a troublemaker. Vic halfway hoped he would start something.

"Come on, Barbara, let's get out of here," the guy said. "This yahoo is crazy."

Vic watched them walk across the floor and out the door. He let go of the Magnum reluctantly. He would just as soon have blown the two of them away.

Goddam this headache.

Norman Hastings sat cramped into a seat in the coach section as the jet waited on the runway at JFK to take off on the flight for Dallas–Fort Worth. It seemed as if they had been stuck there for hours while every other lousy plane in the world was given clearance to take off. When he got home, he would get off a letter to the president of the airline that would blister his ears. It was the last time they would get Norman Hastings into one of their tin cans.

You'd think that at least they could get the cabin pressure

right. It was playing bloody hell with his headache. He massaged his pounding temples and shivered.

"Would you like a blanket, sir?"

He looked up at the smiling face of the young man wearing a blazer with the airline's logo. Boy stewardesses. Flight attendants, they liked to call themselves now. Fags is what Norman Hastings called them.

"A blanket, sir?" the young man repeated.

"No. But you can get me a drink. Wild Turkey. With ice."

"The drink cart will come around after we're airborne," the young man said, grinning, as if he were doing Norman Hastings a great big favor.

"When the hell is that going to be, next Tuesday sometime?"

"We're next in line for take-off. It will only be a few minutes."

A few minutes . . . Oh, sure, Norman Hastings believed that. Like he believed in the tooth fairy. The pilot was probably boffing one of the girl stewardesses up in the cabin and would get the plane off right after he got his rocks off.

The smiley young man moved away up the aisle before Norman Hastings could tell him.

This headache was a bitch. He had the beginning of it when he was checking out of the hospital. He was not about to mention it, though, or they'd want to keep him there another week. As long as he had a medical plan that was paying the bills, the hospital would like to make him a permanent guest. Norman Hastings was not having any of that. He was mostly healed, except for a few raw spots that were still bandaged, and he was not going to spend five more minutes in that shithole city of New York than he had to.

The pitch of the idling engines changed as the plane taxied around into the take-off pattern. About fucking time. The flight attendant made a last trip down the aisle to see that everybody's seat belt was fastened. Norman Hastings unhooked his as soon as the fag had gone past.

His head was killing him.

The greaseball in the next seat looked over as though he wanted to talk. Norman Hastings glowered at him and turned toward the window. The last thing he wanted to do was to listen to a lot of pidgin Spanish gibberish from some bean eater.

The plane surged forward, gathering speed as it roared down the runway. The blue ground lights outside raced by in a stream that stabbed deep into the head of Norman Hastings. He could not remember anything that ever hurt as bad as this.

Jason and Nancy Dahlberg sat in the living room of their house in Seattle's Green Lake district and tried to concentrate on "Dallas." They had not missed an episode since the show went on the air. If they had to be out of the house, as they were the Friday before when they went out to dinner at the top of the Space Needle, they made sure to set the VCR so they could watch "Dallas" on tape when they got home.

Actually, the events at the restaurant the previous Friday had been so exciting that the Dahlbergs did not get around to viewing their tape until the next night. The sight of that girl running crazily through the tables waving a steak knife and screaming was something they would never forget. They hadn't known until it came out in the papers the next day that the young man she left bleeding to death at their table was her husband of only a few hours. Then the most horrible part had been watching in horrified fascination as the girl hurled herself out through the heavy plate-glass window. It took her three runs at the thick double pane to do it. The first time she hit it, only the inner pane cracked. Then, when she did manage to break through, she got hung up on one of the shards of glass and had to rip off one of her breasts before she could fall to the ground six hundred feet below.

During the week that followed, both of the Dahlbergs had been a little under the weather. And that night neither of them could concentrate on "Dallas." The sound was too loud, or the picture was blurred, or the color did not hold, or there was too much noise out in the street. They were both suffering from headaches that were growing rapidly worse.

"What's wrong with the set?" Nancy Dahlberg demanded of her husband.

"Nothing's wrong with it. You must be fooling with the controls while you watch those idiot daytime shows of yours."

"I never touch your precious controls. Besides, I don't have time to watch in the daytime. Don't you think I have anything to do around here?"

"You have plenty to do," he said. "That doesn't mean you *do* it."

"You son of a bitch," she said.

Jason Dahlberg turned in his chair to stare at his wife of twenty-one years. Language like that was simply not a part of her makeup. He decided that she had changed in many ways while he was not paying attention. What a sloppy cow she had become.

"What are you looking at?" she said.

"What the hell do you think, you cow?"

Nancy Dahlberg gripped the arms of her chair. She turned a bared-teeth look of hatred on her husband such as he had never seen on a human face. That was not all that was wrong with her face. Even as he watched, her skin grew blotchy and swollen. God, she was ugly.

Jason Dahlberg's headache threatened to explode inside his skull.

Vic Metzger groaned aloud, but nobody heard him. What with the racket those assholes were making at the pool table and the shit that was booming out of the jukebox, it was a wonder he could hear himself. No way anybody could stand it, especially not with the headache he had.

He planted both hands on the bar and leaned forward. "Hey! Shut the fuck up over there!"

The pool players looked at him in surprise. "What's the matter, Vic? You talkin' to us?"

"You goddam right I'm talking to you. Shut the fuck up or get out of here."

"You're kidding, aren't you?"

That did it. Vic groped blindly under the bar for the gun. He found it and levered himself over the top of the bar, heedless of the drinks he spilled in the process. Holding the revolver out in front of him, he marched toward the pool table.

"I warned you!"

He started shooting.

The screaming began.

Norman Hastings clamped his teeth together to keep from crying out. The agony inside his head had grown worse since take-off. Undoubtedly, the plane was not properly pressurized. Why didn't anybody else complain? When he had suggested to the fag boy stewardess that something was wrong, all he got was some standard bullshit about how the cabin pressure was exactly at its proper level. Then how come his head was exploding?

And the greaser in the aisle seat next to him, sitting there belching tacos and trying to start a conversation. Did he think Norman Hastings had nothing better to do than listen to some wetback's broken English?

He had tried to find some relief by plugging in a pair of those little plastic earphones and turning on some of that stupid music they play on airplanes. All that did was make his head hurt worse. Now he tore out the earplugs and threw them into the aisle.

He must have yelled, too, because everybody turned around to look at him. Stupid idiots. And here came the fag trotting down the aisle to hand him some more airline bullshit. Too much. It was too much!

Umberto Olivares had been uncomfortable with the guy in the next seat since they had got on the plane. The guy didn't want to talk, okay. Umberto generally liked to pass the time in conversation, but he didn't need this guy. For sure.

What ticked him off was the way the guy kept complaining to the kid flight attendant—real nasty and for no reason. When they finally got into the air, the guy kept holding onto his head and moaning and making faces as if something were tearing away little chunks of him. When the kid asked if he was sick, the guy just got nastier. If there had been an empty seat on the plane, Umberto would have gotten up and moved. Just his luck that every seat was taken.

Jesus, what was happening to the guy's face now?

Mike Endersbee had looked forward to the flight. He liked his job a lot, but he liked the Dallas flight best. Dallas was where Lisa lived. He had a week's layover after this flight, and they would have all that time just for themselves. The flight figured to be an easy one. But Mike had reckoned without the passenger in 43A, a Mr. Hastings.

The man had been trouble since the minute he boarded. Clearly, there was something wrong with him, but he had refused any kind of help. Mike had spoken to the captain about 43A, but as long as he was not causing a physical disturbance, there was nothing to be done. Now, at forty thousand feet somewhere over Arkansas, it looked as though the physical disturbance was starting.

The man in 43B, a Mr. Olivares, let out a yell as 43A started to climb over him. Mike hurried down the aisle but slowed suddenly when he saw what was happening to Mr. Hastings's face. The man was pounding crazily at his seat mate as he fought his way out into the aisle. Mike stepped in front of him but was thrown to the deck by a wild backhand blow.

Screaming incoherently, Norman Hastings ran up the aisle, setting off a panic among the passengers, many of whom had been dozing. He reached the emergency exit, threw aside the people who were sitting in the adjacent seats, and began clawing at the release lever.

Mike was not worried about Hastings forcing the door

open; there was a fail-safe interlock to prevent that when the plane was airborne. However, the man was clearly insane and quite likely to do harm to himself and other passengers. Until he got help from up front, it was Mike's responsibility to restrain him. He ran forward and seized the man's shoulder.

Norman Hastings whirled toward him, his face a mass of angry red boils. Before Mike could speak, Hastings smashed him with a fist, breaking his nose and knocking him across the aisle. He fell back against the people sitting over there who were trying to scramble out of the way. As he struggled to regain his feet, Mike saw the crazed man use unbelievable strength and pull loose the safety lever on the emergency door.

The sound was like an explosion. There was a sudden rush of icy wind. Norman Hastings disappeared as though snatched through the gaping doorway by a giant hand. Mike Endersbee's last impressions were of the rush of pillows, carry-on bags, blankets, trays, papers, and human bodies flying out through the opening into the night sky. Then his fingers were torn loose from the metal seat braces he had been holding on to. His body was banged across the empty seat, an ankle shattered against the edge of the open door, and the night sucked him out.

It was difficult to say which one of them attacked first. Jason and Nancy Dahlberg, quiet, seemingly happy, married twenty-one years, came up out of their chairs at the same instant and leaped at each other. They fell to the floor ripping with fingers and teeth at any part of the other's flesh they could reach until they writhed together on a carpet that was soggy with their mingled blood.

On the flickering television screen, J. R. Ewing went about his weekly villainy with no one there to watch.

Vic Metzger, Norman Hastings, and the Dahlbergs were not the only ones to go suddenly, violently berserk that night. Beginning early Friday evening and continuing into Saturday morning, more than a score of normal-seeming citizens exploded into mindless mayhem. The toll of dead and injured mounted steadily. As the reports flashed over the nation's news wires, a terrible pattern began to emerge.

# Chapter 12

Hank Stransky whirled and danced a wild gavotte while his flesh blotched and bubbled and popped and oozed. He was joined by a gyrating middle-aged black man and a slim young girl. Their faces were grinning masks of suppurating boils. They cavorted in an ever-closing circle around a helpless Corey Macklin.

As the wild dancing threesome squeezed in on him, Corey tried to dash between them to freedom, but one or another of them always moved to block him. He struck out at them with his hands, but his blows found nothing solid. Closer and closer they danced, stealing his breath, suffocating him.

Corey fell to the spongy floor, his strength suddenly drained. He tried to rise, but his legs folded beneath him like loaves of soft dough. The three dancers closed in and began to rain blows on his unprotected head.

*Bam!* Stransky hit him.

*Bam!* DuBois Williamson.

*Bam!* Andrea Keith.

*Bam!*

Corey groaned. He fought his way out of the tangled bedclothes. His mouth tasted like old pennies. He blinked at the light streaming through the crack between his window blind and the edge of the frame.

*Bam!*

Gradually, he recognized where the sound was coming from. Who the hell would be hammering at his door at this hour?

"Minute!" he yelled. He swung his feet out of the bed and levered himself to a sitting position. His head hurt. His stomach squirmed.

Brandy. He'd been drinking brandy the night before. Cheap, no-name brandy at some joint he'd never been in before. He should have known better. It served him right. Brandy and he had never been great friends. There was no excuse except that it had seemed like the thing to do at the time.

*Bam!*

"All *right*!" Corey stood up. He caught a glimpse of himself in the mirror over his dresser and winced. He looked just about as bad as he felt. "I'm coming."

After the scene the previous day with Nathan Eichorn, he had needed a drink. He did not want to go to Vic's. Vic's had bad vibes these days. So he went somewhere else where he didn't know anybody. Drank brandy like a damn fool. Came home and had ugly dreams. Now he felt like slow death, and some fool was battering at his door. It promised to be one rotten Saturday.

Without bothering to pull anything on over his underwear, Corey shuffled across the one-room apartment to the door and opened it.

A cloud of cigarette smoke rolled into the room. Doc Ingersoll followed it in. "You look terrible," he said.

"You woke me up just to tell me that at—at—What time is it, anyway?"

"Seven-thirty."

"In the morning?"

"In the morning."

"Balls."

Ingersoll took the crimped cigarette from his mouth, holding it between thumb and forefinger. "You haven't been watching TV or listening to the radio?"

"Hell, no. I've been sleeping. Trying to."

"There have been some developments I think you ought to know about."

"Developments?" Corey's head began to clear.

"You remember those three cases you were asking me about a few days ago? The three citizens who freaked out violently for no apparent reason?"

"Hell, yes. I remember them. I was just dreaming about them. What developments?"

"It seems like the same thing has been happening to a dozen or so other people starting sometime last night."

Corey was wide awake now. His head was clear, his stomach tense but quiet. "The hell you say."

"The hell I do not."

"Any clue as to what's causing it?"

"Nobody's speculated so far. I thought you might want to come down to the plant and take a look at what's coming in on the wires."

"You're damn right I would. Let me splash some water on my face and I'll be right with you."

Thirty minutes later they sat across the table from each other in the *Herald*'s wire-service room. Before them were torn-off sheets of copy from AP, UPI, and Tri-State News Service.

The big story was the spectacular tragedy on board the Dallas-bound airliner out of New York. A passenger—name withheld pending notification of next of kin—had gone berserk and somehow ripped open one of the emergency-exit doors in the coach section. The unnamed passenger and five other people, including a member of the crew, had been sucked out the door before it was blocked by a torn-off panel from an overhead luggage compartment. The pilot had managed to land in Little Rock without further damage or loss of life. Details were to follow.

Corey quickly scanned the airliner story, then shoved it aside to read the local account of the second tragedy in a week at Vic's Old Milwaukee Tavern. Bartender Vic Metzger apparently attacked two or more customers with a revolver. The toll was three dead and two wounded by gunfire; a dozen others had been hurt in the melee. Metzger was subdued only after he had emptied the gun and police reinforcements had arrived. No motive for the attack was known.

Corey set the pages aside gently. He felt a chill along his spine that was not entirely unpleasant. After a moment he picked up more of the wire copy and went on reading.

In Seattle there had been a number of violent occurrences. The people involved were, for the most part, from respected backgrounds. A particularly grisly story involved an administrator of the University of Washington and his wife who apparently killed each other with their bare hands in their own living room.

Milwaukee was hard hit, especially in the neighborhood around Vic's Tavern. Although none of the stories assumed a connection, several pointed out that among those who had freaked out the previous night were a number of people who had been present when Hank Stransky died.

Some of the names Corey recognized. They were men he had laughed with, drunk beer with, and argued sports with. Two of them had bowled on the tavern team. One had gone to pieces while digging in the garden and had attacked neighbors with a shovel. The other had started screaming suddenly at the dinner table. While his horrified family watched, he picked up his two-year-old daughter and threw her against the wall. The man was being held in the violent ward of the Milwaukee county jail. The little girl was in critical condition, with possible brain damage.

"Damn, damn, damn!" Corey said under his breath.

"Pretty bad," Doc Ingersoll agreed.

Corey rose and started for the city room. "I've got to get busy."

Doc Ingersoll glanced down at the scattered wire copy. "Somebody you know?"

"What? Oh, yeah, slightly."

"Sorry," Doc said. "You going out to see them?"

"Later," Corey said. "I've got to get on the phone now."

Ingersoll took a deep drag and coughed for several seconds. "I presume you're not calling to comfort the widows and orphans."

Corey threw a look back over his shoulder. "You want to be Mother Teresa, you go ahead. I'm a working reporter, and this is a story, Doc. This is a capital-S story, and it's right in my lap."

The older reporter watched through a curtain of smoke from his smoldering butt as Corey hurried out.

At his desk in the city room, Corey matched the names of the victims that were mentioned in the wire stories against the telephone book and came up with a list of numbers. He also noted the names of the hospitals where they were taken and added the police and any government agency he thought might be involved. When he was through, he had a pageful of telephone numbers.

He started with the families and friends of the victims. Few of them were willing to talk to the press, but those who were told chillingly similar stories. The victims had shown no abnormal traits in the past. They were usually healthy and in the prime of life. Only during the past week had they displayed any symptoms of illness. Those included a rash or mild infection of some sore on the skin, a brief flulike period of low fever and aching joints, and finally the headache.

Corey scribbled rapid notes as he talked, coaxing answers out of bewildered, grief-stricken people. All part of the job, he reminded himself. At least he wasn't jamming a microphone into their faces.

When he came to a break in his list, he dashed back to the wire room for late input and took a few minutes to plot the reported cases on a map of the United States. It was clear that the attacks were clustered around three population centers—Milwaukee, New York, and Seattle. There were stories of scattered incidents in other parts of the country, including the wild man on the airliner. That one, however,

103

could be counted as New York, since that was the originating point of the flight.

Next Corey went after the hospitals. From them he got little information. Victims who were not killed during their violent seizure had to be put under restraints. No, the patients were not in any condition to be interviewed. No, the hospital authorities were not prepared to offer any theories on what had happened to the people. No, they did not want to talk to him later.

Probably waiting until a camera crew showed up so they could be on television, Corey thought irritably.

Without much hope, he went on to the last batch of numbers on his list—the various governmental health agencies. He got only brusque negatives from the city, county, and state. Finally, he was put through to a U.S. assistant secretary of Health and Human Services in Washington.

"Yes, I've heard the reports," the assistant secretary told Corey when the connection was finally made.

"I'd like your comment," Corey said.

"I don't see that there's anything to comment on at this point in time."

"We *are* talking about the same thing, aren't we? The sudden violent attacks on people here in Milwaukee and on both coasts?"

"Well, now, we're not convinced that there is anything statistically abnormal in the situation."

"I have the reports right here in front of me," Corey said, fighting to control his rising irritation. "There are at least twenty reported cases so far, and more coming in every hour."

"Twenty hardly seems to be excessive. Over any given twenty-four-hour period I can show you figures that would suggest a raging epidemic of anything from measles to bone cancer."

"We're not talking measles here," Corey said. "We're talking about perfectly healthy people who suddenly go crazy. Do you know how many dead there are?"

"I've heard reports. Unconfirmed, I hasten to add."

"You said epidemic a minute ago. Are you willing to call this an epidemic?"

"Nothing of the sort," the assistant secretary said quickly. "I was merely using the analogy to make my point."

"Which is?"

"That the data we have is insufficient basis for any conclusions."

"At this point in time," Corey said sarcastically.

"Exactly," said the assistant secretary, missing the inflection.

"How many of these violent seizures will it take before the government admits that something unusual is happening?"

"That's a speculative question that I can hardly be expected to answer."

"Then the Department of Health and Human Services has an official 'no comment'?"

"I have not been appointed spokesperson for the department."

"My call was put through to you."

"I happened to be in my office when your call came in. My field is personnel administration."

"All right, no official quotes. Do you have any private theories?"

"I can think of one possibility. Mass hysteria."

"You're not serious."

"Of course I'm serious. Do you remember a couple of years ago when we had the big AIDS panic?"

"As I recall, quite a few of those people who thought they had AIDS really did," Corey said.

"My point is that a whole lot more people did not. Here we have a few isolated cases of aberrant behavior in scattered sections of the country. You people of the media scramble to report them, and immediately healthy individuals everywhere start feeling the symptoms. It's called the medical students' syndrome. Show them an exotic set of symptoms and immediately a good percentage will start suffering them. Mass hypochondria, if you like.''

"Is that for publication?"

"Absolutely not." The suave tone of the assistant secretary wavered. "You asked me for a private opinion, and that's it. As far as the Department of Health and Human Services is concerned, the situation has not officially been brought to our attention."

"Goddamit, that's what I'm trying to do," Corey yelled into the phone. "If you're not going to talk to me, then put on somebody who will."

"I'll give you back to the switchboard," said the assistant secretary. "They'll connect you with our chief of public relations."

"Shit!" Corey banged the telephone back into the cradle and sat glaring at it like some loathsome animal.

"How's it shaping up?" Doc Ingersoll wheeled a wooden swivel chair over next to Corey's desk and dropped into it. He laid down another sheaf of wire copy, scattering a light coating of cigarette ash as he did so.

"Nobody will admit anything," Corey said. "The victims who are still alive are in no condition to talk. Relatives and friends are bewildered. Hospital officials aren't saying anything. The Department of Health and Human Services does not admit that a problem exists."

"Sounds like you're on to something."

"Bet your ass I am." Corey consulted his notes. "For some reason, people are going suddenly, violently insane. The only link I have so far is geographical. The victims are adults of both sexes, and all races, as near as I can make out."

"Not quite true," said Ingersoll.

"What do you mean?"

The gaunt reporter leafed through the sheets he had brought with him, pulled out a page of AP copy, and handed it to Corey.

The story had a Long Island dateline. It told of an eight-year-old boy who was being kept in bed, suffering severe headaches. Suddenly and without warning, the child had run screaming into his parents' bedroom and attacked his mother. By the time the father, with the help of several neighbors, could pull the child off, the woman had been blinded.

The boy was taken to a nearby hospital, where powerful sedatives proved ineffective. He was subsequently placed in restraints "for his own safety." Doctors could offer no explanation for the attack. The father reported that the family had witnessed a berserk cabdriver plow into a crowd of pedestrians a week earlier, but the incident had not seemed to affect the boy.

Corey looked up at Doc Ingersoll. "Kids, too."

"So it would appear."

Corey yanked the plastic dust cover off his typewriter. "Let me know if anything else comes in."

"Will do." Ingersoll pushed himself up out of the chair, coughed, and headed back toward the wire-service room.

After a quick check of his notes Corey spun a sheet of copy paper into the machine and began to type. He was working on the third page when he heard a gurgling sound close to his ear. He turned his head and saw the overhanging stomach of Porter Uhlander.

"Didn't expect to see you here so early, Corey," the editor said.

"Why not? It's a working day."

"You aren't due in until noon."

"Doc Ingersoll got hold of me early," Corey said without breaking the rhythm of his typing.

"Ingersoll?"

Corey nodded. He wished the man would go away and let him work.

"I, uh, was wondering if you'd decided about the Houston job."

The clatter of the machine stopped. Corey looked up into the jowly face of the editor. "Houston? Are you kidding?"

"I'm not trying to rush you, Corey, but I'll have to make some staff changes and—"

"Porter, don't you know what's happening?"

"I don't follow you."

"The Stransky story. My story. It's blowing up into something really big, and I'm sitting right on top of it."

Uhlander looked pained. "Mr. Eichorn specifically said he didn't want any more play of the Stransky thing."

Corey grabbed a handful of wire copy and shoved it at the editor. "For Christ's sake, read this."

Uhlander took the sheets reluctantly and read for about fifteen seconds. "Well, um, it does look like there may be something here."

"May be? *May be?* Porter, this story could make me. Make the *Herald.* By tomorrow it will be in every sheet in the country. And on TV. But we'll own it, because we got it first. The rest of the world will come to the *Herald* to find out what's going on. How does that grab you?"

"Don't you think you're making more of this than it is?"

"If I am, it will be forgotten in a week. But if I'm right, and this thing grows— Porter, I've been waiting a long time for this. Don't try to slow me down."

The editor returned the pages of wire copy to Corey's desk. "Before I make any commitments, I want to talk to Mr. Eichorn about it."

"You do that," Corey said, resuming his attack on the typewriter. "In the meantime, you might get makeup to leave me a nice hole on page one."

Porter Uhlander turned and walked heavily toward his office. His stomach rumbled.

# Chapter 13

Dena Falkner spent an uneasy weekend. By Friday she was having second thoughts about her promise to Dr. Kitzmiller that she would say nothing about the accidental spraying from the Biotron helicopter and about what happened to Stuart Anderson. Kitzmiller's forceful personality had blunted the resolve she had built up when she went in to see him, but once out of his aura, her doubts grew.

The night visit of Lloyd Bratz to her house was fresh in her memory. She could not forget the haunted look in his eyes or the appalling story he told of the events in the Biotron infirmary.

Hoping to give her nerves a rest, Dena left the office early Friday and drove north to Shawano Lake where she rented a cabin. There, with no radio and no newspaper, she tried to tune herself into nature and forget for a little while the world's man-made troubles. Early Saturday morning, and again on Sunday, she had rowed out onto the lake and drifted there, watching the fishermen in the other boats.

Always in the past a mini-vacation like that at the lake had refreshed her. This time it did not work. By Sunday evening her nerves were strung tighter than ever.

Now, Monday morning, she walked into her office at the Biotron plant with a gnawing premonition that bad news awaited her. Things began to go wrong almost immediately.

The first thing she noticed was that the agenda for the Monday meeting was not on her desk. The Monday meeting was a ritual at Biotron, with representatives from all operational departments taking part. The agenda was always waiting on the desks of the participants when they came in on Monday. Not this Monday.

The point was not that the meeting was so vitally important. Seldom was anything discussed that could not be handled in the normal course of daily business, but the meeting gave a certain structure to the week, and it allowed the participants to clear away the weekend's cobwebs before tackling new problems.

Dena picked up the phone to call Jimmy Lohnes, the division PR man who usually brightened the meetings with his sardonic humor. She punched out Jimmy's three-digit extension and heard nothing but the crackle of static for a full fifteen seconds before there was a click and an unfamiliar voice answered.

"Switchboard."

"I was trying to get five-three-one."

"Sorry, but there's a glitch in the PBX, and we have to route the calls manually. It *would* happen on the day we're shorthanded for technicians."

"Isn't that always the way," Dena commented.

"Murphy's law. What was that number again?"

"Five-three-one."

The instrument buzzed in her ear, and the voice of Jimmy's secretary answered.

"Mr. Lohnes's office."

"Hi, Adele, is Jimmy in yet?"

"Oh, hi, Dena. No, he called in sick this morning. Flu or something. Anything I can answer for you?"

"I just wondered if he got his meeting agenda. Mine wasn't delivered."

"Uh-uh," said the secretary. "The messenger hasn't been around yet. Some problem in the mail room, I guess."

"Typical Monday. Thanks, Adele."

Dena hung up and doodled aimlessly on her calendar pad. No big deal. They would have the meeting without an agenda; that was all. It wouldn't matter much, but the small break in routine troubled her for some reason she could not name. It was like an itch that was just out of her reach.

Carol Denker, with whom Dena shared the small office, had not come in yet. Carol was never late. It was yet another deviation from the normal day. As the junior in their section, Carol did not have to attend the meetings, but she and Dena habitually took coffee breaks together, swapping complaints about the quality of the company coffee and anything else that popped into their heads. Now Dena would have to have her first cup of the morning alone. It was one more small annoyance.

She walked out of her office and through the open bay to the coffee machine. She dropped in her quarter and walked back with the plastic cup of steaming brew. She thought the office seemed unusually quiet. The muted *jiggety-jiggety* of the Selectric typewriters was softer than usual, and the voices of the young Biotron employees who sat out in the bay were subdued.

Dena went back in and sat down at her desk. She sipped gingerly at the hot coffee and idly scanned the desks outside through her glass partition. She frowned, put down the plastic coffee cup, and leaned forward.

No wonder it was quieter that day. There were a lot of people missing out there. One desk of four was unoccupied.

A chilling thought hit her. She picked up the phone and punched out the extension for personnel. After another delay through the manual switchboard, she heard Personnel Manager Ian McCollough answer the phone himself.

"Hello, McCollough here."

"Hi. Dena Falkner."

"Hi. How are you? Excuse the confusion, but I'm all alone here. Secretary and receptionist both out sick. Must be something going around."

"That's what I was wondering. Are there a lot of people out today?"

"About twenty-five to thirty percent absenteeism," McCollough said. "Every department's understaffed. Have you heard if we're having the Monday meeting?"

"I don't know," Dena said. "Did you get your agenda?"

"Negative. I'll have to miss it anyway, with no one to answer the phone here. Look, I've got to go. All my lines are flashing."

Dena slowly hung up the instrument. Now she was getting worried. The unusual absenteeism that morning might be a coincidence, but she did not think so. It was time for another talk with Dr. Kitzmiller. This time she would not let him put her off the track.

She picked up the phone once more, listened to sixty seconds of crackles and beeps, and dropped it back into the cradle. It would be better handled in person, anyway. She walked out of her cubicle and left the building, heading for Kitzmiller's office. Not the "friendly" office but the spartan quarters back by the laboratories, where he did his real work.

A security guard sat at the receptionist's desk outside the unmarked office door. He stood up when Dena approached and moved casually between her and the closed door.

"Can I help you?"

"I'd like to see Dr. Kitzmiller."

"Sorry, the doctor's not available."

"Would you tell him I'm here, please? Dr. Dena Falkner."

"Sorry, Dr. K was very explicit. He's not available to anybody."

Dena looked at the closed door, then back at the impassive guard. "He *is* in there?"

"Oh, yes. Locked up by himself. No interruptions, he says. Absolutely. If you want to leave a message, I'll give it to him when he comes up for air."

Dena chewed her lip. "Where's the receptionist who usually sits here?"

"Search me. Somebody said she called in sick. You want me to tell Dr. K anything?"

"No," Dena said. "No, never mind."

She stopped back in her own office long enough to lock

112

up her desk; then she left the building and headed for the parking lot.

Automatically, she reached into the glove box but found no cigarettes. She remembered then that as part of her weekend rest cure at the lake she had thrown out the package, deciding it was a good time to quit for good. Like hell it was.

She drove to the Rexall store in Wheeler and bought a carton of Carltons. Very low in tars, she told herself. Next best thing to not smoking. She would get serious about giving them up when things had settled down a bit.

As she took the carton from the clerk, her eye fell on the newspapers stacked on the counter. A small headline at the bottom of the *Herald*'s page one leaped out at her:

### Mysterious Seizures Strike Coast to Coast

Dena took a paper from the top of the stack and noted that the reporter's name was Corey Macklin. She paid for the newspaper and the cigarettes and carried them out to her car. There she lit a Carlton, inhaled gratefully, and read the story. When she had finished, she read it again, then tucked the newspaper down between the seats and started the car. She swung out onto the highway and, after a stop at her house to pack a small bag, headed for Milwaukee.

While most of the operations in the offices of the Milwaukee *Herald* had returned to their normal apathetic pace, Corey Macklin and Doc Ingersoll formed an island of excited activity. Corey sat in shirt-sleeves at his desk, typing furiously as he wrote and rewrote his story to fit the late reports Doc was bringing in from the wire services. He was also busy fielding telephone calls from all over the country. With his original by-lined story on Hank Stransky, then the follow-ups, Corey had become the "authority" on the mysterious wave of violent seizures. He put off most of the callers with vague answers. It was his story, and he was not about to share it.

City Editor Porter Uhlander came out of his office once and started toward Corey's desk. When he saw all the activity there, he changed his mind and retreated, massaging his stomach.

"Porter looks more dyspeptic than usual this morning," Doc Ingersoll observed through a cloud of cigarette smoke.

"It's the story," Corey said. "He was supposed to kill it, but it wouldn't die."

"Like Dracula," Doc said.

"Yeah. What's the total number of cases now?"

"I make it thirty-four verified plus uncounted rumors. There's still a few authentic reports coming in, but the big freak-out seems to have been Friday."

"I wonder if thirty-four is enough for the Department of Health and Human whatever-it-is to take notice," Corey said.

"They'll probably wait until the victims form a political action committee," said Doc.

Corey smoothed out on his desk a map of the United States he had bought on his way into the office. With a red felt-tip pen, he made a dot at the location of each of the new reported cases of violent seizure. Three areas of the map were speckled with the red dots—New York, Milwaukee, and Seattle—but there were isolated incidents in Connecticut, Nevada, Oregon, and Chicago.

"You're probably right," Corey said, "but I'd hate to think our entire government is run by assholes like the one I talked to in Washington."

"When you've been around as long as I have," Doc told him, "you'll learn that the asshole factor in government cannot be overestimated."

One of the high school girls who worked at the *Herald* during the summer approached the desk.

"Mr. Macklin?"

"Yeah?"

"There's a lady outside asking for you."

"Asking what?"

"She wants to see you."

114

"Get her name and number."

The girl hesitated. "She seemed, well, kind of upset."

"I'm upset, too. The whole world's upset. Tell her I'll get back to her."

The girl seemed about to say more, but Doc Ingersoll gave her a tiny shake of the head and she went away.

"Probably wants us to send somebody to cover her garden club," Corey said, intent on the map. "You say the new outbreaks are slowing down?"

"So it seems. We had twenty Friday and Friday night, seven Saturday, five Sunday, and just two so far today."

Corey frowned. "Damn. I kind of hate to see our epidemic peter out."

"You would have loved the black plague," Doc said.

Corey looked at him. "What the hell, I'm not killing these people. I'm just writing the story."

"It's a dirty job, but somebody's got to do it," Doc intoned.

The high school girl returned. "Uh, the lady says it's really important."

"I'll bet," Corey said. "Tell her I'm tied up interviewing the pope."

"She says she's a doctor of biology or chemistry or something like that. From Biotron up by Appleton, you know."

"Oh?" Corey looked up, interested for the first time.

"She says it's about the people who've been going ape. The ones you been writing about."

"Tell her I'll be out in a minute."

When the girl had gone, Corey spoke to Ingersoll. "Biotron—isn't that a fertilizer plant?"

"Also pesticides. It's a division of Global Industries."

"Government contracts?" Corey asked.

"I suppose. Smell something?"

"I'm not sure. Let's go talk to the lady."


His years as a reporter had taught Corey the error of forming preconceived pictures of people he had not met, but he was not prepared for Dr. Dena Falkner. Somehow the

115

combination of chemistry and biology gave him a mental image of an angular woman with a sharp nose, rimless glasses, and sensible shoes. What he found waiting rather impatiently in the outer office was an athletic-looking young woman with great legs, a good chest, and that powerful combination of caramel-blonde hair and brown eyes.

"I'm Corey Macklin," he said, feeling the pull of the liquid brown eyes. "And this is Doc Ingersoll."

"I'm Dena Falkner."

She extended a slim hand and shook with each of them in turn. Corey found her grip firm and cool.

"I've read your stories on the strange seizures people have been having," she said.

"Yes?"

She drew a deep breath and plunged in. "I think it may have all started with an accident at the Biotron facility just over two weeks ago."

Corey stared at her as though his oyster stew had just yielded up a pearl. He said, "Let's find an office where we can talk."

They found an unused conference room and took seats at the table, Corey and Doc Ingersoll on one side, Dena on the other. Corey made scribbled notes as Dena related what she knew of the events at Biotron, and Doc asked pertinent questions. She told of her concern over the sudden disappearance of Stuart Anderson and Dr. Kitzmiller's subsequent evasive response to her questions. She told them about the link between Andrea Olson Keith, the first Seattle victim, and the area sprayed by the Biotron helicopter. Corey added what he knew of Hank Stransky and DuBois Williamson, placing them both in the same area at roughly the same time.

Dena concluded with the nighttime visit of Lloyd Bratz. She repeated what he told her of Stuart's fate in the Biotron infirmary and Dr. Kitzmiller's request for silence.

"I'm glad you decided to talk after all," Corey said.

"As a matter of fact, it was sort of decided for me. This morning there were an unusual number of people missing at the plant. Called in sick, I was told. When I went to Dr. Kitzmiller to ask about it, he suddenly became unavailable. Something is going on, and when I saw your name on a story about the seizures across the country, I thought this might be the place to start checking."

Doc asked, "Do you think there's a connection between the sick calls at Biotron and the botched spraying job?"

"There might be. It seemed worth looking into."

Corey spread out his notes out on the table along with the map of the United States. The three of them sat in silence for a minute, studying the papers. They all looked up at the same time.

Corey said, "Doc, does this sound to you like it sounds to me?"

Ingersoll lit a fresh cigarette from the butt of his last. He inhaled, coughed, and wiped a hand over his face. "What it sounds like is that Biotron sprayed some kind of poison into the air that infected three people who happened to be on the road driving by, or in Hank Stransky's case, working on a construction job. Three people plus one copter pilot, according to Dena's story. Those people suffered this crazy seizure just about a week after their exposure. They, in turn, infected an unknown number of others who were stricken about a week after the original three victims."

"And if those people each infected others," Corey said, "the possibilities are staggering. If this doesn't sound like an epidemic, I'm Rona Barrett."

"Wait a minute," Dena said. "There were other people exposed at the same time. Lloyd Bratz was in the helicopter with Stu. There must have been other men working with Hank Stransky. Andrea Keith was in a car with her grandfather, and the New York man, Williamson, was driving with his wife. As far as we know, the others weren't affected. Why?"

Corey turned to Ingersoll. "Doc?"

"Search me. If it *was* something sprayed into the air at Biotron that caused the initial infection, it just means some people are susceptible and some aren't. Why, I can't tell you.''

"Where do we go from here?" Dena said.

Corey began gathering up his notes. "I don't know about you, but I'm going back to my desk to rewrite this story. I've got something now that even Nathan Eichorn will have to admit is good for a page-one series.''

"Just a minute," Dena said.

Corey looked up, surprised by the sharpness in her tone.

"Is that all this means to you . . . a news story?"

"Well, of course I know people are dying and all that, but my job is to tell the public about it.''

"And maybe build your reputation at the same time?"

"Look, lady, I'm a reporter. This is the way I make my living.''

"Well, I didn't come here just to give you a page-one by-line. I came because I thought you might help me get to the bottom of this and just possibly save a few lives.''

"I'm all for saving lives," Corey said, "but I don't know what you expect me to do.''

"You could come with me to the authorities for a start.''

"What authorities? The police? The first thing they're going to ask is what crime has been committed.''

"There are other agencies . . . The government," she said a little doubtfully.

"Like the Department of Health and Human Services? Let me tell you the response I got from those fine civil servants.''

When he finished relating his conversation with the Washington bureaucrat, Dena looked crestfallen.

"There must be somebody," she said.

Doc Ingersoll spoke up. "What about the EPA?"

"You mean the people who keep our rivers safe for the snail darter?" Corey said.

"Why not? It sounds to me like this falls under the category of environmental protection.''

"It's worth a try," Dena said.

Corey sighed. "Okay, but I don't hold out a lot of hope

118

for government agencies." He checked his watch. "It's too late to get any action out of them today. Are you going to be in town tomorrow?"

"I'll stay over if it will help."

"I'm not going to tackle another bureaucrat by myself," Corey said. "Your degrees may swing a little weight."

"I'll meet you here at eight," Dena said.

"That's a tad early."

"I don't think we ought to waste any more time, do you?"

"Right. Eight o'clock it is."

Dena nodded to the two men and left the office.

Corey looked after her. "She's bossy, but she's cute." He began gathering up his notes.

"Are you going to do that rewrite?" Doc asked.

Corey thought a moment.. "Maybe I'll hold off until we talk to the EPA tomorrow. It's not likely, but they just might give me a new angle."

# Chapter 14

The name of the motel was the Beddie-Bye. That was the kind of thing that normally made Dena Falkner want to throw up. That night she did not give a damn. She had not, as a matter of fact, even noticed the name. The red *Vacancy* sign was lit, and that was all she cared about.

Her room had the usual motel furnishings: queen-size bed, bureau, writing desk with no stationery, bathroom with glasses in waxed Baggies, toilet with a "sanitary" paper strip across the seat, bolted-down television set. On the wall, also bolted, were prints of peaceful landscapes that existed only in the imagination of the uncredited artist.

Dena dropped her bag on the aluminum-tube luggage rack and left the motel to find something to eat. There was a coffee shop adjoining the office, but by that time Dena was aware of the name and was not going to eat in anything called Beddie-Bye.

She drove a mile to a place called Harvey's that looked less offensive than the other eateries along the highway. At least there were no pickup trucks in the parking lot. Inside, it proved to be quiet and unpretentious, with real woodwork and subdued lighting. Dena ordered prime rib and a half bottle of California Burgundy. She was grateful when the waitress left her alone to finish the meal in her own time and think about what she was going to do the next day.

It was still early when she left the restaurant, but the excitement of the day and the half bottle of wine had made her sleepy. She paid the bill with her American Express card and drove back to the motel. Back in her room she got out of her clothes, took a shower, put on a pair of shorty pajamas, and lay down in the bed. Instantly, she was wide awake.

She snapped on the television set but found that it was afflicted with vertical roll. After watching a succession of Merv Griffins slide up and off the top of the screen, she snapped off the set and lit a Carlton. She wished she had bought a paperback to read. A mystery or a good horror story. The only reading material in the hotel room was the Gideon Bible, and Dena was not in the mood for that.

She lay back on the bed smoking, listening to the muffled sounds of traffic outside on the highway. She felt herself sinking into one of those depressed what-am-I-doing-here moods. Definitely counterproductive.

To snap herself out of it, Dena examined her motives in coming to Milwaukee specifically to see Corey Macklin. He was really not a very likable man. She had no way of knowing how capable he was other than to recognize that he was the only one who early on seemed to realize the importance of what happened to Hank Stransky and the others. Even so,

120

Dena suspected him of using the story of the seizures for his own enrichment. Or hoping to do so.

But where else was there to go? Dr. Kitzmiller, whom she had always respected, was too deeply involved himself, in one way or another, to be of any help to her. And as for the police, she had already come to the same conclusion as Macklin had—they were not going to get involved unless there was a crime. As far as Dena was concerned, there assuredly *was* a crime here somewhere, but she would need more solid evidence before she considered going to the police.

There was nobody else. Oh, given time, she might convince someone that all was not kosher at the Biotron plant, but how much time did she have? Dena had a feeling there was not much, and she needed action now, not words.

So she was left with Corey Macklin. Not exactly a knight in shining armor, but all she had. And maybe, after all, he was not as shallow as he seemed on first meeting. Underneath the sophomoric cynicism, maybe there was a man hidden somewhere. Dena could only hope so. She would watch him closely the next day when they went together to the local office of the EPA.

Dena snubbed out her cigarette and lay back, using auto-relaxation techniques to will herself to sleep. Sleeping had seldom been a problem for her. There had been some restless nights during her affair with the doctor in Chicago, but nothing serious. However, during the past two weeks, since Stu Anderson disappeared and especially since Lloyd Bratz showed up at her house, she had slept only fitfully.

She concentrated on thinking about her work. Not the new conflict with Dr. Kitzmiller about the accidental spraying but about her regular assignment on developing a pesticide for the gypsy moth. That project had languished as Dena's concern grew over Stu and the violent fate of disparate people who had had the misfortune to be on the old county road outside Biotron at the wrong time. She wondered who was working on the gypsy moth now. She wondered if anyone cared. She imagined huge gypsy moths gobbling up everything green in sight, then starting on the people. On that fantasy she drifted into a troubled sleep.

While Dena was settling in at the Beddie-Bye Motel, Corey Macklin was preparing the turndown speech he was going to give Nathan Eichorn on the Houston job offer. He had worked himself into a fine righteous indignation when a telephone call informed him that Mr. Eichorn had been called back to Houston on an urgent personal matter. His business with Mr. Macklin would have to wait.

Corey went home to bed with a profound sense of relief. He took comfort in the thought that even if his reasons were partly selfish, he had been prepared to do the noble thing.

In the tenth-floor suite of the San Francisco hotel Anton Kuryakin sat at a writing desk poring over a stack of American newspapers. He had marked several stories with a felt-tipped pen. Viktor Raslov sat on the opposite side of the room talking in low tones into the telephone. The two thick-bodied men sat at a small table playing chess.

When Raslov hung up the telephone, he came over to where Kuryakin was sitting.

"You are very busy, Anton."

Kuryakin spread out the newspapers before him. "Look here," he said. "I have marked the stories. Here . . . here . . . and here. Stories of sudden, unexplained violence. Random violence directed against anyone at hand. These attacks have spread rapidly in diverse parts of the country." He looked up at Raslov. "There can no longer be any question of what has happened."

"Good. Our assignment here is finished."

"Our assignment was to learn what progress the Americans have made in their version of Project Romanov."

"I know our job as well as you, Anton, and I say we are finished here. Our local consulate and the embassy in Washington concur."

"In the name of humanity, can we remain silent?"

"Humanity was not mentioned in our new orders."

"What new orders?"

"To return home."

"Comrade, knowing what will happen here, how can we go?"

Raslov put a hand on the other man's shoulder. "Anton, my friend, knowing what will happen, how could we stay?"

Kuryakin grew thoughtful. "How soon must we leave?"

"As soon as practicable. I should say within the week. Aeroflot will have transportation ready for us in Washington. I should not have to remind you that we will be closely watched until then."

"No," said Kuryakin. "You do not have to remind me."

# Chapter 15

Corey got to the *Herald* office at ten minutes after eight the next morning. Dena Falkner was sitting at his desk, smoking a Carlton, looking annoyed.

"You're late," she said.

"Ten minutes?"

"To me eight o'clock means eight o'clock."

"Well, mark me tardy and keep me after school."

"That's very cute."

Doc Ingersoll, hacking dryly around his Camel, came over to the desk before Corey could get off his next crack. "Telling jokes?" he said.

"I'm just getting chewed out for being ten minutes late," Corey said.

"If eight o'clock was too tough, you should have told me," Dena said.

"What difference does it make? We're not going to find any bureaucrat in his office before nine anyway."

"I thought it would be a good idea if we got our act together before we went in to talk to the people."

"Mine's together," Corey said testily. "Have you got a problem?"

"Why don't you two stop bickering," Doc said, "until we finish our business."

"Who's bickering?" Corey said.

Dena glared at him, then said, "Doc's right. Let's organize what we want to present to the EPA. Then, later, you can do your macho routine, and we'll all applaud."

Corey gave it a beat, then turned to Doc Ingersoll. "Anything new on the wire?"

"The AMA finally admits that something is going around. They say it may be a new strain of flu."

"Flu!" Corey shouted. "Man, I *saw* what happened to Hank Stransky. If what he had was flu, I'm Prince Charles."

"Just quoting the AMA," Doc said. "It seems there have been flulike symptoms connected with some of the cases they've been able to trace."

Dena said, "The flu, or something like it, is what kept people home at Biotron yesterday."

"Baloney," Corey said. "The AMA is under pressure to put some name on what's been happening to people, so they make it something familiar . . . something curable. They'll probably recommend everybody take two aspirin and call them in the morning. If they're able to call anybody in the morning."

"Do you think we'd better get started?" Dena asked.

"Might as well. Ready to go, Doc?"

"You two can handle the EPA," Ingersoll said. "I want to stay on top of the wire so we'll have the big picture. Also, I've got another idea I want to follow up on. I'll fill you in when you get back."

Corey looked at Dena. "Your car or mine?"

"I'm parked in a loading zone, so we'd better take mine. That is, if you don't mind riding with a woman."

As they went out, Corey turned to wink at Doc. "Cute, though," he said.

Doc Ingersoll watched them go with a shake of his head. He dragged on the Camel, burned his fingers, coughed, and picked up the telephone to call his friend Dexter Horn, a pathologist for the county of Milwaukee.

Dena and Corey arrived at the Federal Building at a quarter after nine. The offices of the Environmental Protection Agency were on the third floor. They rode up in the elevator without speaking.

It took fifteen minutes to get past the receptionist, and after sitting another quarter of an hour in a cramped waiting room, Corey was grinding his teeth while Dena paged nervously through a pamphlet on auto-emission control.

"Excuse me?"

They looked up with a start to see a thin woman with large glasses who had come silently into the room.

"Mr. Macklin?" she said. "Dr. Falkner?"

They nodded in turn.

"I'm Mr. Zachry's secretary. He would like to see you in his office."

"About time," Corey said, standing up. "Lead on."

"Mr. Zachry is on the eighth floor," said the woman.

Dena looked at her sharply. "Is he with the EPA?"

"Well . . . not exactly."

"What does that mean?" Corey demanded. "Who *is* he with?"

"And how do you know our names?" Dena added.

"Mr. Zachry will explain," the woman said, "if you will come with me."

Corey and Dena looked at each other and shrugged. They followed the woman out of the EPA offices and down the hall to the elevator.

On the eighth floor, the secretary led them down a dimly lit corridor where none of the doors had names. The office they entered was small, sparsely furnished, with a single window that looked out over a drab rooftop next door. A colored photograph in a clear plastic frame on the desk showed an attractive dark-haired woman in shorts and a blonde little girl about ten years old. They were standing together in front of a suburban house, squinting into the sun.

The man seated behind the desk might have been fifty. He had the blocky build of a college football guard who had kept in shape. His light hair was short and neatly brushed. He gave them an all-American smile when they entered and came around the desk to shake hands.

"I'm Lou Zachry," he said. "Thanks so much for coming up."

Corey looked around the bare office. "You're not with the EPA," he said.

"No, I'm not," Zachry said. He pulled two chairs over close to the desk. "Thank you, Miss Peters."

The secretary nodded to everyone and withdrew.

"I'm with an agency you probably haven't heard of," Zachry continued.

"Try me," Corey said.

"The IDI."

Corey repeated the initials and shook his head. Dena shrugged.

"Inter-Departmental Intelligence," Zachry said.

Corey looked bored. "That means nothing to me. You people come up with new sets of initials every day."

Dena said, "Could you be a little more explicit?"

Zachry leaned back in his chair and grinned. "I'm not surprised you haven't heard of us. Our budget doesn't allow for a public-relations operation like some of our better-known colleagues have. And to tell the truth, we're not all that eager for publicity."

"Just what is it that you do?" Dena asked.

"You've probably heard the old wheeze that the government has grown so big and diverse that one department no longer knows what another is doing."

"I've heard it," Corey said.

"Well, unfortunately, it's true. And there is a kind of secrecy fetish in some of the agencies that keeps the situation from changing. Sometimes it can lead to expensive duplication of effort and sometimes to dangerous ignorance among different branches of the government as to what's going on. It's the job of IDI to keep an eye on what everybody is doing and to try to minimize the problems.''

"How does that concern us?" Dena asked.

"We've been watching the action out at Biotron for some time," Zachry said. "Specifically, we're curious about some government contracts that people are reluctant to talk about. Some of us have the feeling that there's more going on out there than it looks like in the official reports.''

"Amen to that," Dena said.

"So when I heard you two were here with some information, I sent Miss Peters down to see if she could steer you up here.''

"And just how did you know about us?" Corey asked.

Zachry chuckled. "We have a sort of word-of-mouth telegraph in the building that gets the news around faster than the telephones.''

"Then maybe you already know what we came here about," Dena said.

"Rumors only. I'd like to hear your version.''

Taking turns, Dena and Corey told their story of the events of the past three weeks. Zachry listened intently, nodding now and then. When they had finished, they sat back and looked at the government man.

Finally, Corey spoke. "I hope you're not going to ask us to fill out some forms.''

"Nope," Zachry said. "But I am going to ask you to let me work with you.''

"What will that involve?" Dena asked.

"I'd like you, Dr. Falkner, to return to Biotron, keep your eyes open, and let me know everything you can find out. In turn, I'll fill you in on any reports I get from other sources. Agreeable?''

"So far," Dena said.

"What about me?" Corey said.

"What were you planning as your next move?''

"I thought I'd go out to Biotron myself, talk to this Dr. Kitzmiller. It looks like he's the key to what's going on."

"You may be right," Zachry said, "but I'd like you to concentrate for now on following the other angles of the story. Run down what you can on the victims, look for similarities or differences. Hold off a bit on hitting Biotron."

"Why?"

"If they know they're under investigation, they'll be on their guard. With Dr. Falkner on the scene, we'll know what they're up to and be ready to move when the time is right."

"We may not have a lot of time," Corey said. "If some sort of disease has been released from Biotron, the sooner we know everything about it, the sooner it can be stopped."

"Quite right," Zachry said. "I'm not talking about extensive delays. A matter of days at most, to learn as much as we can. Then we can take direct action."

"Mr. Zachry," Dena said, "I like your style."

"Thank you. And since we're going to be working as a team, how about using first names? I'm Lou."

"Dena."

"Corey."

"Are you two going together?"

"Is that an official question?" Corey asked.

"Nope. Strictly personal. Curious about my teammates." Zachry nodded toward the photograph. "Divorced myself. My wife didn't like Washington, for which I can't blame her. Ten years ago she took my daughter and left." His eyes clouded for a moment, then quickly refocused.

"We're not going together," Corey said. "Not yet."

Dena shot him a look that Corey pretended not to see.

"None of my business, anyway," Zachry said. He scribbled a telephone number on two slips of paper and gave one to each of them. "You can get me at this number twenty-four hours a day. Don't hesitate if anything comes up. Anything at all."

"What if you want to reach us?" Corey said.

Lou Zachry smiled. "I'm not in intelligence for nothing."

# Chapter 16

Dena Falkner drove back Tuesday evening to the town of Wheeler. She drove slowly, her mind occupied with thoughts of the people and conversations of the past day in Milwaukee. She brought the three men out one at a time on her mental stage to sort out her opinions about them.

Doc Ingersoll was all right in kind of a used-up way. There was an intelligence in the man, and the glimmer of a moral sense. Doc's trouble was the long years of boozing, and the continuing assault of tars on his lungs may have burned the man out.

The uncomfortable thought made Dena mash out the Carlton she had just lit, low tar or no low tar.

Lou Zachry, the government man, seemed to be sincere in his promise to work with them, but Dena was not completely at ease with government spying agencies. Also, she wondered about Zachry's reluctance to publicize what they knew so far. He had his reasons, no doubt, but were they the reasons he gave them? All in all, compared with bureaucrats she had known, Zachry was a plus.

Corey Macklin she saved for last. There was no denying he was sharp and energetic, and maybe attractive, if you liked the type. But Dena was not sure she could trust him. He had an overdeveloped streak of machismo, but she could handle that. It was his overdone cynicism and his looking-out-for-number-one attitude that might cause trouble.

So maybe they weren't the A-Team, but they were better

than nothing, and nothing was what Dena had going in. She would have to make the best of it.

The little house where she lived looked good to Dena after the restless night in the Beddie-Bye Motel. She heated a can of Campbell's vegetable soup, read the newspaper, and found she was exhausted. She climbed gratefully into her own bed and slept straight through until the alarm woke her at seven-thirty.

She showered, breakfasted, and felt fine until she drove into the Biotron parking lot and a sense of foreboding began to build. It did not feel like the same place where she had worked more or less contentedly for the past two years. Somehow the neat white buildings had an ominous look. The people walking on the paths between buildings all seemed bent on some sinister mission.

She parked the car and told herself to cut out the fantasizing. It did not help, however, to see that there was an unfamiliar man at the guard post where she entered. She wondered if Ralph, the regular guard, was one of the plant's many "flu" victims.

She entered the building not knowing what to expect and was relieved to see that things were almost back to normal. Only a few of the desks were empty that day, the noise level of machines was back up, and in the scattered conversations there was an occasional stutter of laughter. Almost normal. And yet something was not right.

Dena was greeted as she came in by half a dozen people, some of whom had been among the missing on Monday. She looked at them closely for any sign of illness but saw little. She stopped Jimmy Lohnes, the PR chief, as he emerged from his office, looking none the worse for his sick day.

"Welcome back," she said.

"Thanks. I see the place managed to operate reasonably well without me."

She did not smile. "Jimmy, don't you think there was something odd about Monday?"

"Odd? How do you mean?"

"So many people being out. And just for one or two days."

"Were a lot of people out?"

She gave him a rueful grin. "Yeah, but then how could you know? You were one of them."

He looked around in an exaggerated parody of guilt. "And the plant ran on without all of us. If it happens again, management might start handing out pink slips."

"Yes, well, so long, Jimmy." Dena continued pensively along the hall, trying to sort out her thoughts and her worries.

She entered her small office, sat down at her desk, and looked out through the glass partition. Here and there, out in the open bay, somebody sneezed or coughed lightly, but overall the work force seemed in good health.

"Hi, Dena."

She had not seen Carol Denker aproaching the office. Now she turned and watched as her assistant came in, hung up her jacket, and sat down at the other desk in the small office.

"Hi." Carol put a box of Kleenex out on the desk, extracted a tissue, and blew her nose. Dena swiveled her chair around to face her.

"Did you have it, too?" Carol asked.

"Have what?"

"Whatever it is. The one-day awfuls. I was out Monday; you were gone Tuesday."

"I had to go into Milwaukee."

"Whatever, I'm glad to see you back. Coffee breaks are no fun alone. I only took two all day."

"How are you feeling?" Dena asked.

"Pretty good, actually. Monday I thought I was really coming down with a good one—sore throat, achy joints, upset stomach. This morning all I've got is a little sniffle. It must be some kind of twenty-four-hour virus."

"Must be," Dena said. "A third of the plant called in sick on Monday."

"No kidding? Something must be going around."

"Yeah, I guess," Dena said.

As the morning progressed, she began to wonder if maybe the multiple absences could have been just a wild coincidence. With Lloyd Bratz and his bizarre story so much on her mind, might she not have projected an onslaught of the twenty-four-hour flu into something more sinister? She picked up the phone and dialed the extension of the personnel director. The call went through without any switchboard trouble that day and was answered by Ian McCollough's secretary.

When McCollough came on the line, Dena felt a little foolish. "I was just curious," she said, "about the absenteeism today."

"I'm happy to say the situation is pretty well back to normal," McCollough said. "Two-thirds of the people who were out Monday came back yesterday. Most of the rest are here today. One thing the experience did was make me appreciate my secretary and my receptionist all the more. I came close to a breakdown trying to do their jobs."

"They're both back today?"

"Back and apparently recovered. It seems like Monday was just an aberration. One of those unexplained peaks in the chart. You having any problems?"

"No," Dena said. "No problems. Just curious."

She and Carol went out together as usual for their coffee. Carol sneezed once but seemed otherwise to have shaken off any effects of the illness that had kept her home.

"Have you any idea where you caught whatever it was you had?" Dena said.

"Beats me. I haven't been anywhere except here and home. Neither Ken nor the twins had any symptoms, so I guess it was just me. It came and went so fast . . . like nothing I've ever had."

Dena pointed to an adhesive bandage on Carol's wrist. "What's that?"

"Oh, I got careless playing with the cat, and she scratched me a little. It didn't seem like much, but about Friday night it was itching like crazy. I put some Bactine on it and a Band-Aid. It's all right now. No big deal.''

"That's good."

Dena went to work, trying to concentrate on the problem of the gypsy moth, but her attention kept returning to the large room full of desks beyond the glass. What was it that bothered her about the people out there? She fancied that there was some kind of shadow over them. And over Carol, who was sitting quietly at the desk just behind her, sniffling. Why did she keep seeing the face of Stuart Anderson?

The telephone rang, making Dena jump. She grinned self-consciously at Carol and answered. On the other end was Dr. Kitzmiller's longtime receptionist.

"If you have time, Dr. Kitzmiller would like to see you about ten o'clock," the woman said.

"I'll be there. How are you feeling?"

"Oh, I'm fine today, thanks. I had a touch of something Monday and yesterday and thought I'd better stay home. Two days off seem to have done the trick."

"That's good." Dena said thoughtfully. The people's stories all had a chilling similarity. They were sick enough on Monday to stay home from work but feeling fine today. What kind of a "flu" was that?

She exchanged a couple of meaningless remarks with the receptionist and hung up.

Dena arrived at Dr. Kitzmiller's promptly at ten and was admitted immediately. The chief biochemist wore a grimace that was apparently intended as a smile when she entered his office. He waved her into a chair across from him.

"Ah, Dena, good of you to come."

She took a seat and waited for him to state his purpose in summoning her.

"I, ah, understand you came to see me on Monday."

"That's right. I was told you were 'unavailable.' "

"Yes, it was something I could not avoid. One of those tiresome meetings with customers that are usually handled by the sales department. Unfortunately, some of the key

133

sales people were out, so I had to be there. Was there some problem you wanted to discuss?''

''I thought there was at the time, but now I'm not so sure.''

''Oh?'' Kitzmiller seemed genuinely interested.

''There were a lot of people out sick Monday.''

''Were there? I didn't notice.''

''Well, there were. Most of them seem to be back today, though.''

''Good, good. A big weekend, perhaps?''

''I don't think so.''

''You have another explanation?''

''I'm not sure. They all had symptoms like the onset of flu, but today they seem to be cured. I was wondering if it might have some connection to what happened to Stu Anderson and Lloyd Bratz.''

Kitzmiller looked pained. ''I don't think we can jump to that conclusion.''

''I thought it would be worth mentioning,'' Dena said. ''When one unusual occurrence follows another, a scientist is trained to look for a connection.''

''I'll certainly have someone look into it,'' Kitzmiller said. ''As I believe I told you, we are monitoring the situation very closely.''

Dena sat until the silence between them began to grow uncomfortable; then she moved to rise.

''I understand you, too, left the plant Monday,'' Kitzmiller said not quite casually. ''You were not among the ill, I hope.''

''No. I had some business in Milwaukee.''

''Oh?''

This time the pause was almost audible. Dena held a polite smile but said nothing.

''Ah, well,'' Kitzmiller said finally, ''I suppose you will be wanting to get back to your work.''

''If there was nothing else.''

''No, no, nothing else. Please feel free to come to me

with any questions you may have. I am sorry I was not here yesterday."

She left Dr. Kitzmiller's office with her nerves jumping. Something was definitely troubling the man. What?

While Dena Falkner worried about Dr. Kitzmiller, Eddie Gault, in another part of the plant, was worried about a number of things.

He, too, had noticed the unusual absence of Biotron personnel on Monday. That most of them returned on Tuesday and on this day did not ease his mind. Some were still missing. Just as the two helicopter pilots were missing.

He had not seen Dr. Kitzmiller since the interview right after the canister switch. Not that Eddie was anxious to see the chief of biochemistry again just now, but he was worried. Somebody had been following him. Watching him. Eddie could tell. He was relieved when it was quitting time and he could take the worry home to Roanne.

After work, she was waiting for him outside in the van as usual. And as usual, she looked so beautiful with her white-blonde hair all soft and shiny and her blue eyes smiling at him that his knees went watery and he felt the familiar pleasant ache in his groin.

He climbed into the van beside her. She kissed him. Her lips were soft and moist. Eddie began to relax.

"How was your day?" she asked.

"Slow. They've put a temporary hold on all testing, so there isn't much for me to do."

"That must mean they're worried," Roanne said.

"Maybe. And so am I."

Roanne's eyes blazed. "We've been all over this. Those bastards are getting what they deserve."

Eddie's mouth fell open. He stared at her with the hurt eyes of a little boy whose mother has struck him for the first time.

"Ah, baby, I'm sorry, but you mustn't bother yourself about these things. What we did was right. It's going to save lives in the end. You'll see."

135

"I hope so."

"Trust me, baby. Trust Roanne."

"One thing—most of the people who were out sick yesterday came back."

"There, you see? You were worried for nothing."

"I've still got to wonder what made them sick. The infirmary's full; I know that much. They've closed it off and put guards outside."

"That's typical Establishment thinking," Roanne said, turning down the corners of her lovely mouth. "They ignore a situation until it's too late to make any difference; then they overreact."

Eddie scratched at the soft flesh on the inside of his elbow. Roanne reached out and lightly touched the reddened patch of skin.

"What's this?"

"It's nothing. I got a scratch from a thorn when I was pruning the roses last week. It must have gotten a little infected."

Roanne started the van's engine and pulled out of the parking lot. "I'll put something on it for you when we get home. Then we can take a shower together. Would you like that?"

Eddie looked over at her. She moved her hand to his thigh and squeezed gently.

"Yeah," he said. "I'd like that a lot."

# Chapter 17

Corey Macklin and Doc Ingersoll sat with their heads close together at Corey's desk in the Milwaukee *Herald* office. Corey was trying to pay attention to what Doc was saying while watching the ash on the older man's Camel grow longer and droop precariously over his chin.

"It's all set up for you and me and a photographer at St. Bartholomew's, one o'clock," Doc said.

"Why a private hospital?" Corey asked. "Why not the county morgue?"

"Because they've already cut up a couple of these people at the morgue and they're getting nervous about it, for reasons that we will see. Or so Dexter Horn tells me. What's the matter?"

"Would you for Christ' sake flick the ash off that cigarette?"

As Doc removed the Camel from his mouth and examined it, the three-quarter-inch ash let go and filtered down to the papers on Corey's desk.

"Oops."

Corey rolled his eyes as Doc blew ineffectually at the gray flecks. "Never mind. Shall we get some lunch before we go?"

"We'd better. From what Dexter tells me, we might not feel much like eating afterwards."

"I'll go rustle up Jimbo."

Corey found the bearded young photographer in the lounge sitting on one cracked plastic chair with his feet up on another. His eyes were half-closed, his hands jammed into his pockets.

"Ready to go, Jimbo?"

"I'm ready, but I'm not going."

"What do you mean?"

"The man's got another assignment for me. Hot story."

"What's that?"

"They're handing out citizenship awards at the city-council luncheon."

"You're kidding."

"Would I kid about this? You think I want to be shooting up good film on one suit handing a worthless plaque to another suit when I could be getting shots of a cut-up corpse? To me this is not a kidding matter."

Corey believed him. Next to big chests on women, Jimbo Tattinger liked best to take pictures of gore. Nobody loved a head-on collision more than Jimbo.

"Did Uhlander personally tell you this?"

"Personally and in the bulging flesh."

Corey's first impulse was to rush into the city editor's office and ask what the hell he thought he was doing, but he thought better of it on the way there. Nathan Eichorn had warned him there would be obstacles if he persisted in the story. Knowing the owner's reputation, he guessed the reassignment of Jimbo would be only the beginning. No point in escalating the battle. He settled for throwing a scowl at Uhlander's closed door as he passed on his way back to the city room.

"There won't be a photographer," he told Doc Ingersoll.

"No?"

"It seems Uhlander wants to use Jimbo on the citizenship awards at the city council."

"That's ridiculous."

"Sure it is."

Doc stared at him for a moment, then nodded. "I see."

Corey said, "You and I had better get out of here before one of us gets tagged to go along with him and write the captions."

They stopped for lunch at Heinkel's Bratwurst Gardens, then drove in Corey's car out to St. Bartholomew's Hospital in Wauwatosa.

The pathology lab in the basement of St. Bartholomew's was small but well equipped. It smelled sharply of disinfectant. There was only one dissection table, a stainless-steel contraption with a drain at one end for escaping body fluids. At the other end was a sink and a hanging scales.

On the table lay the nude, drained body of a white female. The gray flesh across her stomach sagged in loose folds. Her lower belly bore the navel-to-pubis scar of an old hysterectomy. High on the inside of her right thigh was an open slash four inches long. The severed end of a rubbery artery protruded from between the lips of the wound.

The hair on the woman's head and her pubis was curly black with wiry gray strands running through it. She had a mole with a hair growing from it on one earlobe. But it was her face that commanded attention. The flesh was covered with raw, puffy lesions like boils that had burst. The woman's dead eyes were mercifully closed.

Dexter Horn stood by silently while the reporters looked over the body. The little pathologist clutched a linen handkerchief in one hand. He used it nervously to blot his scalp where the few strands of black hair looked drawn on.

Doc Ingersoll introduced the pathologist to Corey.

"I've been reading your stories in the *Herald*," Horn said.

"I'm glad somebody has."

"I think a lot more people will be reading you pretty soon. You've maybe got a bigger story than you know."

Corey looked down at the dead woman. "What's the background on this one?"

Horn consulted a clipboard. "Helena Gotch, Caucasian female, age fifty-four, married. Lived in West Allis. Friday night, while cooking dinner, she came screaming out of the kitchen with a cleaver and went after her brother. He'd been staying there since her husband went crazy and scalded himself to death in their shower a week before."

"Jesus," Corey said softly.

"It doesn't get any prettier. She lopped off part of the brother's ear before he ran out of the house and jumped over a fence. She took off up the street screaming. Couple of motorists thought she was in trouble and tried to help. She left one of them with a broken jaw, the other with internal injuries. Finally died when she tried to run through a plate-glass window and sliced open her femoral artery."

"That's the wound on her leg?"

"Right."

"What happened to her face?" Doc Ingersoll asked.

"The brother said it just bloomed like that all of a sudden. The blisters swelled up and popped while she ran around screaming. Her husband had the same face. They all do."

The picture of Vic Metzger rose up in Corey's mind. That triggered another association.

"You say her name was Gotch?"

"That's right."

"Who was the husband?"

"Let me see." Dexter Horn flipped back a page on the clipboard. "Karl Gotch. Sheet metal worker. Age fifty-five."

Karl Gotch, beer drinker, member of the bowling team, and destroyer of the pinball machine at Vic's Old Milwaukee Tavern. Now he had been destroyed by an affliction like the one that had hit Vic and Hank Stransky before him. And now his wife. Corey saw a chilling pattern begin to emerge.

"Did you do the autopsy on the husband?"

"Yeah, and half a dozen others."

"What did you find?"

"I'll give you a copy of my report, but first I want to open this one up so you can see for yourself."

"Okay, go ahead."

Dexter Horn pulled on a pair of surgical gloves. He selected a knife from a tray beside the table and cut the scalp from one ear down along the back hairline to the other ear. He grasped the flap of detached skin like a bathing cap and pulled it forward over the woman's face. Then he used a rotary bone saw to slice off the top of the skull. He set it aside and revealed the yellow-gray mass of the brain. With a curved knife he cut through the connecting tissue, then lifted the jellylike brain out of the skull and plopped it on the enameled surface of the table.

"Come here." He beckoned Corey closer. "Take a look."

Corey and Doc Ingersoll leaned over the exposed brain where Horn was pointing. Corey began to wish he had passed up the bratwurst and sauerkraut lunch.

"What are we supposed to be looking for?"

Horn touched the brain with the point of a knife. "Here's one."

Corey squinted and saw a dark speck on one of the ridges of the dead brain.

The point of the knife shifted. "Here's another."

Corey followed the steel point and saw the second speck.

"And another."

"What are they, maggots?"

The pathologist was offended. "Of course not. You think we leave these stiffs lying out in the alley or something? This baby's been in the freezer since they brought her in. Anyway, flies don't breed under the skull."

"Okay, so what are they?"

"I'll be able to show you better under a microscope," Horn said. He selected an area of the cerebrum and sliced off a wafer of brain tissue. He examined it and smiled, holding it up for the others to see.

"Got one of the little suckers here." He carried the tissue sample to a binocular microscope mounted on a table along the wall and sandwiched it between two glass slides. He adjusted the instrument, then beckoned Doc and Corey over.

Corey peered through the eyepieces and felt a chill ripple down his back. What he saw looked like a short, segmented worm. With teeth. It seemed to be emerging from a tunnel in the spongy brain tissue. He raised up and looked at Dexter Horn while Doc Ingersoll took his turn at the microscope.

"What is it?"

"My best guess is that it's a parasite of some kind. It's like nothing I've seen before. I've been trying to classify it ever since I opened up the first head and found a bunch of them. So far, no luck. None of my references list anything like it."

Doc straightened and backed away from the microscope. His face was paler than usual. "God, that's ugly. Is it alive?"

"Not now," Horn told him, "but it was. Apparently it feeds on living brain tissue. When the brain dies, it dies."

Corey took another look. "There are clusters of little black dots around it. What are those?"

"Eggs," said Horn.

The impact of what he had just heard came gradually to Corey. For a moment he thought the bratwurst was coming up, but he swallowed hard and kept it down.

"You mean these things eat their way into the brain and lay eggs there?"

"Stripped to the essentials, yes."

"How do they get there?"

"From the victims I've looked at, traces in the blood vessels seem to indicate the eggs—they're much too small to be seen by the naked eye—are carried to the brain by the circulatory system. There they hatch, and the parasites start eating their way through cerebral cortex. That's the outer layer of the brain . . . the well-known gray matter."

"Could that cause a headache?" Corey said, remembering the last moments of Hank Stransky's life.

"The brain itself has no feeling," Horn said, "but as these things eat through blood vessels, it causes multiple cerebral hemorrhaging, and that—let me tell you—can bring on the king of headaches."

"What about the violence? These people lash out at anybody and anything close to them."

"It's entirely possible that the nervous system is affected as bits of the brain are consumed, bringing on the irrational acts of violence."

142

Doc Ingersoll swallowed audibly. "Is it okay to smoke in here?" he said.

"I don't care," the pathologist said. He nodded toward the brainless corpse on the table. "And she doesn't care. So go ahead."

Doc gratefully set fire to a Camel and sucked in the smoke. He exhaled with a long "ahhhhh!"

"Someday let me show you the lungs of a guy who smoked like you do," Horn said. "They look like chunks of anthracite."

"I'll pass," Doc said. "There are things a man's better off not knowing."

Corey was leaning over to stare at the brain of Helena Gotch. With no support from the protective skull, it was flattening out like a pudding under the force of gravity.

"How do these things get into the bloodstream in the first place?" he asked.

"You understand we haven't had a lot of time to study this," Horn said, "but I'll show you what I think."

The pathologist turned back to the dissecting table. Corey and Doc stood behind him, looking over his shoulder. He pointed out several tiny nicks on the now-bloodless shins of the woman. The skin around them was dotted with tiny scabs.

"Bites?" Doc asked.

Horn shook his head. "Little breaks in the skin caused when she shaved her legs. Barely noticeable ordinarily. But an insect bite would do just as well. That's all the opening the eggs would need. In other cases I've been able to trace the travel of the eggs through the bloodstream from some skin break to the brain, and I'll bet that's what happened here."

"But where do the eggs come from? How do they get into the skin break?"

"Hey, I'm just a pathologist. Once you get outside the body, you're in somebody else's territory. I know those eggs can be carried for short distances in the atmosphere, but like all parasites, they won't live long without a host. I

143

thought maybe you guys would have an idea about where they come from.''

Corey looked at Doc Ingersoll. ''Maybe we do,'' he said.

''What causes those broken blisters on her face?'' Doc asked. ''You said the other victims had the same thing.''

''In the other cases I've found eggs adhering to the edges of the ruptured flesh. Probably will on this one, too. This is just another guess, you understand, but they could have been carried from the brain, back through the bloodstream, into the tiny capillaries of the face. There they produce some kind of an irritant that causes the flesh to swell up and burst.''

''Like a seedpod,'' Corey said.

''More or less.''

''Blowing the eggs out into the atmosphere to get into anybody nearby who's got a cut finger or a scraped knee.''

''I suppose it could happen that way,'' Horn said.

Doc said, ''Why go to all that trouble? Why wouldn't they just hatch there in the brain where there's plenty of food?''

''Once these things start eating at it, the brain and the brain's owner are not going to last very long. Survival of the parasites requires that they find a new source of food or perish.''

''Ergo, the exploding face,'' Doc said.

For a long moment the three men were silent, staring down at the violated corpse. Finally, Corey said, ''How come all this hasn't been published?''

''There's been pressure to keep it quiet.''

''Pressure from where?''

''I don't know, but from high enough to clamp a lid on the whole department. But we can forget about that now. After this latest batch it won't matter if the pressure comes from God; the story's going to come out. Your paper's already touched on it, so I figured you might as well get it first. Besides, I owed Doc a favor.''

''Consider it paid in full, pal,'' said Ingersoll.

''Want to watch me open up the rest of her?'' Horn said.

"No, thanks," Corey said quickly. "We've got work to do."

As they rode up in the elevator from the chilly basement, Doc said, "If Dexter Horn is right, we could all be into some real heavy trouble with this. What do you think?"

"I think," Corey said, "that we've just been handed the greatest headline you ever saw."

"Headline?"

Corey held up both hands, framing the invisible banner headline. "Just picture it, Doc: *Attack of the Brain Eaters!*"

# Chapter 18

The headline that appeared in the Thursday edition of the *Herald* read: SCIENCE BAFFLED BY BRAIN EATERS. The impact was everything Corey Macklin had hoped for. The story was picked up by AP and UPI with full name credit to Corey. The news departments of all three television networks were trying to reach him before the ink was dry.

A major publisher offered a generous advance on a book. Corey declined. Agents from both coasts were suddenly eager to represent him. Corey refused to take their calls. Celebrities, crackpots, government officials, and just plain folks jammed the telephone lines to the *Herald*. Everybody wanted to talk to Corey Macklin, but Corey was not talking. Not yet.

Wednesday night, when they had returned to the office from St. Bartholomew's, Corey had offered to share the by-line on the brain eaters story with Doc Ingersoll. "After all," he said, "it was your connection that got us into the autopsy. And most of the medical input comes from you."

Doc had fallen into a coughing spasm and come out of it shaking his head. He slapped his pockets until he found a fresh pack of Camels, stuck one in his mouth, and lit it.

"No, thanks," he said. "I'm happy with things as they are. It feels good to be involved in a real story again, and I'll stick with it as long as you want me to. But you can leave my name off of it. I don't want to be famous. And that's what you're going to be, buddy, like it or not."

"I think I'll like it," Corey said.

Doc squinted at him through the smoke of a freshly lit Camel. "Maybe."

Doc Ingersoll proved to be a prophet. After the early Thursday edition of the Milwaukee *Herald* and the wire-service pickups of his story, Corey Macklin became at least semifamous. And if his name was not yet in the Woodward-Bernstein category, his coinage was rapidly becoming a household term. Health officials tried hard to come up with another, less threatening name for the deadly parasites, but it was "brain eaters" that caught the public imagination.

There were the inevitable jokes—Hear about the Polish brain eater that starved to death?—but they did not last long once the seriousness of the situation became known.

During the taping of his show Thursday afternoon, Johnny Carson included a reference to brain eaters in his monologue. Actually, the mention came during an ad-lib exchange with Ed McMahon. By the time the show was aired that night, reports of the latest wave of seizures were coming in from all over the country. Switchboards at NBC were inundated with protesting calls, and the network was forced to insert an editorial apology into the show. For the later broadcast to the West Coast, the offending exchange was bleeped out.

NBC's was not the only switchboard jammed with incoming calls on Thursday. Telephone lines into the Milwaukee

146

*Herald* were blown out as the number of callers wanting to speak to Corey Macklin overloaded the circuits. To his own surprise, Corey was suddenly recognized as the "authority" on the brain eaters. While the phone company worked to unsnarl the lines, Corey, along with City Editor Porter Uhlander, was isolated above the furor in the rarely used top-floor office of Nathan Eichorn.

The diminutive publisher was not his usual dapper self. There was a scuff on one of his lizard-skin boots, the collar of his shirt was wilted, and there was a patch of whiskers on his jaw that the razor had missed. He pulled his tie loose and unbuttoned the collar as he paced to and fro on the thick office carpeting.

While he paced, Eichorn kept his eyes on a television set that was built into the wall. On the screen a network anchorman was talking to field reporters in various cities around the nation. The volume was turned down to a murmur, but the on-screen activity had an air of great urgency. The network news people had that look of somber elation they reserve for the reporting of disasters.

Porter Uhlander stood next to the window and followed Eichorn with his eyes, avoiding the events on the television screen. The city editor looked as though at any moment he might throw himself through the double pane of safety glass to the concrete twelve stories down.

Corey Macklin was the calmest of the three in the room. He stood with his arms folded, leaning against the publisher's desk while he tried to catch his name from the turned-down sound of the television set.

Every few steps Nathan Eichorn would stop his pacing, turn from the television screen, and glare in turn at Uhlander and Corey. He would mutter "Brain eaters" under his breath, shake his head, and resume his travels. Finally, he planted himself in front of the city editor, glared up at the taller man, and said in tightly controlled tones, "*Brain eaters*. How in the name of all journalism did you let that abomination get into our headline?"

"I didn't know," Uhlander admitted. "It wasn't cleared through me."

"I'm responsible," Corey said. "I got the story late yesterday and had to go straight to composing with it. The headline was my idea."

Eichorn turned and regarded him sadly. "Brain eaters. Not only did you insist on following this story despite everything I said; you stick a head on it that belongs in the *National Enquirer*. Balls."

"Mr. Eichorn, I didn't create the story. It was happening whether I wrote it or not." Corey could not resist a small grin. "As for 'Brain Eaters,' it sold papers. We couldn't keep them on the streets."

"Why not. If you put 'fuck' in a headline, it would sell papers, too." Eichorn dropped into the tall chair behind his polished mahogany desk as though he were suddenly exhausted. He frowned at a smudge on one shirt cuff, then licked the ball of his thumb and rubbed at it. "Did you know there are maybe a hundred people downstairs looking for you? That's not counting all the crazies trying to get through on the telephone."

"Looking for me, you say?" Corey found it impossible to hide his pleasure completely.

"Yes. Most of them seem to expect you to tell them how to escape the brain eaters."

"How the hell should I know that?"

"Why not? As far as they're concerned, you invented the little suckers, and now you can call them off."

"That's crazy."

"Of course it is, but that has nothing to do with public behavior."

For the first time, Corey lost some of his composure. "All I did was write the story."

"I know that, Corey." The publisher seemed to shrink even smaller in the high-backed chair. "You're a professional newspaperman. Overambitious, maybe, but still a pro. I was wrong in trying to pull you off the story. I didn't

148

know then what we were up against. You see, there was pressure being put on me, too.''

''Pressure from where?'' Corey said.

Eichorn looked up at him sharply. ''This has to be off the record.''

Corey nodded.

The publisher grinned without mirth. ''I never thought I'd have to say that to one of my own employees. The pressure came from Washington. Maybe you know that the Justice Department has been building an antitrust case against me for about eighteen months.''

''I've heard,'' Corey said.

''Well, the people back there let me know that the whole thing would be dropped if the *Herald* would back away from this story. The story you wouldn't let go of.''

''What were they hoping to accomplish?'' Corey asked.

''I don't know. I didn't ask. I've worked long and hard to build up what I have, and I'd have done almost anything to keep it from being taken away.'' He slumped even deeper into the heavily padded swivel chair. ''Now I don't know what's going to happen.''

Porter Uhlander cleared his throat. ''How do you want it handled from here on, Mr. Eichorn?''

The little publisher threw up his hands. ''What choice do we have? Pandora's box is open. The story's out. Keep on it. Maybe the brain eaters will get us all and it won't make any difference.''

While the *Herald* was besieged by people clamoring for more information about the brain eaters, the Biotron plant outside Appleton was having its own problems. The announcement was made on Friday morning that all labs and offices would be closed at the end of the shift and would remain closed until further notice. No explanation was offered.

There was no organized protest by the nonunionized employees of Biotron, just a sort of stunned confusion. They were assured that the plant would reopen as soon as possi-

149

ble; they should hold themselves in readiness to return to work.

After she read Corey's by-lined story in the Thursday *Herald,* Dena Falkner tried without success to reach Dr. Kitzmiller. When she heard the announcement of the plant closure, she tried again. However, there was still no response on his private extension, and when she went in person to his office, she found it locked and a company security guard outside.

"Is Dr. Kitzmiller inside?" she asked the guard.

"Sorry, miss, I have no information."

"It's vital that I talk to him."

"If you want to leave a message—"

Dena did not wait for the rest of the brush-off. She walked through the building to the office of Jimmy Lohnes. The usually genial PR man was hunched behind his desk when she arrived, seemingly fighting off an angry pair of telephones that were ringing without letup. As Dena hesitated in the doorway, Lohnes swept an arm across the desk, knocking the instruments flying. They hit the carpeted floor with a muffled clang and were silent at last.

"Nice backhand," Dena said.

Lohnes gave her a pained half grin. "Oh, hi, Dena. Excuse the outburst, but those damn things were giving me a world-class headache. Everybody seems to think I'm the man who can explain why the plant is closing. Hell, I just got the news the same time as everybody else. I haven't a clue as to what's going on. What can I do for you?"

Dena looked at him sideways. "As a matter of fact, I thought you might explain why the plant is closing."

"That figures," Lohnes said, massaging his temples. "What does the grapevine say?"

"That it has something to do with the brain eaters."

"That's not bad, as rumors go. Still, I haven't seen anything about us in the news."

"I have a feeling you will."

"Do you know something I don't, Dena?"

"Nothing important."

Lohnes's secretary entered looking distraught. "Excuse me, Mr. Lohnes, but there seems to be something wrong with the tele— Oh!"

"They fell on the floor," he explained.

Dena left the public-relations chief picking up his telephones and returned to her own office. There she found Carol Denker searching through desk drawers.

"Lose something?" Dena asked.

"I was sure I had aspirin in here somewhere. You haven't got any, have you?"

"Sorry."

"Damn. My head feels like there's a spear through it. If they hadn't closed up the plant, I'd probably have had to go home anyhow."

"Migraine?"

"If it is, it's a first. I've never had one like it before."

Headache. Dena thought of Corey's description of the bartender in Milwaukee who complained of a two-day headache just before trashing his own tavern. She thought of the carefully worded story in the *Herald* about the tiny parasites that ate into your brain. Suddenly, she could no longer look at Carol Denker. She was seized by a sudden violent shudder.

Carol looked up from her search of the desk. "Something wrong?"

Dena shook her head. "I guess somebody walked over my grave." Twenty minutes later she was driving grimly toward Milwaukee.


Eddie Gault did not go to work Thursday, so he did not get the message and witness the confusion that resulted. Eddie Gault had the flu. So he thought.

He lay in bed shivering under the blankets while Roanne Tesla brought him soup and felt his forehead and fed him a mixture of honey and wheat germ. When she had the television set on in the living room, she kept the volume turned way down. In his present condition, it would not do Eddie any good to hear about the brain eaters. She did not much like to think about them herself. Probably, she reasoned, it was just another instance of national paranoia.

Two thousand miles away, in San Francisco, the four-man delegation claiming to represent Soviet agriculture was glowering at a hapless assistant to the manager of the airport. The assistant, an earnest young man named Henderson, was sweating profusely as, in the absence of his chief, he passed along the orders he had been given to these dangerous-looking Russians.

"This is outrageous!" Viktor Raslov stormed. "We are emissaries of the Soviet Union, traveling on diplomatic passports."

"I'm very sorry, sir, but there has been a delay in your flight."

"Delay? What kind of delay?"

"Uh, well, mechanical, I believe." Henderson was not a good liar. As he well knew, the delay in the Russians' flight was prompted by a call from the San Francisco office of the FBI. Henderson wished fervently that the local agents would arrive as promised and take him off the hook.

"I want to speak to the Soviet consul," said Raslov.

"Yes, sir," Henderson said, relieved to be taking action, any action. "If you will come with me, you can use the telephone in my office."

The public concern over the brain-eater scare had brought crowds far above normal to the airport—people looking to get out of the city or coming to meet friends who were fleeing from some other locale. By the time Henderson had steered his group through the crowd and upstairs to his office, it was discovered that the foursome had become a threesome. Anton Kuryakin was no longer with them.

By Friday night nobody was making jokes about the brain eaters. The wave of new seizures that began on Thursday grew to a flood on Friday. Hospitals were filling rapidly not only with bona fide victims of the parasites but with almost everybody who had a headache, or thought he did. Some

152

medical personnel were reluctant to treat the people brought in as rumors spread about the contagious nature of the brain eaters.

The public, now afraid and confused, clamored for action. Health authorities were urged to do something. Anything. A quarantine was suggested. The health authorities would have been happy to oblige, but they had no idea where to start. From the original concentration of attacks around New York, Milwaukee, and Seattle, the seizures had spread to all parts of the country. The authorities could do little more than issue calming reports that calmed no one.

It soon became evident that the parasites could strike anyone, regardless of age, sex, race, economic circumstances, or geographic location. Nevertheless, with the dearth of hard facts, rumors sprang up like toadstools in manure. Calamity is easier to face when there is someone to blame it on.

The homosexual community was an early target. Remembering the recent AIDS scare, groups of men marched on gay bars and community centers with guns, clubs, axes, torches, and fists. They did not stop to ask themselves how beating up a few homosexuals would protect anybody from the brain-destroying parasite.

In Detroit the blacks blamed the Jews. In Los Angeles the Jews blamed the Arabs. In Berkeley a feminist leader blamed men. In St. Louis the conservatives blamed the liberals. In Miami the Jews, blacks, Cubans, Haitians, and WASPs blamed one another.

Before the weekend was over, hardly a group had not been accused by some other group of bringing the new plague upon the nation. Communists, Hare Krishnas, Orientals, union members, meat eaters, nuclear plants, Indians, doctors, politicians, poor people, the media, and visitors from space had all taken their share of heat from a frightened and frustrated populace.

Throughout the weekend the appalling stories continued.

In Manchester, New Hampshire, a Sunday school teacher broke off in mid-sentence, ripped a wooden chair apart, and attacked his class with the jagged legs. Two of the children were killed and six injured severely before the teacher was subdued by half a dozen men from an adult class in the next room.

In Santa Monica a body builder suddenly began to scream and rush about the gym, attacking people with a forty-pound dumbbell. He caved in the skulls of the gym owner and his best friend, then ran out onto Pacific Coast Highway and threw himself under the wheels of a Gray Line tour bus.

In New Orleans a customer complained to the bartender that the music was blowing his mind, then, without waiting for a response, leaped on the bandstand and killed a seventy-year-old trumpet player with his own instrument as the rest of the band watched in impotent horror.

In Los Angeles a well-dressed woman driving a bronze Mercedes inexplicably swung her car broadside near the junction of the Harbor and Santa Monica freeways, causing an accident involving two hundred cars and tying up traffic for many miles in all directions. When rescuers reached her, they found her face a mass of raw lesions and her throat ripped out by her own hands.

On a Caribbean cruise ship the captain, two crewmen, and a middle-aged woman passenger went berserk at approximately the same time and ran screaming through the ship attacking anyone in their path. The radio operator managed to get off an SOS before his neck was snapped and the ship set afire. By the time a Liberian tanker reached the scene, more than a hundred people were dead.

The list of dreadful seizures continued until a public numbed by horror upon horror no longer responded to fresh stories. Published reactions, official and otherwise, provided little relief.

From Washington came a message from the surgeon general assuring the populace that there was nothing to worry about. He would have had a hard time convincing the crowd of baseball fans watching the Portland Beavers shut out Salt Lake City on Thursday as almost simultaneously a dozen people in the stands and one catcher in the Portland bullpen went berserk and created bloody mayhem in the park.

On Thursday night in Biloxi, Mississippi, Reverend Cadwallader of the New Faith and Final Judgment Church proclaimed it the end of the world and led thirty followers to the top of a nearby hill, the better to be close to heaven when the big transfer began. On Sunday evening they were still waiting.

On Sunday night the president spoke to the nation. Everyone who was still unaffected by the terrible new plague was in front of a television set, tensely waiting for some word of assurance.

"My fellow Americans . . . without warning our country has been struck by an insidious, invisible enemy. As in the past, when the American people have been threatened and have rallied to defeat those who would destroy us and our way of life, I must call on you tonight to join with me in meeting this new, terrible crisis. . . ."

Corey Macklin, Dena Falkner, and Lou Zachry, the government man, were among the millions watching the president's telecast. They were wedged with about fifty others into a narrow Milwaukee bar that was built to hold half that many.

"This is a time calling for personal sacrifice as we mobilize all the forces at our command to repel this invader."

"I don't believe it," Corey said. "He's going to declare war on the brain eaters."

Zachry gave him a hard look.

"Hush," Dena said. "Let's at least hear what the man has to say."

The president was not reassuring. His usual robust tan seemed to have paled several shades. One eyelid had developed a twitch, and his rich, practiced voice had a quaver that reflected more than his age.

The essence of his message was to remain calm. Local authorities were bringing the situation under control.

155

"Bullshit," Corey muttered. Several men standing nearby grunted their agreement. Dena kicked him in the shin.

The people were asked to report all suspected cases of the new epidemic. The president avoided using the term "brain eaters." Stay out of crowds, they were told. Do not attempt to leave population centers. Stay tuned to radio or television for late developments. Obey law-enforcement officers. Help was on the way. Trust in God.

As the president concluded his short message, Corey swallowed the last of his beer, which had grown warm in the glass. He said, "For a minute there I thought he was going to leave out the Almighty."

"Like it or not, the Almighty may be our only hope," Dena said.

"No atheists in foxholes, right?"

"Something like that."

Back out on the street, Corey, Zachry, and Dena stood in a little protective knot while scattered pedestrians hurried by, eyeing each other furtively.

"I'd like to go out to Biotron tomorrow," Corey said. "Meet the famous Dr. Kitzmiller."

Dena made a face. "Lotsa luck. Dr. K can be hard to find when he doesn't want to be found."

"He hasn't had me looking for him. What about you, Lou? Want to come?"

Zachry shook his head. "I've got too much to do here. Touch base with me when you get back."

Corey consulted his watch. "I'd better get up to the city room now and see what Doc's pulled off the wire. I want a fresh story for tomorrow's early edition."

"If you don't mind, I'll come with you," Dena said. "Right now I don't want to walk the streets alone."

# Chapter 19

They found Doc Ingersoll in the wire room at the *Herald* with stacks of wire copy littering the table where he sat and Camel butts spilling out of the ashtray. Doc was bent over a pad of copy paper on which he was making notes, his head tilted to keep the smoke out of his eyes.

He looked up and grunted when Corey and Dena came in. "Learn anything new from Zachry?"

"Not much," Corey said. "How about you?"

Doc waved at the untidy stacks of torn-off wire-service copy. "Plenty. Too much. I read so much of this crap I started to imagine *my* brain was being chewed on."

The other two looked at him sharply.

Doc fanned away the cigarette smoke. "Just kidding."

Dena flipped through some of the wire stories and read the datelines. "They seem to come from all over."

"They do," Doc said. There isn't a section of the country that hasn't been hit. God knows how many cases have gone unreported."

"Any good hook to hang tomorrow's lead on?" Corey asked.

"You read 'em. After a hundred or so I felt like I was reading the same one over and over."

"That bad?"

"Worse."

"Anything out of Washington?"

"Transcript of the president's speech. Inspirational."

"We heard it."

"Also, they're talking about a ban on international travel. Other countries don't want our brain eaters. Imagine that, after all of their wretched refuse we took in."

Dena lay down the wire stories and leaned over to look at the notes Doc had been working on. "What's this?"

"From the stories coming in, I've been trying to put together a profile of the brain eaters. Symptoms, duration, chances for survival—that kind of thing."

"And what did you come up with?" Corey asked.

"Bad news and worse news." He dug through the jumbled papers until he came up with the one he wanted. "The first symptom seems to be a skin irritation at the point of entry. Dexter Horn showed us at the autopsy how the parasites apparently get into the bloodstream through some small break in the skin. In the reports I've read tonight, there seems to be a fair number of cases where the victim reported a rash or low-level irritation following a small cut or abrasion of the skin."

Corey frowned in thought. "DuBois Williamson's wife said he was stung by a bee sometime before they drove past Biotron. She thought he might be allergic, the way it swelled up later."

"That fits," Doc said. "In the cases where they've traced symptoms at all, they usually start with a skin irritation of some kind."

"What else?"

"A sort of bad cold or onset of the flu feeling. Only lasts a day or two, then suddenly goes away."

"Like what I saw at Biotron last week," Dena said.

"Sounds like," Doc said.

"I can understand the skin irritation," Corey said, "but why the false flu?"

"Damned if I know," said Doc. "Maybe the parasite brings some kind of virus with it. If you want a clinical explanation, you'll have to go to somebody else. All I'm doing is tabulating, looking for a pattern."

"Okay, go ahead."

"The last stage before the flip-out seems to be the headache. We know about that, too, from the autopsy."

"I've seen the effect," Corey said grimly.

"How long do they last?" Dena asked.

"One, two, three days. Probably seems a lot longer if it's your head. They get progressively worse. No treatment helps."

"And the pain drives them crazy?" Corey said.

"Something sure as hell does. Once the victim goes into the violent stage, there's no communication with him. He starts trashing anything and anybody around him. Finally, there are the facial eruptions like we saw on the corpse. These are followed shortly by violent death—sometimes by the victim's own hand."

"They *all* die?" Dena asked in a hushed tone.

"Apparently. There are reports where the victim has been subdued, but ordinary restraints aren't strong enough to hold them. They break loose and continue their rampage until something kills them. The lucky ones die early, of cerebral hemorrhaging."

"How long does the whole thing last?" Corey asked. "From the time it gets into the bloodstream to the end?"

Doc Ingersoll pulled out another sheet on which he had drawn a graph that resembled a graduated series of mountain peaks. He said, "As near as I can figure, the average duration is seven days, with some deviation to either side."

He pointed to the undulating line of the graph. "The beginning point here is June first, the date of the helicopter spraying at Biotron. And here, seven days later, we have Stransky, Williamson, and the girl in Seattle blowing up."

"Also, Stu Anderson, the helicopter pilot," Dena put in.

"Then," Doc continued, "we have nothing until the next peak, a week later. That's when we had outbreaks that were centered around the locations of the first three. The tallest peak here, just beginning to round off, is this weekend. It started Thursday, with Friday the highest point and a slight downturn Saturday and Sunday.

"You'll notice how the peaks get blunter and the valleys

159

shallower. Project this for another couple of weeks and you'll have a steady line going thataway.'' Doc Ingersoll pointed toward the ceiling.

"You're not very encouraging," Corey said.

"You want encouragement, read Mary Worth."

Corey studied the graph for a minute, then laid it aside. He shuffled through the stacks of wire copy, selected several stories, and stuffed them into a pocket. "I think I'll save the doomsday report for later in the week," he said. "I don't want to spoil anybody's day."

"Besides, statistics make dull stories," Doc said.

"Exactly." Corey selected one of the sheets from his pocket. "This one about a little kid in Boston who tore up his nursery school before diving into a dry swimming pool will make a better headline than statistics on a thousand deaths."

"That's a fact," Doc agreed.

"Sometimes you guys make me sick," Dena said.

"Sorry. Just shoptalk. Why don't we all go out and get some dinner?"

"I'll pass," Doc said. "I want to keep an eye on the wire. I've got candy bars here and coffee in the machine."

"A diet like that will kill you," Dena said.

Doc removed the Camel butt from his mouth and looked at her. "None of us going to live forever, honey."

Corey and Dena left the building and walked around to the parking lot. They got into Corey's car and sat for a moment looking at the near-deserted street.

"Not many people out tonight." Corey observed.

"Can you blame them?"

"I guess not. Any special place you'd like to eat?"

"To tell you the truth, Corey, I don't feel much like going to a restaurant. Have you got anything to eat at your place?"

"Sure. Frozen pizza. Chicken pot pie. Hot-dog buns. Half a dozen eggs, I think. A little milk, if it's still good. Pork and beans. Beer."

Dena made a face. "That's what you eat?"

160

"That's what's left over."

"Have you got a market nearby?"

"Yeah."

"Let's stop there and pick up something."

With Dena making the selections and Corey pushing the cart, they purchased two well-marbled Spencer steaks, baking potatoes, butter, sour cream, asparagus, lettuce, onions, tomatoes, and salad dressing. From the liquor department Corey picked out a couple of bottles of California Burgundy.

When they unloaded the bags in his kitchen, Corey said, "This may be the most unfrozen food I've ever had in this place at one time."

"Poor, deprived fella," Dena said, patting his shoulder. "Does the broiler on your stove work?"

"I don't know."

"Let's find out." She turned the proper knob on the gas range, and after a moment there was a *whoomp* of flames in the broiler. "It works. Can you make a salad?"

"I think so, but why don't we relax for a minute first. I've got bourbon."

"Bourbon is fine. I'll put the potatoes in the oven. It takes them a while to bake."

Corey poured the drinks, adding ice and a splash of water to generous shots of Wild Turkey while Dena scrubbed the potatoes and put them into the oven. Corey was waiting for her when she came into the small living room. She sat down next to him on the couch and picked up her drink. They maintained a careful space between them.

"Let's make a deal," Corey said.

"What's that?"

"Just for tonight, let's forget all about the brain eaters. Tomorrow we'll be back in the real world, but tonight I'd just like to relax and pretend we haven't a thing to worry about."

"I'm not very good at pretending."

"Try."

"Okay, if you say so."

They touched glasses and drank. Corey appreciated the fact that Dena did not question the strength of the drink.

"I assume you're not married," she said.

"Nope. I was when I was twenty-three. She was a cocktail waitress. Looked great in black net stockings. Six months later I was in Vietnam, and she was back hustling drinks. I got the divorce papers while I was in the hospital."

"Leave you bitter, did it?"

"Nah, I figure I got off easy. Anyway, bitter people are a pain in the ass. Everybody makes mistakes."

"Have you made any more? Do you mind talking about it?"

"Not as long as it doesn't dominate the conversation. While I was working in San Francisco, there was Barbara. She was a dancer. She thought it was kicky to live with a hotshot reporter. Kicky. That was one of her words. Imagine her chagrin when the hotshot husband got himself fired and asked if she wanted to come with him to Milwaukee, of all places. *Adios*, Barbara."

"Sad story," Dena said.

"Not really. I only asked her to come along because I knew she wouldn't."

"So you've survived."

"Sure. How about you?"

"I came close once to getting married. Or so I thought, to a doctor in Chicago. Trouble was, he already had a wife. I knew that, of course, but like the little simp I was, I thought he'd leave her."

"They never do," Corey said.

"So I found out."

"What about the copter pilot?"

"Stu? He was fun, and I liked him a lot, but there was no commitment there. Neither of us wanted it. We were both more interested in our work than in starting a heavy romance."

"Do you like what you do?"

"Biochemistry? Sure I like it. Why?"

"Just curious. I get a bad taste from people who hate their

162

jobs. Hell, nobody's chained to his machine. If they hate it, let them find something else. Do 'em good to know what it feels like to be out of work for a while.''

"Do you like what you do, Corey?"

"Hell, yes. What I don't like is not being as successful at it as I ought to be."

"You've still got time."

He sobered for a moment. "I hope so." Then he brightened. "Want another drink?"

"Are you going to make a move on me?"

"Maybe. I can't promise anything."

"My life is full of men who can't make promises." She handed him her empty glass. "Easy on the water."

By the time they were well into their second drinks, both were feeling the effects. Corey had put on an old Johnny Mathis album, Dena had kicked off her shoes, and they were dancing awkwardly on his living room carpet.

"I think it's time to put the steaks on," she said.

"How can you tell?"

She tapped her head with a forefinger. "Women's intuition. Besides, I can smell the potatoes."

"Amazing," he said. "I'll open the wine. Let it breathe. Whatever that means."

"Don't forget the salad."

The steaks were done rare, really rare, the way Corey liked them and was never able to get them in a restaurant. For some reason restaurant chefs thought "rare" meant "medium rare." The asparagus in butter was tender, the potatoes fluffy with sour cream topping, and the salad was crisp and cold. They finished one bottle of wine and started on the second.

"Delicious dinner," he said.

"Anybody can cook a steak."

"No they can't. I'm living proof."

"You give great salad, though."

"Just lucky."

After dinner they sat again on the couch, this time with no space between them. What was left of the wine sat on the coffee table in front of them. Corey had Mose Allison on the turntable, the volume turned low.

"I know we had a deal," Dena said, her head against his, "but . . ."

"But . . ." he prompted.

"Corey, how serious do you think this is?"

"You and me?"

"No, damn it, the brain-eater thing."

"It's serious," he said, "but not critical. At least I hope not. I give it a couple more weeks; then people will find something else to worry about."

Dena drew back and looked at him. "Just how do you see this coming to an end in a couple of weeks?"

He shrugged. "Everything ends."

"Sometimes I think . . ." She hesitated, searching his face.

"You think what?"

"That all the brain eaters mean to you is a story. Your story. Something that will make you famous. And maybe rich."

"Hey, like I told my publisher the other day, I didn't invent the damn things. I just named them. If the story brings in a few bucks for me, why not? Who loses?"

Dena sighed. She did not protest when Corey put an arm around her shoulders. "I don't know. I guess I'd feel better if you showed a little more concern for the victims."

"Dena," he said, "I put in some time as police reporter in San Francisco. I've seen babies left in trash cans after their little heads were twisted around so they'd stop crying. I've seen a teenaged heroin addict who drowned in her own vomit. I've seen a man who raped and murdered two little boys and was then turned loose by a judge because the police questioned him before his lawyer got there. I had so much concern for the victims I damn near became one myself. You never get used to it, but you learn to lock it away until there is time to cry."

"Do you cry, Corey?"

"I kind of mist up at movies about the crusty old grandfather who goes all soft and chuckly when the cute little kid climbs in his lap.''

She gave him a punch on the shoulder. ''Okay, tough guy, I shouldn't have brought it up. But if we're going to have a relationship, we'll have to sit down sometime and tell each other where we stand.''

''Are we going to have a relationship?''

''That depends on what we learn about each other.''

''Fair enough,'' he said. ''Shall we go to bed?''

''Just like that?''

''What the hell, I bought you dinner.''

''All right.''


He sat on the bed and watched her undress. Her movements were as graceful and unself-conscious as a Degas ballerina. She laid her clothes over a chair and turned to look at him. Clearly, she was proud of her body. Justifiably.

She slipped into the bed and pulled the covers up. ''Are you going to join me, or are you having second thoughts?''

He grinned and shook his head. ''Be right with you.'' He moved toward the living room.

''Hey, no fair,'' she said. ''You watched me; now it's my turn to watch you.''

''I was just going to change the record.''

''Do you have to have music?''

''No.''

''Then get out of those clothes and into this bed before *I* have second thoughts.''

He did as he was told, and they made a music of their own far into the night.

# Chapter 20

Corey awoke at dawn. It was a habit from his army days that he had never been able to break. He reached down sleepily to scratch an itch and discovered he was naked. He usually slept in the bottom half of a pair of pajamas.

He frowned, still half-asleep, trying to remember what had been different when he had gone to bed the night before that would cause him to forget the pajamas. A second later he discovered he was not alone.

She lay on her side, facing away from him. The caramel-blonde hair lay in a soft tangle across the pillow. Corey lay his hand on the smooth curve between the woman's rib cage and hip, and with a relieved smile he remembered who she was and why they were in bed together naked.

Dena stirred in her sleep and moved closer to him. He put an arm around her, letting his hand rest on her breast. The nipple stirred under his fingers. He nuzzled the back of her neck, inhaling the floral scent of her hair, mingled now with the tang of her sweat.

He drifted off again into a pleasant semisleep, always aware of the woman's body next to him. Increasingly aware.

About seven o'clock Dena rolled over. With her face an inch away from his, she said, "Did you bring a gun to bed, or are you just glad to see me?"

For the next hour Corey showed her just how glad he was to see her.

For breakfast he scrambled eggs with what was left of the onions chopped into them. Dena found a jar of instant coffee in the rear of the refrigerator, and they ate together comfortably, making small jokes and smiling a lot.

With her second cup of coffee, Dena lit a cigarette.

"Do you know, this is my first one since yesterday afternoon? How about that?"

"You trying to quit?"

"Cut down, anyway. You don't smoke?"

"I used to. Tried a pipe for a while, but I couldn't keep the thing lit. Kept losing them."

"You're better off if you don't," Dena said.

"I've got other vices."

"So I've observed."

They sat silently for a minute, drinking their coffee, Dena smoking. Finally, Corey spoke.

"It's been nice, but I guess we'd better reenter the real world."

She nodded, watching him.

He got up, kissed her once, and went into the living room where he turned on the radio.

"Corey?"

He turned and saw that she had come out and was standing behind him. He straightened up and faced her.

"Last night was good," she said.

"Yeah," he said. "Me, too."

"It just occurred to me that it might not happen again."

"Why wouldn't it?"

"Because of what's going on outside. Because of the brain eaters. Because we might lose this fight."

He stepped toward her and took her in his arms. "We might win, too."

"Do you think so?"

"Hell, think any other way and you're finished. What's more, I don't intend to lose you."

"Do you mean that?"

"You're damn right I mean it." He kissed her hard and long, and she believed then that he really did mean it.

He turned on the radio, and the news hit them like a bucket of cold water.

167

Unrest was growing as people across the country continued to suffer attacks by the brain eaters. However, the number of reported cases was down from a high on Friday. This was interpreted as a hopeful sign, but Corey remembered Doc Ingersoll's graph with the projected line that climbed steadily up and away.

There were disturbances in the cities ranging from a gay people's protest march in West Hollywood to a full-fledged riot in Detroit. There was looting in the Bronx and vandalism in Atlanta. A sociologist in Boston suggested that the brain eaters were just an excuse for release of tensions. There were always people ready to pounce on any excuse for rioting or looting.

A conference of mayors had been hastily called to discuss evacuation of the cities. The trouble was that there was no safe place to go. Rural and suburban areas were as hard hit as the population centers.

One area where the brain eaters had not yet struck was the prisons. To protect their isolation, inmates demonstrated against the admission of any new convicts. They even demanded a moratorium on visitors. The result was a greater glut than ever in the courts and dangerous overcrowding in county and municipal jails where the new criminals were held awaiting transfer.

Prisons were not the only places where newcomers were unwelcome. Everywhere strangers were met with hostility. The feeling was that anything as foul as the brain-eating parasites had to be brought in by the other guys. However, as more people saw their own friends, neighbors, and family members stricken, it became harder to deny the terrible truth—anyone could be a carrier. The national paranoia continued to grow.

When the stories on the all-news station started to repeat, Corey snapped off the radio.

"How long will it take us to get up to Biotron?" he asked.

"Three hours, more or less, depending on the traffic."

"It's nine now. We'd better get going."

"I left my car in the *Herald* parking lot."

"Leave it there. We can take mine."

"And my bag is at the Beddie-Bye Motel."

He grinned at her. "Cute name."

"Yeah, isn't it. I'm starting to think of it as my home away from home."

"We'll stop on the way and pick up your things."

As soon as they were outside, they could sense the tension that hung over the city. Traffic was sporadic, with a sudden jam at an intersection one minute, empty streets the next. Pedestrians were few. People moved in small clusters, as though staying close to friends could protect them.

Many small businesses were closed and shuttered. Corey tried three gas stations before he found one open. The surly young attendant seemed reluctant to stand too close as Corey proffered his credit card.

"Cash only," the boy said.

"Since when?"

"Since now. Who knows if anybody's gonna be around to pay their credit-card bills?"

Corey started to argue but thought better of it when he saw the young man scratching at a rash under his chin. He paid for the gas and got quickly back into the car with Dena. They headed north on Highway 41.

The traffic out of Milwaukee was neither heavier nor lighter than normal, but the flow was uneven, tentative. There was a nervous, uncertain feel to it. The faces of the people in the other cars were set in tense lines. They gripped their steering wheels as though holding on to sanity.

Corey kept the car radio on but soon turned the volume down. The voices of the newscasters droned on gravely about the brain eaters. There were continuing new outbreaks and wild speculation on where they came from and how they could be banished. It soon became clear that nobody knew anything. Or if somebody did, he was not talking. It gave Corey a perverse sense of relief to know that the story still belonged to him.

They skirted the city of Appleton and headed northwest on a narrower state highway.

"What are the chances of Kitzmiller's being at the plant when we get there?" Corey asked.

"Chances of his being there are excellent," Dena said. "I've never known him to be anywhere else. He has living quarters in the biochem lab building. The chances of his seeing us are something else again. I told you about the brush I got last time I tried to talk to him."

"One way or another, we'll run him down," Corey said.

"My hero."

Dena gave his arm a playful squeeze. He grinned at her and drove on.

The chain link gate at the main entrance to the Biotron plant was closed and locked. A guard in the company's tan uniform stood beside it, a heavy-caliber revolver prominently holstered at his side.

The guard walked up to the window on the driver's side when they drove up to the gate. Corey rolled down the window. Dena leaned across him to show her ID badge.

"I'm Dr. Falkner," she said. "We'd like to go inside to talk to Dr. Kitzmiller."

"Sorry, miss . . . uh, doctor, but the plant's closed. Nobody gets in."

"I'm a reporter," Corey said, fumbling for his credentials.

"Reporters included," said the guard.

"He's Corey Macklin," Dena put in. "He's been doing the story on the brain eaters. Maybe you've heard of him."

The eyes of the guard ran coldly over Corey. "I've heard of you, but my orders were—"

Dena cut him off. "Is Dr. Kitzmiller inside?" Her tone snapped with authority.

"He, uh, well, I . . ."

"Call him. Tell him Dena Falkner is here with the man who's writing about the brain eaters. Now, please."

"I suppose I could do that." The guard was still hesitant.

"Thank you." Dena sat back and folded her arms in an attitude that said the matter was settled.

The guard edged off to the wooden building beside the gate. They could see him using the telephone inside while he kept his eyes on them. After several minutes he laid the receiver down without hanging up and came back to the car.

"I can let one of you go in," he said, "but not both."

"No deal," Corey told him. "We're together."

Dena touched his arm. "You go in, Corey. I have nothing new to say to Dr. K."

"What'll you do, wait out here?"

"If I can borrow your car, I want to pick up some things at my place. It's just a few minutes from here."

Corey frowned. "Be careful, will you?"

"It's my own house. What could happen to me?"

"I don't know. Just watch yourself, okay?"

She looked at him for a moment, then smiled. "Okay."

He got out of the car, and Dena came around and got in behind the wheel. He reached in through the window and squeezed her hand, then walked toward the wooden building where the guard was again talking on the phone.

"There'll be someone out to take you inside," the guard said.

"Thanks." Corey watched Dena drive off up the road in his car. He tried to rid himself of the uneasy feeling that he should not have let her go.

The man who came out to get Corey was tall and slim with a 1950s Ivy League cut to his suit and his hair. He put out his hand and gave Corey a brief, dry grip.

"I'm Baldwin Edge. Department of Health and Human Services."

The guard relocked the gate behind the two men, and they walked through the executive parking area toward the main building.

"Are you connected with the company?" Corey asked.

"No. That is, not officially. I was sent out here the end of last week when the plant was ordered closed. I've been reading your stories."

They walked into the deserted lobby, past the glassed reception area where no receptionist waited. Their footsteps echoed in the empty building.

"They've given me an office here to use temporarily." Edge indicated an open door. "If you'd care to come in and have a seat . . ."

Corey looked into the empty office. "It was Dr. Kitzmiller I wanted to talk to."

"Yes, but if you don't mind, there are a couple of things I'd like to discuss first."

Corey shrugged and preceded the Department of Health man into the office. He dropped into a chair and waited while Edge took his place behind the desk.

"You've become rather famous in the past week."

"My moment in the sun," Corey said, wishing the man would get to the point.

"And you have certainly made these, uh, brain eaters famous."

"I think they could have been just as big without me."

"Perhaps. But the fact is, people look to you for authoritative news on these parasites."

"Rather than to, say, the Department of Health?" Corey suggested.

Edge gave him a chilly smile. "That *has* been a matter of concern to some of my colleagues."

"I'm glad to hear that your colleagues are getting concerned. I talked to one of them more than a week ago about the strange series of deaths. His opinion, as I remember, was that the whole thing was a case of mass hysteria."

"Yes, I know about the incident," said Baldwin Edge. "Unfortunate. The man has since been reassigned to other duties."

"So you people are now ready to admit that the brain eaters really exist?"

"It seems we have no choice."

"So it seems," Corey agreed. "What can I do for you?"

"Actually, it's the other way around. I'm here to offer you our assistance."

172

"You're about a week too late."

Edge's manner chilled. "I've already apologized for that."

"Save it."

"I don't have to point out the effect your stories have had on the general population."

"No," Corey said, "you don't."

"In our department we have specialists on the use of the media in relation to mass psychology. When improperly used, the results can be devastating."

"I don't see where you're taking this," Corey said.

Baldwin Edge continued as though Corey had not spoken. "For instance, the publication of news about herpes probably did more than any single thing to reverse the so-called sexual revolution of the sixties and seventies."

"Then the media's got a lot to answer for."

"In the same manner, just as homosexuals were gaining a measure of public acceptance, reports of the AIDS breakout gave people a legitimate reason to be antigay without losing their liberal credentials."

"Mr. Edge, this is all interesting as hell, but I've got work to do."

"In any disease story certain words can trigger a panic re-action in the public. Words like *epidemic*. And *plague*. In your case, the unfortunate coinage *brain eaters* is a glaring example. People reading the stories picture tiny creatures literally eating out their brains."

"Then they've got a pretty accurate picture."

"Mr. Macklin, I don't seem to be making my point with you. What I'm saying is that if you continue to write your stories in such alarmist tones, you could be responsible for a national panic that will dwarf anything in our history. I am not in any way suggesting that your work be censored, merely that one of our media people work with you to mini-mize the fright quotient of your prose."

Corey let several long beats go by before he answered.

"Okay, Mr. Edge, your point is made. You want me to submit my stuff to you before it goes to print. Not to censor

173

it, of course, but to—what was your phrase?—minimize the fright quotient.''

''Essentially, that's it.''

''Well, you can kiss my essential ass.''

All of Baldwin Edge's Ivy League aplomb fell away like a broken shell. His face turned dark; his hands balled into fists. Corey had a wild happy moment when he thought the man was going to swing at him. However, Edge brought himself under control, breathing hard.

''Now you can take me to Dr. Kitzmiller,'' Corey said. ''He *is* here, I suppose.''

''He's here,'' said Edge through clenched teeth.

Without further conversation, he rose and marched out of the office. Corey followed, feeling good.


# Chapter 21


Dena drove away from thé Biotron plant with a feeling of relief. There was something about an empty office building that gave her the creeps. Ghosts seemed to lurk in the shadowy corners and behind the empty desks. Ghosts of the people who spent so much of their lives there.

She pulled to a stop in front of her own little house and sat for a moment looking at it. The house looked lonely. Dena exhaled sharply through her teeth and told herself to stop personalizing buildings. She had enough to occupy her mind without cluttering it up with silly fantasies.

She got out of the car, walked up the short path to the front door, and let herself in. Although she had been away only three days, the house seemed to Dena to have a musty, uncared-for feel to it. A fine layer of dust covered the polished hardwood surfaces. A spider had begun a web at the edge of the mantel. She let it be.

Moving with a practiced efficiency, she packed a large suitcase with clothes and enough personal articles to sustain her for a couple of weeks. She tried to think of it as going on a vacation trip, but she could not rid herself of the unsettling thought that she would never return to this little house.

As she went through the door, Dena could not resist turning for a last look. The place held no really powerful memories for her. She had lived there for two years in relative comfort but without any sense of fulfillment. There had been a few good times, but there had been loneliness, too.

She closed the door decisively behind her, locked it, and walked briskly back to the car. How silly, she told herself. I'll probably be back there in a few days dusting off the furniture and wondering what all the fuss was about. She keyed Corey's engine to life and pulled away down the quiet, elm-shaded street.

The clock in the dashboard told her that only twenty minutes had passed since she left Corey at Biotron. He would not yet have had time to learn anything from Dr. Kitzmiller. She was not eager to sit outside the gate and wait for any length of time. Not under the cold eyes of the security guard.

For a moment she considered going back to the little house to wait there but rejected the notion almost immediately. Then it occurred to her she was only a mile or so away from Carol Denker's house. She could kill a few minutes by stopping in to see how Carol was feeling.

Dena had already turned up the short street that led to the Denkers' place when she remembered the circumstances under which she had last seen Carol. The brief flulike symptoms that kept her home from work, the headache when she came back. Maybe going out to see Carol now was a bad idea.

Dena was disgusted with herself. She was falling victim to the paranoia that had people locking their doors against

175

neighbors and refusing to answer their telephones for fear they could catch something over the wire. Carol was her friend. Besides, if anything *were* wrong, she could simply turn around and drive back to meet Corey.

Like most of the houses in the small town of Wheeler, the one where the Denkers lived was more than sixty years old. It was a boxy two-story frame building with a wide front porch and a brick fireplace chimney running up one wall. It was too big for the family of Carol, her husband, and two small children. However, the rent was half of what they would have to pay in Milwaukee, where Ken was working for his doctorate at the university. So Ken commuted back and forth from Wheeler while Carol worked at Biotron.

The street was quiet under its heavy green canopy of shade trees. Nothing unusual about that. All the streets in Wheeler were quiet, all the time. Dena was a little surprised to see Ken's pickup in the driveway. He would normally be at school now. In the garage she could see the Ford that Carol drove. Something wrong?

Stop being silly.

She parked in the street and started toward the big house. A tricycle was overturned in the walk at the foot of the porch steps. It must belong to one of the Denker children. The boy. He was five, wasn't he? And the girl was what? Two? Close enough. Now, what were their names? Oh, what did it matter? Dena was not there to have a conversation with the children.

She had not really been social friends of the Denkers; her contact with Carol was almost entirely at the office. Their friendship was based on their mutual profession and shop-talk. Dena had been invited out there for dinner a couple of times. She had reciprocated, but that was it. She knew Ken as a quiet, pleasant man who looked something like a scholarly Robert Redford, but she had never talked with him about anything serious. The kids were always clean and well behaved. Thinking about it as she approached their house, Dena was surprised at how little she really knew these people.

Actually, Dena would not have minded seeing more of Carol's kids. She liked children and once in a while regretted not having any of her own.

She climbed to the porch and rang the bell, then waited nervously for someone to come.

Silence.

The window shades were pulled down behind the lacy living-room curtains, so she could not see inside. That was another odd thing. Shades were not drawn at that time of day. Dena felt a tiny prickle of apprehension.

To satisfy herself that she had really tried, Dena gave the bell key another jab. When there was still no response, she turned with relief and started off the porch.

A scream.

Dena froze, her foot on the top step. Unmistakably, it had been a scream. Thin, high-pitched, and terrified. And it came from inside the Denkers' house.

Again.

A child's scream of eye-popping terror.

Get out of here, Dena's good sense told her. You don't know what might be happening in there. Anyway, it's none of your business. It might be just one of the kids getting spanked.

And yet she did not move to leave.

"Help me! *Helllp!*"

That was not a kid getting spanked. That was a kid in deadly fear.

Now she could not go. A human being needed help. Dena looked quickly at the neighboring house, separated from the Denkers' by a wide yard. Nothing doing there. She turned toward the house across the street. Quiet and lifeless. From the urgency in the little voice calling for help, Dena feared she might be too late if she ran to one of the houses to try to get somebody.

She turned and walked slowly back across the porch. Her movements were stiff and wooden, as in a dream. But this was no dream, the sick dread in the pit of her stomach reminded her. She walked across the thick welcome mat to the heavy front door. She tried the old ornate doorknob. It was cold against the flesh of her palm.

The knob turned.

The door opened.

The hallway was dim, even with the light that came in through the open door and the fan-shaped window above it. Dena left the door open and moved cautiously into the living room. The furniture was contemporary in light wood and fabrics, contrasting with the house, which was dark wood and gloomy wallpaper.

There was light in the living room, but the angle of illumination was wrong, throwing shadows crazily where no shadows should be. Dena looked around and saw why. A floor lamp had been knocked over, the shade tilted so its light shined upward from the floor.

A fight? An intruder? What am I doing here?

*"Help me!"*

The cry came from upstairs, muffled but unmistakable. Dena started for the stairway.

As she stepped through the archway from the living room, she stopped, sucking in her breath. At the bottom of the stairs Ken Denker sat on the floor with his back against the wall. His fine blond hair was tangled. His glasses hung drunkenly from one ear. From his stomach protruded the black wooden handle of a butcher knife.

Dena put a hand to her mouth to keep from crying out. Her stomach contracted. From upstairs came the scream again and a thumping sound. The children must be locked in up there, she thought, and started up the stairs.

There was no light on the second floor other than what filtered past the window blinds. Dena did not take the time to search for a switch but continued in the direction of the child's cries. She made her way cautiously down the dim hallway; then suddenly she stopped.

Someone was there.

A shadowy figure stood motionless ahead of her, outside a closed door. The paneling of the door was splintered and

178

slick. Blood dripped from the hands of the standing figure. Fat red pustules broke out on the face as Dena watched. The face was contorted and swollen with the boils but still recognizable. Carol Denker.

Dena turned and started back for the stairs. Helping a child out of a room where he was trapped was one thing, but facing this wild wreck of a woman was something else. Bravery and cowardice were meaningless terms. Dena had only one thought—get the hell out of there.

She was not quick enough. Carol exploded away from the battered door and came at her like something out of a nightmare, her mouth gaping, uttering an incoherent growl. Dena stretched out for the railing at the top of the stairs, but she was hit in the back and knocked staggering against the far wall. She bounced off and hit the floor. Fireflies danced in the darkness before her eyes.

When her vision cleared, she saw Carol coming at her, hands extended, fingers bent into claws. Saliva oozed from her mouth and hung in a swaying, silvery thread from her chin as she advanced.

"No!" Dena cried. "Carol, don't! It's Dena!"

No flicker of comprehension showed on the mad face coming toward her.

Painfully, Dena pushed herself to her feet, back against the plaster wall. One elbow tingled where she had scraped it in her fall. She put out her hands defensively, knowing as she did so how impotent she was against the maniacal strength of the woman.

Carol was close enough for Dena to hear her wheezing breath and smell the stink of her sweat. Then a dark shape rose behind her in the stairwell. Dena stretched to look over the woman's shoulder and was shocked to see Ken Denker coming up behind her.

The knife was still buried in Ken's stomach. The front of his pants was glistening dark with blood. He walked unsteadily toward his wife, who was still reaching out for Dena.

"Carol!" Ken's voice had a gargling sound as blood welled up in his throat.

In some recess of the woman's tortured mind, the voice registered. Carol Denker turned away from Dena to face her husband. He took a lurching step toward her and grunted with the effort.

Carol suddenly clapped both hands to her head and screamed. The nails dug into her flesh and tore it away in bloody strips. Her cry was a banshee wail like nothing that should come from a human throat. Still screaming, she lunged at the stumbling, oncoming figure of her husband.

They came together with a thud. Carol's body drove the knife still deeper into the man's stomach. With their arms about each other in a bloody last embrace, they lurched together to the top of the stairs. Then, in grotesque slow motion, they toppled over and fell bumping and crashing down the uncarpeted steps to the hardwood floor in the hallway below.

For a long moment Dena continued to stand where she was, her back pressed against the wall. There was no sound from downstairs, only the whimpering of a child behind the door that had been battered by the mad mother.

When she got her breathing and heartbeat under control, Dena went to the stairs and slowly descended, one cautious step at a time. Ken and Carol Denker lay together in a tangle of limbs at the bottom. Mercifully, Carol's face was turned away, hiding the ugly broken pustules. She might have been in repose, were it not for the unnatural angle at which her head lay on one shoulder.

Ken Denker's eyes were open and unblinking. He seemed to look off to the corner of the ceiling and beyond. One arm lay over his wife's back in a last cold caress.

Dena hurried back up the stairs. It took her several minutes to tear the broken paneling loose so she could reach in and open the bedroom door. Inside she found the children. They were huddled on the bed, the little girl crouched behind her brother. Tears rolled from the girl's eyes; the boy stared. His narrow chest heaved with strangled sobs.

"It's all right," Dena said, keeping her voice soft. "Don't be afraid of me."

The children edged back away from her on the bed as she approached.

"I won't hurt you."

"Mommy will," the boy said. "She hurt Daddy."

"It's all over now. Come, I'll take you out of here."

"She was trying to hurt us, too," the boy said. "I wouldn't let her in."

Moving slowly as though approaching frightened wild animals, Dena reached out to the children. Cautiously, they let her take their hands. The boy looked around with frightened eyes as she led them into the hall. The little girl continued to cry without making a sound.

Dena led them to the back stairs and down to the kitchen.

"Where's my mommy and daddy?" the boy said, looking around.

Dena's throat closed, and she could not answer him. She led the two children out the back door and around to the front of the house. The boy kept looking back toward the blank windows and the open front door of his home. The little girl looked at nothing.

The commotion had finally roused a neighbor, a stout, gray-haired woman wearing an apron.

"What's happened?" she said, her mouth tight with fear.

"Can you take the children?" Dena asked.

"Yes, of course. Where are the parents?"

"They're inside." Dena looked quickly down at the boy, who was watching her. "Please call the sheriff."

"The sheriff? But what—?"

"Please." Dena cut her off.

The woman looked down from the children to the open door, then back at Dena. She nodded her understanding. "Come along, kiddies," she said. "I have some cookies over at my house. I think they're still warm."

Dena looked her thanks at the woman and hurried out to the car. She started it up and drove wildly back toward the Biotron facility. She wanted nothing so much at that moment as to be in the arms of Corey Macklin.

# Chapter 22

Baldwin Edge took Corey into an office that was furnished in a manner designed to make it look comfortable, yet somehow it missed the mark. The tweedy sofa, the relaxing prints on the walls, the antique hat rack with the mirror, the flowers on the low table, all seemed too artfully arranged. Even more out of place than the furnishings was the thin, bony man seated behind the desk. There were no soft edges to him. He did not belong at all.

"Hello," he said without getting up. "I am Dr. Frederich Kitzmiller." He had just the trace of an accent.

Corey approached the desk. "Corey Macklin, Milwaukee *Herald*."

"Yes, I know," Kitzmiller said.

The man from the Department of Health stood uncomfortably behind Corey's shoulder.

"I don't think there is any need for you to stay, Mr. Edge," said Kitzmiller.

"I should know about any action that is decided upon," he said uncertainly.

"I will see that you are informed."

"Yes, well, there *are* other things I should be attending to." Baldwin Edge made an awkward exit, closing the office door behind him.

"I dislike dealing with government people," Kitzmiller said, "but it seems unavoidable, no matter what field one is in. I suppose you have your own problems with the government, Mr. Macklin."

"Some. Your friend Mr. Edge, for one."

"How so?"

"He wanted to censor my stories."

"Indeed? When did he make this suggestion?"

"Just now, before he brought me here. He prettied up the language, but that's what he wanted."

"And what was your response?"

"I told him to forget it."

Kitzmiller removed his glasses, breathed on the lenses, polished them, and laid them down on the desk. "I did not authorize Mr. Edge to conduct any discussion. He was to bring you directly to me."

"It doesn't matter," Corey said. "I'm here now."

"So you are. Shall we get to the point, then, Mr. Macklin? I assume the reason for your visit is to talk about your, ah, brain eaters."

"I'd rather you wouldn't call them *my* brain eaters, but that is why I'm here."

Kitzmiller watched him impassively. The blue eyes were bright and cold.

"I have evidence that they originated right here at Biotron," Corey continued.

"What kind of evidence?"

"Eyewitness reports."

"How does it happen that I have not seen Biotron mentioned in your stories?"

"It's not the kind of a thing we would print without authentication. I wanted to talk to you first. Get your side of the story. You do have a side?"

Kitzmiller studied him across the desk, the blue eyes like chips of ice. "May I talk to you off the record?"

"Sorry, but I can't accept that. If you won't talk to me for publication, I'll go to other sources, but I won't make any promises."

"I see. Well, then, what is it you want to know?"

Corey pulled a wad of copy paper and a pencil from his jacket pocket. "To begin with, were these parasites, the ones that have been attacking people's brains, developed here at Biotron?".

"Yes."

Corey blinked, surprised by the sudden directness of the answer.

"But not, I hasten to add, deliberately," Kitzmiller continued. "They were an accident. An unfortunate result of our research on a pesticide project. One we called in-house TCH-nine."

Corey made rapid notes in his personal shorthand. "When was this project begun, doctor?"

"A little more than a year ago."

"Is this TCH-nine still in production?"

"No. It was never used. The entire project was abandoned as soon as the potential dangers were recognized."

"When was that?"

"Approximately two months ago."

"And what was done with the stuff that had already been produced?"

Kitzmiller regarded Corey shrewdly. "Apparently, you have already heard that story."

"I'd like to hear it from you."

"The existing TCH-nine, which was no more than two liters in a pressurized canister, was scheduled for disposal in the usual way prescribed by the Environmental Protection Agency. Unfortunately, there was . . . an accident."

"What happened?"

"The canister of TCH-nine, which was marked for disposal, was switched with another that contained purple dye being used for a dispersal test."

Corey stopped writing and looked at him. "An accident, doctor? Switching a deadly substance for a harmless one? Don't you have controls to prevent something like that?"

"We have always had an adequate control system."

"Really?"

"Mr. Macklin, are you here for an interview or a debate?"

"Sometimes there is a fine line separating the two," Corey said. "I'm not trying to get on your case, Dr. Kitzmiller, but people are going to want to know *how* the brain eaters got turned loose and who was responsible. Frankly, I find it hard to believe that it was an accident."

"So do I," Kitzmiller said.

It took Corey a beat to react. "Would you explain that?"

"My theory is not a popular one."

"Nothing about the brain eaters is popular."

"Your newspaper will probably put me down as an alarmist."

"We'll see."

"Very well." Kitzmiller sat more erect in his chair. "In the week prior to the exchange of the canisters, we had visitors."

"Here at Biotron?"

"That is correct. It was a tour arranged by our State Department." He mouthed the words as though they left a bad taste. "The visitors represented themselves as a delegation of agricultural specialists from the Soviet Union."

"So?"

"Russians."

"Yes, I understand. You said, 'Represented themselves.' Don't you think they were authentic agricultural experts?"

"I know they were not." He ticked off the names on his fingers. "One of them was Viktor Raslov, a high official in the Communist party. Another was Anton Kuryakin, a biochemist of considerable accomplishment in his own country. The other two I am certain were assigned by the KGB to ensure the loyalty of the others. They had the look."

"The State Department didn't know this?"

"Of course they knew. However, given the current political climate, they deemed it wise to pretend they believed the Russian's transparent masquerade. This month we are friends."

Corey stared at him. "Let me see if I understand this. Are

185

you suggesting that these Russians who toured your plant are somehow guilty of unleashing the brain eaters?''

Kitzmiller gave a little snort of disgust. ''I was sure you would react this way. The liberal press has turned a justifiable fear of the Russians into a joke. Russkies. Commies. These are the words of the liberal press. People who know the true nature of the Soviet Union and the men who rule there do not use cuddly nicknames for them.''

''I'm sorry, but you took me by surprise. Is it your position, doctor, that the Russians, whoever they are, during their visit to your plant, managed to switch the brain-eaters canister with the harmless one? That presumes an awful lot of knowledge for the Russians of your activities here and your procedures. It also presumes an incredible lack of security on your part.''

''That is not what I mean at all,'' said Kitzmiller. ''Although it is not unlikely that they had the knowledge of what we are doing, our security was at least adequate for keeping an eye on them while they are on our premises.''

''How, then, are they to blame?''

''Someone here is working for them. Their inspection tour was an opportunity to give the order for switching the canisters.''

''A spy in Biotron?'' Corey tried unsuccessfully to keep the disbelief out of his voice. Kitzmiller did not seem to notice.

''Such a thing is not unheard of. Facilities with much tighter security than ours have been infiltrated. You must remember the case of TRW out in California.''

Corey made rapid notes. ''Have you any idea who the spy is?''

''I am sorry to say that I have not. We had a suspect, but he does not seem likely now.''

''Who was that?''

''Rather an obvious candidate—the man who had the responsibility for disposal of the TCH-nine canister. We interrogated him at some length; however, I do not think he has the intelligence the Russians require of their people.''

186

"What's his name?"

Kitzmiller hesitated a moment. "Are you going to print this?"

"Not unless it's critical to the story."

"I suppose it can do no harm to tell you now. He has been under surveillance since the accident. His name is Edward Gault."

Corey wrote the name on the wad of copy paper. "There's nobody else you suspect?"

"Our investigation was just getting under way. Unfortunately, because of this business"—he waved a hand to indicate the empty plant—"we had to suspend it."

"Yeah, that's unfortunate," Corey said dryly.

He looked up from his notes and followed Kitzmiller's glance over to the hat rack. There was something not right about it. The reflection in the glass was a shade too dark. He started to say something about it but was interrupted by the sound of running feet outside the office.

The door opened without a knock, and a young security guard stepped into the room.

"Excuse me, Dr. Kitzmiller, but there's some trouble at the gate. I think maybe you'd better get out of the plant."

"Trouble? What kind of trouble?"

"Some people are trying to break in."

Corey got out of his chair and started for the door. The guard stepped into his path. He looked at Dr. Kitzmiller.

"It's all right," Kitzmiller said. "Mr. Macklin is with the press. He would like to see what is happening. So would I, for that matter."

He came around his desk, and he and Corey walked swiftly with the young guard through the lobby and out to the executive parking area. A distraught-looking Baldwin Edge hurried out of the office he was using and joined them.

Across the asphalt at the fence, the older guard was standing inside the locked gate as a dozen or so people clamored to get through. The people outside screamed and gabbled incoherently. Their faces were twisted into mindless masks of agony, their eyes wide and rolling, their mouths agape. The facial skin of many of them had begun to blister and pop in the deadly telltale of the brain eaters.

Corey stared in disbelief. "My God, who are they?"

"I recognize some of them," Kitzmiller said. "They are people who work here."

"Look at them," said Baldwin Edge. "They're like . . . wild animals!"

As he spoke, a car skidded to a stop at the gate, and two more wild-eyed men stumbled out to join the others. A pickup came. Another car. It collided with the pickup, but the occupants paid no attention as they spilled out and stumbled toward the gate. From both directions on the road others came staggering on foot. Across the field they came. Out of the small stand of beech trees across the road.

"What do they want?" said Edge. His voice quivered with emotion.

"Some instinct must have brought them here," Kitzmiller said. "Obviously they are not in rational control of their behavior."

The guard at the gate had his revolver in his hand, the barrel pointing to the sky. The younger guard unholstered his own weapon as he ran to join him.

There were now more than twenty of the crazed victims outside the gate, screeching and yammering. Their clawed fingers grasped the mesh; their ruined faces pressed against it. They put their combined weight against the gate and pushed. It began to buckle inward.

The older guard fired his pistol in the air. The report had no effect on the growing crowd outside. There were more than twenty of them now, pushing and jostling one another to get at the gate.

Baldwin Edge began making a strange sound. Corey looked at him and was surprised to see that the man was crying.

"We had better go out the back," Kitzmiller said. "There is an exit there that will take us back toward the laboratories."

Before they could move, the latch holding the steel gate

188

shut snapped with a bang. The two guards fell back, brandishing their pistols as the wild, screaming people lurched in through the breech. One of them, a young woman, reached the older guard. Her fingers dug into his face. From where they stood, Corey and the other two men could see the blood spurt out over the woman's hands as the guard screamed. His pistol clattered to the ground.

The younger guard fired. The woman dropped. The older guard stumbled away, both hands to his torn face. A man from the crowd hit him with a wild swing of his fist. The guard staggered sideways and fell. The younger guard fired again. The man who had hit the guard grabbed at his stomach.

Edge gave a little cry and started to run toward the gate. The younger guard was now firing at random into the writhing crowd.

"Stop it!" called Edge. "Stop! These people can't help themselves. You're killing them!"

The hammer of the guard's revolver clicked on an empty chamber. Two of the men who pushed through the gate hit him, and he fell. They began kicking at his head and his stomach.

Baldwin Edge ran up to the fallen guard, gesturing and trying to talk to the people who were kicking at him. Then Edge, too, was knocked to the ground. His screams were cut off abruptly as a middle-aged man with the strength of madness crushed his throat.

"Can't we do anything?" Corey said.

"Don't be foolish," Kitzmiller said. "Come."

He took Corey's arm and began to lead him back into the building. They stopped abruptly as they saw coming toward them through the lobby two men and a woman dressed in the white smocks of laboratory technicians. They reached out toward Corey and the doctor. They were close enough for Corey to see their faces erupting in bloody sores.

As Corey and the doctor turned back, they saw the knot of people from the gate leave the fallen ones and start toward them.

"Here is your story, Mr. Macklin," Kitzmiller said in a tone of lifeless irony. "Unfortunately, it looks as though you may not have the opportunity to write it."

The sound of a revving automobile engine made Corey look beyond the crowd of babbling victims to a black Buick that turned off the road and was picking up speed as it headed for the broken gate.

"More of them coming," Kitzmiller said.

"No," Corey said. "That's my car."

He could clearly see Dena at the wheel, her mouth compressed into a grim line, her eyes intent on the scene before her. The Cutlass hit what was left of the gate, shattering a headlight and carrying the twisted chain link segment completely off its hinges. Dena swerved to avoid the stumbling people, letting the shattered gate fall away from the car as she did so.

She skirted the milling crowd and slammed the car to a stop in the parking area in front of the entrance where Corey and Kitzmiller stood. Corey yanked open the door on the passenger side and shoved Kitzmiller into the car. He started to climb in himself but was pulled back by something clutching at his jacket. He turned and saw the crazed, blistered face of one of the lab technicians. The man had a fistful of Corey's jacket. In his other hand was a broken glass laboratory flask. As the jagged edge of glass was thrust toward his face, Corey shrugged out of his coat, leaped into the car, and slammed the door. The flask shattered against the safety glass of the side window.

Dena tramped on the accelerator and spun the car back around toward the gate. Corey saw her wince as they bumped over something yielding that lay on the asphalt. Dena set her jaw and drove on, picking up speed. They roared back out through the gate and onto the road, heading away from the shrieking crowd that was spilling into Biotron.

# Chapter 23

Dena slowed the Buick as they passed through the suburbs of Germantown and Menomonee Falls into Milwaukee. The traffic was sporadic and unpredictable. Corey sat beside her, leaning tensely forward.

"Do you want me to drive?" he asked.

"No, I'm okay."

Dr. Kitzmiller sat slumped in the back seat, saying nothing.

Dena watched the seemingly aimless progress of the other drivers. "I don't think people know where they're going," she said. "Being out in their automobiles gives them a sense of being in control, but once in the car, they feel they have to move, to go somewhere. And there isn't anyplace to go."

"The place for us to go right now is a hotel," Corey said, ignoring the philosophical observation.

"I detest hotels," Dr. Kitzmiller volunteered.

"It's only temporary," Corey told him, "until we find out what's happening."

Kitzmiller was unappeased. "I should be back at the laboratory. There is much to do."

"It will be a day or so before anybody can go back there," Corey said. "You remember how it was when we left. We were lucky to get out."

"The police should have the situation there under control by now."

"We can't rely on the police," Dena said. "They are no

more immune to the brain eaters than the employees of Biotron.''

Kitzmiller groaned in the back seat. ''I wish we did not have to use that term.''

''We can call them anything you want, doctor, but thanks to Corey here, in the mind of the public they will forever be the brain eaters.''

Kitzmiller sat frowning for a minute. Finally, he shrugged. ''After all, what does it matter what they are called? They exist.''

''Even the surgeon general will have to admit that now,'' Corey said sourly.

''There must be an antidote,'' Kitzmiller said. ''Some way to destroy them. I should be working now to find it. All my notes are back there at Biotron. I am useless in a hotel.''

''We can at least do some preliminary planning,'' Dena said. ''I'll stay and work with you while Corey finds out what he can about any official moves.''

''I detest hotels,'' said Kitzmiller, returning to his original complaint.

''Holiday Inns are very nice,'' Dena assured him as a sign loomed ahead of them.

''And it's only temporary,'' Corey said again.

''I suppose there is no choice,'' the doctor said gloomily. ''I hope you will hurry with whatever you have to do, Mr. Macklin. I should not have to remind you that time grows short.''

Something was critically different at the *Herald* building. There was the feeling of urgency as people strode in and out of the building with an air of grim purpose. But the difference was more than that. It was more than the missing laughter, the almost total lack of idle conversation among employees and visitors. Something vital to the building was missing. It took Corey a moment to recognize what it was. The heartbeat was stilled. The mighty presses down in the basement were not running. At a time of day when the rumble of the machinery should send a pulse through the entire twelve floors of the building, no papers were being printed.

The city room, usually a scene of semiorganized confusion, looked like a ship in the last stages of abandonment. Fewer than half the usual crew was there, cleaning out their desks. Each was absorbed by his own personal drama. They acknowledged Corey, if at all, with a distracted nod.

He hurried past the worried-looking staff and into the office of Porter Uhlander. The city editor sat behind his desk, hands clasped over his stomach, a vacant look in his eyes.

"What's going on?" Corey demanded.

"Going on? Oh, hello, Corey. How're they hanging?"

Corey walked closer and peered at the editor. "Are you on something, Porter?"

"Valiums, son. Wonderful little pills no bigger than a BB. Makes everything bearable. I should have discovered them long ago."

"Shit," Corey said.

Uhlander smiled beatifically. "You ought to try them yourself. You're too tense. Take everything too seriously. You need to mellow down."

"Damn it, Porter, I don't want to mellow down. I want to know what's going on here. Half the people who work in the city room are missing. The rest are cleaning out their desks."

Uhlander smiled at him.

"And the presses have stopped."

For the first time, the editor showed a little emotion. He said, "You noticed that. The *Herald* has suspended publication until . . ." The vague smile returned as Uhlander's gaze drifted back toward the ceiling.

Corey waited. Finally, out of patience, he snapped, "Until when, Porter?"

"Until the disappearance of the brain eaters or the end of the world—whichever comes first." The editor giggled.

"How many of those happy pills did you take, anyway?"

"Two or three. Maybe six. It really doesn't matter, does it?"

"I suppose not," Corey said wearily. "Is Mr. Eichorn still here?"

"Noooo," Uhlander drawled. "He beat it back to Houston. It seems his daughter is feeling poorly. The Eich is afraid it might be"—he tapped his forehead—" you know."

The editor focused on something beyond Corey. He raised a hand in a cheery wave. "Come right on in. Don't be shy. The more the merrier."

Corey turned to see Doc Ingersoll coming through the open door to the editor's office. He looked even more haggard than usual. His shirt was badly wilted, and the front of his suit was peppered with cigarette ash.

"Thank God somebody's here who can talk sense," Corey said. "You're not popping goofballs, too, are you?"

"That's not my vice," Doc said. "But our friend Porter just might have the right idea."

"What's the story here. What's all this suspend-publication shit."

"That's the new rules from Washington. Like everybody else, we are now operating as part of a media pool. Every population center has one newspaper printed and one radio and TV station on the air. You can bet that in Milwaukee the newspaper ain't us."

"A pool? What the fuck is the reason for that?"

"Attrition, for one thing. There aren't enough people on their feet to keep everything going."

"Jesus. That bad?"

"Worse. You remember that graph I drew up? The one that showed the brain-eater attacks growing geometrically? I think I was too optimistic."

"Who's giving the orders?"

"Harv Gehrman from over at the *Journal* was made the pool captain."

"At least they put a real newspaperman in charge," Corey said.

"Don't get overconfident. A man from the Department of Commerce is on his way to take over."

Corey groaned. "I should have known."

Porter Uhlander spoke up, startling the two reporters, who had forgotten for the moment that he was there. "You boys might as well take the rest of the day off. Enjoy yourself. Nothing to do around here."

"Thanks, chief," Corey said.

"Don't mention it."

As they left the office together, Porter Uhlander smiled benignly at their departing backs.

"I hear there was some trouble up at Biotron," Doc said.

"Where did you hear that?"

"UPI."

"The wire services are still operating, then?"

"Tri-State shut down, but we're still getting AP and UPI, along with Reuters and Tass."

"Let's go take a look at what they've got. On the way I'll fill you in on the Biotron business."

The wire-service reports were full of bad news and more bad news.

The number of victims struck by the brain eaters was mounting faster than the names could be recorded. Hospitals were running out of beds, due largely to people who had nothing more than simple colds or the flu or uncomplicated headaches. They had read enough about the brain-eaters symptoms to be justifiably scared out of their wits. Conversely, many who had been legitimately attacked by the parasites refused to accept the fact and screamed their way into madness and death, denying all the while that the brain eaters had them.

In view of the situation, the surgeon general had grudgingly admitted that there was indeed something to be worried about. He announced the setting up of a national task force of physicians to come up with a solution. Since there was so far no effective treatment for the victims, this news did little to calm the populace.

The story of what was now called the Biotron Massacre was reported merely as one more incident in a time of madness. Two security guards, an official of the Department of

Health, and an unknown number of brain-eater victims, said to be Biotron employees, had died before state police and National Guardsmen were able to restore order.

The guard had been called out elsewhere, too, primarily in large cities where looting was on the rise. It seemed that for some the lure of an unguarded color television set could overpower any concern about having their brains chewed out. There was a growing clamor for martial law. So far the president was noncommittal.

Commerce and industry were closing down all across the country as people grew reluctant to leave their homes.

The commissioner of baseball announced the suspension of the season until further notice. Fans paid little attention except in Seattle, where the Mariners had the best record of their history and were already talking about the playoffs. The manager hinted darkly that the whole brain-eaters panic might have been a plot by the California Angels, who were in a horrendous batting slump.

Theaters, concert halls, schools, even churches— anyplace where crowds of people gathered—were closed. Stores were locking their doors, bringing on a rash of hoarding and a sudden shortage of consumer goods. Emergency plans for rationing were under way in Washington.

The reactions from other countries were as varied as might be expected.

Great Britain offered help in the form of medical personnel and supplies.

The USSR suggested that the affliction was an expected result of the decadent Western life-style.

France hinted that the decay of American brains had begun long ago.

Mexico lined the border with troops to keep out would-be immigrants.

Cuba threatened a missile reprisal if the brain eaters were spread to Havana.

Canada offered assistance as long as U.S. citizens did not try to move up there.

Central America and the Middle East were too absorbed

in their own wars and revolutions to pay much attention to what happened in the United States.

And the horror stories continued. The reports of bloody rampages by victims of the parasites had lost their power to shock, owing to the sheer number of such incidents.

A schoolteacher in Orlando . . .

A farmer outside Des Moines . . .

A pensioner in Albuquerque . . .

A nine-year-old girl in Portland . . .

As Corey shuffled through the repetitive stories of mayhem and death, he suddenly laughed.

Doc cocked an eyebrow. "Something funny?"

"Not really." Corey handed him the sheet with the story he had been reading.

### DOOMSDAY WATCHERS FLEE HILLTOP

Some thirty members of the New Faith and Final Judgment Church fled in panic from the hilltop outside Biloxi where they had been awaiting "judgment day" when one of their number attacked the Reverend Clayton Cadwallader with a ceremonial crucifix. Witnesses describe a behavior pattern in the assailant similar to victims across the country of the "brain eater" parasites.

Doc Ingersoll let the sheet fall onto the pile. "You're right," he said. "It's not really funny." Then he laughed. "But what the hell; you can't cry all the time. Do you suppose the reverend is still sitting up there on the hill?"

"I don't know, but if his follower got in a good one with that crucifix, he'd better be on good personal terms with the Lord."

"Amen," said Doc piously.

"*Here* you are!" a voice accused from behind Corey in the doorway to the wire room.

He turned to see Lou Zachry looking like a 1950s college boy dressed for a date, in a checked sport jacket and knitted tie. Zachry's all-American face was flushed.

197

"Here I am," Corey admitted.

"What have you done with Kitzmiller?"

"I haven't *done* anything with him except check him into the Holiday Inn. Dena's with him. What's the problem?"

Zachry paused for a deep breath. "No problem. I just expected you to touch base with me when you got back from Biotron."

"So I came here first. What's the big flap?"

"You've heard of the president's task force on the brain eaters."

"Yeah."

"Well, I'm heading up the local chapter."

"You? Why would they pick somebody from the—what was your agency again?"

"IDI—Inter-Departmental Intelligence."

"Right, so what are you doing on a brain-eater task force?"

"In an emergency like this there's always lots of departmental crossover. And I was on the scene and had already gotten my nose into this business with you. Anyway, I'm it. Like a lot of government decisions, the logic of it doesn't matter."

"Okay, so what do you want with me?"

"I have a job for you. I understand you don't have a functioning newspaper here anymore."

"So they tell me. We're all part of a pool now."

"Not you. You're the task-force press liaison."

"Sounds impressive. What do I have to do?"

"Keep the rest of the media off Dr. Kitzmiller's back. I want him to head up remedial research."

"Well, that makes sense, anyway." Corey checked his watch. "We'd better get over there. He detests hotels."

"Let's go," Zachry said.

"Want to come, Doc?" Corey asked.

"No, thanks, I'm not feeling too red hot."

Corey looked at him sharply.

Doc grinned. "No, nothing like that. Just lack of sleep

catching up with me. I'll grab a few hours' shut-eye and be frisky as a colt again.''

Corey nodded. He turned reluctantly and left the building with Lou Zachry.

As they entered the Holiday Inn, Corey was immediately hailed by a reporter and a female cameraman he recognized from the *Sentinel*. Lou Zachry faded into the background as they approached.

"Well, Corey, you got this one staked out early, didn't you," the reporter said. "Where you keeping him?"

"Keeping who?"

"Come off it, hotshot. There's no more exclusive on this story. We got a tip that you checked Dr. Kitzmiller from Biotron in here this afternoon. We all know what happened at Biotron today, and it's not hard to figure that it has to do with the brain eaters. Okay, I'm the designated pool reporter, and Lisa here is my cameraman, so let's have the room number."

"Well, why didn't you just ask for it?" Corey said. "He's in eleven-twenty-one."

"Thanks." The *Sentinel* pair started toward the elevator; then the reporter turned back. "Too bad about you not being the star anymore, buddy, but that's show business, right?"

Corey showed his teeth and went back to join Zachry.

"There wasn't much you could do, I suppose," Zachry said, "but I wish you hadn't given them the room number. I'd like to have some time with Kitzmiller before they turn him into a media event."

"Who said I gave them the right number?" Corey asked. "Kitzmiller's in two-oh-five."

Zachry grinned. "I can see I picked the right man for press relations. I suggest we get him the hell out of here."

The government man's suggestion was just fine with Dr. Kitzmiller. "The sooner I get back to my laboratories, the sooner I can begin the search for an antidote," he said.

"I'm certainly agreeable to that," Zachry said. "By to-

199

morrow the National Guard should have the plant secured so you can go back in there. How much of a staff will you need?''

"For the moment Dr. Falkner here and I will be able to handle the research. Then I will need medical personnel—chemists, biologists, laboratory technicians, and clerical help.''

"You'll get them. Are there facilities at the Biotron plant so the four of us can stay there? I'd like to make that our nerve center.''

"Brain Eater Control,'' Corey said.

The others looked at him. No one smiled.

"You could stay there, I suppose,'' Kitzmiller said without enthusiasm. "The accommodations will not be terribly comfortable.''

"We'll make do,'' Zachry said.

"What about tonight?'' Kitzmiller asked. "You said there are already reporters here looking for me?''

"Yes, and I'd just as soon they didn't bother you with a whole lot of questions just now.''

"I detest hotels,'' Kitzmiller reminded them.

"You can spend the night at my place,'' Corey said. "Besides the bedroom, I've got a sofa that can be slept on.''

"I do not sleep on sofas,'' Kitzmiller said.

"So you can have the bed.''

"I suppose that will have to do.''

"Fine,'' said Zachry. "Tomorrow afternoon we'll rendezvous at Corey's apartment at one o'clock and head for Biotron. In the meantime, I'll make sure they're set up to handle us there.''

"What about you?'' Corey asked Dena.

"No sweat. I'm beginning to feel at home at the Beddie-Bye Motel.'' She snapped a salute in the direction of Lou Zachry. "See you at thirteen hundred hours, captain.''

# Chapter 24

Viktor Raslov saw that Kuryakin was missing at the same moment that he was handed the telephone by Neal Henderson, the young assistant to the manager of San Francisco Airport.

Accident? A wrong turn? Or—O hated word—defection?

Raslov could not very well change his mind now about talking to the embassy, since he had made such a point of it with this nervous young man. However, he did not want to call attention to Kuryakin's absence before it was absolutely necessary. Such things could be quite embarrassing. The head of a delegation was responsible for the safety, not to mention the loyalty, of its members.

He signaled the KGB men with his eyes, and one of them slipped out of the office to scan the terminal. While Henderson stood by perspiring lightly, Raslov punched out the number of the Soviet consulate. He identified himself and after some delay was put through to the chief consul.

"Yes, yes, Raslov, what is it?" The chief consul was senior to Raslov in the party and had no need to be polite.

"There seems to be some delay here in our flight," he said in Russian. "Nothing serious, but I thought you should be informed."

"If it is nothing serious, why did you call me? You must have heard about the trouble we are having down here with some right-wing protest group that is blaming us for these so-called brain eaters. The police seem in no hurry to disperse them."

"No, I had not heard," Raslov said.

"Everything here is confusion," the chief consul said. "There is nothing I can do for you."

"I understand," Raslov said. "Please do not concern yourself."

He hung up the telephone and said to young Henderson, "The consul says if the delay of our flight is prolonged, he will expect a full report from your superior."

"I'm sure it won't be long," said Henderson. "Would you care to wait in the VIP lounge?"

"VIP?"

"It's for . . . dignitaries and important travelers."

"We will wait out there," Raslov said, pointing back toward the terminal. "Where the people wait."

"Yes, of course, whatever . . ." Henderson finished the sentence lamely as he saw he no longer had the Russian's attention.

The KGB man came back into the office and gave a small shake of his head. Raslov swore under his breath and started out, the two KGB men flanking him.

"We'll page you," Neal Henderson said to their departing backs, "as soon as there is any word."

"You did not see Kuryakin?" Raslov said to the KGB man who had left the office.

"No, sir."

"Did you look in the lavatories?"

"No."

"Well, do so." To the other he said, "Search the other terminals. If you see Kuryakin, detain him. Do you understand?"

"Of course."

Raslov's eyes met those of the KGB man. They did not like to be given orders by anybody except one of their own. Not even a party official. Raslov resolved to be more diplomatic. It was never a good idea to get on the wrong side of the KGB.

Anton Kuryakin did his best to blend in with the other

people milling around San Francisco Airport. It was not so difficult in the international terminal where he had slipped away from Viktor Raslov and the thick-necked men from the KGB. There the babble of foreign tongues was louder than the English, and the people were dressed in all manner of costumes. Indeed, Kuryakin, in his dark conservative suit and his bland peasant face, looked more American than the Latins and Asians who made up the bulk of the crowd.

Once he moved on through the other terminals, he began to feel more conspicuous. It was the first time he had been alone among Americans. He felt sure his foreignness would call attention to him, but no one seemed to be looking.

How colorfully they dressed in this country, he thought. And with so little formality. There were more women wearing pants than dresses. None of the men wore a hat. Kuryakin was glad he had left his own packed away. He saw also that there were very few neckties in evidence. Kuryakin considered removing his but reasoned that his suit and starched white shirt would be even more conspicuous without a necktie than they already were. Furthermore, he would feel decidedly undressed without it. He left it on.

The airport held a bewildering array of shops and services that seemed to Kuryakin to have nothing to do with air travel. It was in stark contrast to Moscow, where an airport looked like an airport and not a department store. Given the choice, Kuryakin would have taken the Russian way.

Here there were restaurants, bars, clothing stores, a barbershop, a beauty parlor, a medical clinic, a flower store, and stands selling sourdough bread. All manner of attractions to make a man forget what his business was. Kuryakin resisted the temptation to inspect the variety of goods available to anyone who had the price. He reminded himself that he had a mission, and he knew they would be looking for him soon—Raslov and the other two. Probably, also, the American authorities. He had no time to waste.

There were decisions to be made. Which airline should he take? He passed up the one called American as seeming disloyal to his own country. The same went for Pan American.

Continental suggested that it might somehow deposit him in Europe, and Trans-World was a longer jump than he wanted to make. How much simpler it was in Russia, where the joke was that when you wanted to fly, you either went Aeroflot or grew wings.

Finally, after studying a map board showing their routes, he settled on United. He got into a line at the counter, glancing around to be sure no one was yet coming for him. With the general excitement over the brain-eater business, no one was paying any attention to him. He relaxed and moved slowly with the queue. Standing in line was one thing he understood.

After ten minutes he reached the counter, where a harried black man explained that the line was for people who had already purchased their tickets and wished to check their luggage. Kuryakin sighed and moved out of line. Such frustrations were not uncommon in Moscow either.

By careful observation he found the correct line where people were buying tickets and took his place behind a Latin-looking woman with a very noisy baby. That line moved more slowly than the other, and tempers were fraying on all sides by the time Kuryakin again reached the counter.

"I wish a ticket to Milwaukee," he pronounced carefully when it was his turn at the counter. He understood English quite well, but speaking the language made him uncomfortable. So much of it seemed to be pushed through the nose.

"Everything is full," the clerk told him. "The best I can do is put you on standby on flight eight-fifty-nine for Chicago."

"Cheecago . . . is it close to Milwaukee?"

"Practically next door. There are shuttle flights every hour. I mean, there used to be. Maybe they're still operating, but I can't promise you. Everything is a mess."

"Yes, big mess. I take the 'bystand.' "

"Standby."

"Yes, that one."

The clerk explained to him how it worked, and Kuryakin

carefully counted off some of the American bills he had been given for the trip. It left him with very little money, but if he got where he was going, that would not matter.

The lounge where the standby passengers waited was extremely comfortable by Moscow standards. There were individual padded chairs for sitting, a huge window through which one might watch the planes taxiing by outside, and an immaculate public rest room. But what seized his attention was a fascinating machine into which young Americans fed an unceasing stream of coins.

The machine featured a televisionlike screen on which a voracious little head sped through a maze gobbling up white dots and blobs of various shapes until an even more voracious creature caught the tiny head and gobbled it up in turn. The progress of the gobbling head was apparently controlled by whoever put the coin into the machine, while the opposing blobs seemed to operate on whim. The whole process was accompanied by melodious electronic bleeps, blats, boops, and honks—altogether an amazing device. A microcosm of the capitalist system.

*"Mr. Karloff, you may board Flight eight-fifty-nine for Chicago immediately at Gate Twenty-one."*

So intent was Kuryakin on the machine that he almost did not hear his name called over the speaker. More specifically, the name he had chosen to use for concealment purposes. It was the first American name that popped into his head when the ticket agent asked. It pleased him to travel under the name of his favorite American motion-picture actor. Moreover, one whose name was pronounceable.

He found the behavior of the flight crew admirably calm, considering the emergency situation. Kuryakin had thought a self-indulgent society such as the United States would rapidly come apart when faced with imminent destruction. Although he generally considered Westerners to be weak and indecisive, he was not a man to withhold approval where it was due.

One of the female attendants leaned down over him suddenly, and Kuryakin thought for a moment he had been discovered.

"Would you like something to read, Mr. Karloff?" She fanned a display of American magazines.

She was an attractive young woman with a husky voice. Rather like his daughter, Natalia, back in Moscow. Thoughts of Natalia and home tightened his throat for a moment, making it difficult to speak.

"Sir?"

"No, thank you," he said. "Nothing to read." He did not want to be distracted from his thoughts during the flight.

"We will have sandwiches once we're under way," the young woman said. "I'm sorry, but due to the emergency there will be no hot meal on this flight."

"Is all right," he said.

"But I'll be around with the cart if you'd care for something to drink. They're free this flight."

"Good." Kuryakin made himself smile. Americans, he had observed, smiled at one another constantly without reason. Maybe not so much now as before the brain eaters came.

There was a delay of half an hour before the United flight was cleared for take-off. Kuryakin sat tensely all the while, expecting at any moment to be grasped by rough hands and pulled off the plane. It still amazed him that it was so easy to travel in this country without so much as being asked for one's papers. How could the Americans possibly keep track of their people?

He had a momentary pang of conscience about leaving Raslov. Viktor would have to do some powerful explaining about the disappearance of his countryman. Kuryakin would gladly have included Raslov and even the KGB thick necks in his plan if he thought they would be amenable. He knew, however, that his thinking in that matter was unorthodox, and he was not likely to find any support from the others.

The decision to act had been made impulsively when he saw the opportunity offered by the confusion in the airport. Once he had decided what he must do, there was no question in Kuryakin's mind of where to go. The American authorities were out of the question. He had heard of the prisons into which people like him were thrown. The political authorities there were no more to be trusted than they were in Russia. They were as bad as the police or the army.

The only people he felt free talking to were other men of science. Theirs was an international language that transcended politics. They could be trusted. True, there were scientists who had gone bad. Nazi Germany was a prime example. It was possible that he was making a mistake, but he had made his choice, and there was now no turning back.

When they were airborne, the young woman came as promised, pulling a cart loaded with liquor. Kuryakin selected a tiny bottle of vodka. The name sounded Russian, but it was an American product. Nevertheless, Kuryakin felt it was a small gesture of loyalty on his part.

Eddie Gault woke up feeling better. Much better. He decided he had not had the flu after all.

He got out of bed, pulled on a bathrobe, and went looking for Roanne. He found her in the living room watching TV with the sound turned low. She snapped off the picture when he came into the room.

"Well, you're looking chipper," she said.

"Feel fine." He nodded toward the blank television screen. "Was that the news?"

"News is about all that's on nowadays. Just the same old stuff."

"What's happening at the plant?" he asked. "Have they opened up again?"

Roanne eyed him strangely. "No. They're going to be closed a long, long time."

"You mean they shut everything down?"

"Almost. They say Kitzmiller is back. He and a few others are staying out there and doing something in the laboratories. Nobody else except security."

"What's he doing there?—Dr. Kitzmiller?"

"The television says he's trying to find an antidote for the brain eaters."

"Brain eaters? Oh, God." Eddie moaned and sank into a chair. "For just a minute there I forgot about them. It seemed like a fever dream."

"No dream, Eddie," she said.

"Oh, God. God."

"It won't do you any good to carry on that way. What's done is done."

"What's been happening the last couple of days? I felt so lousy I wasn't paying attention."

"Some people were killed at the plant."

"Jesus, how did that happen?"

Roanne told him about the Biotron massacre as gently as she could, minimizing the role of the brain eaters as the cause of it all.

As she spoke, she watched Eddie carefully.

He sucked at a raw hangnail on his thumb.

"Are you sure you feel all right, Eddie? Do you think you should be up?"

"I told you, I feel fine. I've got to think. I've got to do something."

"You'll just give yourself a headache." Roanne's expression changed suddenly. "You don't *have* a headache, do you?"

"No." He eyed her suspiciously. "Why do you ask that?"

"I'm just worried about you."

"Did you think maybe those things, those brain eaters, had gotten to me?"

"No, of course not."

"Might serve me right if they did."

"Don't talk that way."

"I mean it. I'm the one let 'em loose. Serve me right if they got into my brain, too."

A sharp retort formed in Roanne's throat, but she swallowed it. She went over and stood in front of Eddie's chair.

In a voice that caressed him, she said, "Baby, I don't want to hear you say that. You're too important to me."

"Am I?" he said listlessly.

"You know you are."

She moved closer, gently pushing his legs apart and stepping between them.

"I got to think," he said.

"There's plenty of time to think," she said.

"People are dying. Lots of people. And it's my fault."

"Everybody dies, Eddie." She tried to lighten it up. "Besides, a little depopulation wouldn't hurt this country. We've talked about that."

"I don't know. I just feel it's wrong."

She went down to her knees. "There's nothing you can do now, baby. Nothing."

"I can at least take the responsibility for what I did."

"That wouldn't help anybody. They'd only hurt you. And me."

With deft fingers she started working on his belt buckle. Eddie covered her hands with his own. "Not now."

She looked up at him, her blue eyes half-closed, pale lips barely parted. It was a look that had always got him hot before, but now he only shook his head.

"Don't, Roanne. I don't feel like it. I got to think."

He stood up and walked into the kitchen, leaving Roanne kneeling before the empty chair. She looked after him and frowned.

# Chapter 25

Viktor Raslov's search of the San Francisco terminals had barely gotten under way when he froze at the sound of a polite voice behind him.

"Mr. Raslov?"

He turned to see one of those smooth-faced young men with the old eyes who were favored by the United States as police operatives.

"Yes?"

"I'm Kyle Taylor, sir. I'm with the Federal Bureau of Investigation."

Big surprise, thought Raslov sourly.

"So?"

"Would you mind coming along with me?"

What if I minded? Raslov wondered. Would Agent Taylor shoot him down there in front of all these witnesses? No, the Americans were more devious than that. More probably, the other agents now edging casually closer through the crowd would seize him, and they would take him to some quieter locale to be shot. Discretion. The Americans were always discreet.

Aloud he said, "I think you have made a mistake. I am a Russian citizen." A token show of indignation would be expected.

"It's a routine matter, sir," Agent Taylor said. The old eyes in his young face scanned the crowd. "And would you ask your . . . associates to come with us?"

There was just enough of a pause to let Raslov know that Taylor knew exactly who the "associates" were. It was all part of the game. The elaborate game of pretense and deceit upon which the ultimate fate of the world might depend.

Raslov sighed and signaled the KGB men to accompany him and the FBI agent.

They returned to Neal Henderson's office, from which the young assistant airport manager was, for the moment, absent.

"What I want to do," said Agent Taylor with a hard-edged smile, "is to apologize to you for the delay in your flight."

"We were told it was a mechanical problem," Raslov said. "Is your bureau now involved in the field of aircraft maintenance?"

Taylor's lips compressed in a cool smile. "We may as well admit there was no mechanical problem."

"So?"

"What with the national emergency, there have been communications breakdowns. What happened was we received conflicting orders from Washington. Your flight was held but, as it turned out, unnecessarily. A bureaucratic mistake. You probably know how that goes."

Raslov said nothing. Let the young FBI man squirm a little bit.

Taylor went on quickly. "That's the bad news. The good news is that your flight is cleared for immediate departure."

Surely, Raslov thought, this glib young man has not failed to notice that there is one fewer in our party than when we arrived. Now that we have misplaced Kuryakin, the Americans are suddenly anxious for us to depart. Why?

He said, "By strange coincidence my orders, too, have been changed. We will not require the airplane for immediate departure."

"Oh?" Taylor could not completely hide his displeasure. "When *will* you be leaving?"

"That has not been decided. In any event, is this not a matter for your State Department?"

Point for Raslov. The FBI man could not question him further without stepping on diplomatic toes, and he could certainly not now detain him, having claimed that it was only "bureaucratic bungling" that had caused the delay in the first place.

After an exchange of meaningless pleasantries, the Russians were permitted to leave while the FBI agents attempted, unsuccessfully, to lose themselves in the airport crowd. Raslov and his men resumed their search, but the delay in Henderson's office would have been just enough to let Kuryakin slip away. Raslov was muttering darkly to himself when one of the men beckoned to him from the counter of United Airlines.

Considering the volatile personalities involved, the brain-eaters task force operating at the Biotron plant got off to a surprisingly smooth start. Dr. Kitzmiller, in charge of the operation, asked for specific people from across the nation whose expertise would be valuable in the search for an antidote. With Lou Zachry pulling the strings, the people Kitzmiller wanted were speedily brought out if they were available. The crucial nature of their job was further pointed up by the fact that a number of Kitzmiller's specialists had themselves fallen victim to the parasites.

Dr. Jason Everett, specialist in diseases of the brain, was flown in from Denver. Parasitologist Dr. Dorothea Knight came from Boston. From Honolulu they brought epidemiologist Dr. Luke Chin. Dr. Marcus Pena, who knew all there was to know about blood diseases, came from San Diego. Under the direction of Dr. Kitzmiller and with the consultation of Dena Falkner, these temperamental specialists managed to work together in something resembling a team.

Corey Macklin, sulking in the spartan quarters provided for him adjoining the laboratories, admired the work being done but fretted continually about his own contribution, or

212

lack of same. While Dena, Kitzmiller, and the others worked long, tiring hours in the labs, Corey felt he was accomplishing nothing.

"You're doing a fine job, Corey," Lou Zachry told him. "Without you the place would be crawling with reporters and other snoopers, all getting in the way and slowing down any progress we might be making in the labs. And if it weren't for your releases, God knows what kind of crazy stories they'd take out of here."

"I'm a newspaperman, not a PR flack," Corey complained. "I should be writing this story myself, not passing out vaguely worded bullshit to pacify the so-called reporters in this so-called media pool."

"If we can lick this thing, you'll have the biggest story of them all," Zachry said. "And if we don't . . . Well, then, it won't matter, will it."

Corey grumbled, but he had to admit the government man had a point.

The pool reporters, for their part, were not enthusiastic about being kept away from Kitzmiller and the others and allowed to interview only Corey Macklin. The television people, especially, were unhappy. Their reportage depended on pictures, and there was nothing there to take pictures of.

"Believe me," Corey told them. "If I could bring one of the brain eaters out here in tiny handcuffs for you to put on camera, I'd do it."

Nobody thought that was very funny.

"I want to go into Milwaukee," he told Zachry after the morning briefing was concluded.

"What for? This is where the story is."

"The story is in the whole country," Corey said, "and I'm cut off from it. All there is here is a bunch of doctors who might as well be talking a foreign language for all I know of what they're doing."

"Your job here is important. The fate of God knows how

many people depends on what happens in these laboratories.''

"I'm going into Milwaukee," Corey said stubbornly.

Lou Zachry kept the all-American boy grin, but his eyes hardened. He said, "I don't think it's a good idea for you to leave."

"I don't think I give a damn what you think," Corey said. "I still go where I want when I want. Unless you're putting me under arrest."

"No, no, nothing like that, but I wish you'd think about it."

"I have thought about it. I need a day off. Let the pool reporters interview one another this afternoon."

Corey could tell that Lou Zachry was not pleased, and he almost hoped he would make an issue of it.

But the government man grinned and gave him a playful poke to the shoulder. "Go ahead, then, but don't play cards with strangers."

In spite of his irritation Corey grinned back. "Don't worry, Mom," he said, "I'll be good."

The drive from the Biotron plant into Milwaukee was no longer the routine trip it had been just a month before. During the early days of the panic, people had rushed off in their cars, thinking somehow to put distance between themselves and the brain eaters. Accidents had multiplied with the number of distraught and ill drivers on the road. Before long, all efforts to clear away the wreckage were abandoned. Now people were forced to drive more slowly to be alert for chunks of wrecked automobiles on the road.

Some of the freshly painted, well-kept farmhouses along the way were deserted. In most cases the cows and the dogs of a stricken family were taken in by neighbors, but chickens were too much trouble, and flocks of the abandoned birds could be seen flapping along the shoulders of the highway.

Another problem in driving was the absence of operating

gasoline stations. Not since the gas shortage of the early 1970s had filling the tank been such an iffy proposition. Highway-station operators, because of their contact with people from all points, were early victims of the brain eaters. Others had closed down when supplies from the refineries were slow in coming. The lush Wisconsin countryside through which Highway 41 passed had become a pastoral no-man's land.

The city of Milwaukee, although torn by illness, death, and fear, still had life on the streets, but that was not necessarily good news. As he drove slowly along with the doors locked and the windows up, Corey saw bands of shouting youths smashing the few windows that remained intact and carrying out anything portable from the buildings.

Sirens wailed continuously. No one walked the streets alone. Furtive faces peeked from behind shuttered windows. The police and National Guardsmen attempted to maintain some semblance of order, but as their own ranks were thinned by the parasites, they fought a losing battle.

The clamor for martial law was nationwide now as fear of the brain eaters surpassed fear of a police state. However, the president was strangely silent. There was a rumor that he and several cabinet members were themselves victims of the brain eaters. It was questionable, anyway, what good martial law would do as the parasites decimated the troops who would have to enforce it.

The *Herald* building was a ghost—cold and empty and silent. A man sat out in front on the sidewalk with his arms wrapped about his knees. Corey recognized him as one of the *Herald*'s pressmen and started to get out of the car to speak to him. Then he saw the terrible pain and incipient madness on the man's face and quickly drove off. He headed for the apartment building where Doc Ingersoll had lived for almost thirty years.

The Dorchester Apartments, on the fringe of downtown, were housed in a weather-stained brick building constructed in the solid square lines of the early part of the century. The residents were as permanent as the building. The only vacancies appeared when someone died.

There were plenty of vacancies now.

An old building like the Dorchester had none of the security frills of the 1980s. When it was built, the caller at your door would be someone you knew, not a killer or rapist.

Corey entered the building, climbed two flights of stairs, and made his way down a hall of oft-painted doors where the odors of meals past lingered like cobwebs in the air. He found the number of Doc's apartment and knocked on the brown-painted panel. Inside there was a thump, a muttered curse, and shuffling footsteps approaching the door.

Doc Ingersoll opened the door and squinted through a curtain of cigarette smoke. He wore the pants of his dark gray suit and an undershirt. On his feet, a pair of worn leather slippers. He badly needed a shave.

"Corey?"

"Who else? You look terrible."

Doc's apartment consisted of a combination living room and bedroom, with a curtained-off kitchenette. It had the seedy, comfortable look of the home of a man who has lived alone a long time. There were dishes stacked in the sink, and the ashtrays were in their usual state of overflow, but the place was reasonably clean.

Doc spoke in a strained voice. "What are you doing in town?"

"I needed a day off. Curious about what's happening in the world."

"I thought most of it was happening up there at Biotron. From what I read, you people are expecting to come up with an antidote any day now."

"That's just the standard bullshit I put out for the pool reporters. 'There are no suspects at present, but an arrest is expected momentarily.' "

"I thought it sounded familiar." Doc walked back into the room and eased himself down on the edge of the unmade pull-down bed. What's the real story?"

"Not much. They think they may have discovered a blood test to show whether the brain eaters are into you. But even if they know you've got 'em, they can't do anything about it."

"I didn't read about that. The test."

Corey snorted. "Dr. Kitzmiller doesn't want it published before they're sure it works. Give the people false hope or some damn thing. If you ask me, false hope is better than no hope at all."

"Yeah." Doc started to cough. He reached automatically for a fresh cigarette.

"Are you all right?" Corey said. "You really don't look good."

"When did I ever look good?" Doc growled. He lit the new cigarette, inhaled, coughed.

"You wouldn't have a beer, would you?" Corey said.

"Help yourself." Doc gestured in the direction of the noisy old Philco refrigerator.

Corey took a can of Heileman's from the refrigerator. He held one out toward Doc, who shook his head. Corey returned the second can and came back to sit in a worn chair next to the bed.

"So what are you doing to keep busy these days? I see the *Herald*'s buttoned up."

"I got myself assigned to the press pool. There isn't much work for me with so many newspaper guys out of a job, but at least I can keep in touch with the action."

"What *is* the action, Doc? All I get is the same kind of shit I hand out."

"You saw the city when you came in?"

"Yeah. Depressing."

"That's about the way it is everywhere. Vital services are still operating, but for how long, nobody knows. Only a few stores are open. The emergency rationing program is working about as well as expected. Meat is in short supply. Gasoline is the biggest headache. What did you drive in on, by the way?"

"They have their own underground tanks at Biotron."

"You've got it made, buddy. Your own gas supply, plenty to eat, medical help all around you, the government taking care of you . . . What are you doing back here, anyway?"

"I don't belong there, Doc. I think Zachry gave me the job just to keep me out of the way."

"Count your blessings. Did you hear Eichorn's dead?"

"No. How?"

"Burned to death in his house in Houston. Nobody used the story, but his daughter was a brain-eater victim. Went crazy and attacked the family with a hatchet. Then she set fire to the place. They think Eichorn was dead before the flames got to him."

"Jesus," Corey swore softly.

"Porter Uhlander, now, he's gone fishing."

"You're kidding."

"Nope. He loaded his gear along with a case of Tums and a lifetime supply of Valium into his camper and took off for that cabin he kept up on Pelican Lake. He plans to ride out the emergency right there."

"That's the silliest thing I ever heard."

"I don't know. It makes as much sense as what a lot of other people are doing."

"Are you going into the pool headquarters?" Corey asked. "I'd like to see the operation."

"Nah, they don't need me there."

"Then what do you say we find a bottle somewhere and get drunk? I'm locked up with a bunch of white-wine drinkers at Biotron."

"I'm going to pass, Corey. I just don't feel like doing a damn thing. You go on down to the pool. You might find some laughs."

Corey looked at the older reporter curiously but said nothing. He got up and started for the door. "I'll give you a call before I leave town."

"Sure. You do that." Doc Ingersoll made no move to get off the bed.

Corey left the apartment and closed the door softly behind him. He walked down the steps feeling depressed. Behind one of the doors on the first floor a woman sobbed.

The headquarters of the media pool had been set up in the Civic Auditorium. As he drove carefully across town, Corey wondered about Doc's deteriorating state of mind. It was especially unlike him to turn down a drink. Corey resolved to call him again before leaving town, but now he needed his full attention on his driving.

Desks and portable partitions had turned the auditorium into a haphazard maze. There was much activity, with people rushing back and forth, but Corey got the impression that little was being accomplished. He searched out newspaper people he knew and from them got a little clearer picture of the national situation.

Cures were the current rage. Quacks of all kinds were trumpeting that they had discovered the one and only cure for the brain eaters. The cures ranged from simple electric shock and exotic herbs to various mystical foolery. Although they were not even reported by the pool, these self-proclaimed healers were doing a booming business on word-of-mouth. The Food and Drug Administration had too many other problems to worry about shutting them down.

There was a one-paragraph story on the UPI wire about a delegation of Russian agricultural experts who had changed their plans to fly home from San Francisco and were delaying their departure for unstated reasons. The item caught Corey's eye only because of Kitzmiller's charge that these same Russians were somehow to blame for loosing the brain eaters. He tucked it away for future consideration.

Corey soon tired of the pointless bustle at the pool headquarters. He understood now Doc Ingersoll's reluctance to come down. On his way out he got on a telephone and dialed Doc's number.

He heard the burr of the phone ringing on the other end, but there was no answer. After ten rings Corey hung up and left the building feeling vaguely uneasy. Maybe the phone wasn't working properly. He decided to drive over and see if he could change Doc's mind about tying one on.

The ringing of the telephone was like a red-hot knife blade stabbing through Doc's head. He clapped both hands over his ears and stood hunched over the bathroom sink, whimpering until the ringing finally stopped. The pain continued. He looked up at his reflection in the streaked mirror.

Corey had been right. He didn't look good. It had taken immense effort not to show the terrible pain of his headache while Corey was there. He had swallowed a full bottle of a hundred aspirin tablets since that morning, but they had done no good. Nothing was going to do any good.

Doc had not let himself admit what he had until there was no longer the faintest hope he was wrong. Now he fancied he could hear the ugly little creatures chewing their way through his brain tissue, popping the blood vessels as they went, creating the unbearable pressure under his skull. He knew he could stand it no longer than a few more minutes; then he would go screaming into madness, lashing out at everything and everyone around him. His face would erupt in those festering boils and spew the seed of the diabolical parasite into the air.

He walked back to the bed and pulled open the drawer of the nightstand. Lying on top of a John D. MacDonald novel was a Smith & Wesson .38-caliber revolver. It was well oiled and loaded. Doc picked up the gun, jammed the muzzle against the roof of his mouth, gagging at the oily taste. He pulled the trigger.

# Chapter 26

All the way back through the littered streets to the Dorchester Apartments, Corey had a sense of foreboding, like a cold, moist hand clamped on the back of his neck. He repeatedly told himself to snap out of it, that there could be any number of reasons why Doc had not answered his telephone. But the cold grip would not loosen.

He left the Cutlass out in front of the building in a no-parking zone. Interesting, he thought, how insignificant our minor laws become in a time of mortal danger. He would have given a lot to know he would come back and find a cop ticketing his car, just as though it still mattered where anybody parked. He irritably pushed the thought away. The cops had other worries, and so did he.

The woman somewhere on the first floor was still sobbing. She seemed to have been frozen in her lament since the beginning of time.

As Corey topped the second flight of stairs, he detected another smell mixed with the stale cooking odor. It was the old Fourth of July smell of exploded gunpowder.

He quickened his step down the hallway and knocked at the door to Doc's apartment. There was no response. In his heart Corey had not expected there would be one. He tried the door. It was unlocked. Somehow he had expected that, too.

Corey stepped inside. The gunpowder smell was

sharpest in there, cutting through the memory of a thousand cigarettes. A layer of blue haze hung in the room at eye level.

Doc lay with the lower part of his body on the bed, the upper sprawled down to the floor. Beneath his head the rug was soaked with dark, drying blood.

Corey knelt beside his friend. He saw the revolver still gripped in Doc's hand. He saw the beginning of the red welts on the old reporter's sallow face. Welts that would now not erupt to blow out the eggs of the brain eaters.

He stood up quickly and walked into the bathroom. There he braced his hands on the edges of the porcelain sink and leaned his head over it while his stomach lurched. In a few seconds the churning in his gut eased, and Corey looked up into the mirror over the sink. What did Doc see in this glass, he wondered, before he ate the bullet? Corey looked into his own eyes and did not much like what he saw there.

"This is it, hotshot. The Big Story," he told his warped reflection. "The one you've been waiting for. Now that you've got it, how do you like it?"

He turned away from the unanswering image in the glass and went back into the living room—bedroom. He walked over and eased Doc's feet down off the bed and arranged them so he was lying on the floor. Making the corpse more comfortable. Doc would have laughed at that.

He spread a blanket over his friend and walked to the refrigerator. He popped the top of a can of Heileman's and raised it in the direction of the body.

"So long, Doc," he said. "Rest easy."

He drained half the can of beer, set the rest down on the table, and walked out of the apartment. Downstairs the woman was still crying.

"I wish I could join you, lady," Corey whispered, and continued out of the building.

On the street a teenager with a scraggly moustache was trying to break into the Cutlass.

"What the hell are you doing?" Corey yelled at him.

"Fuck you, old man."

That was exactly what Corey needed. With an open-mouthed cry of pent-up rage, he started to run at the would-be car thief. The youth stared for a moment, then turned to flee. Corey caught him with a punishing tackle at the knees and brought him down hard on the pavement.

"Hey, don't, mister . . ." the teenager protested.

But Corey could not stop. He rolled the boy over onto his back and drove his fist again and again into the frightened face. The boy's nose broke, his teeth gave, he blubbered through the blood that filled his mouth.

With his fist drawn back for one more blow, Corey suddenly stopped. The black rage drained away, and he relaxed, unclenching his hand. He rose and walked back to the car, paying no attention to the whimpering boy, who still lay on the sidewalk. His thoughts were somber as he started the car and headed north, but the terrible anger was gone.

Dr. Kitzmiller leaned forward across the desk in his Spartan office adjacent to the laboratories. His cheeks were sunken, and there were purple shadows under his eyes. Fatigue lay heavy upon him, but his eyes blazed with the bright blue light of a Bunsen burner.

"I am tired of carrying on the pretense," he told the man standing across the desk from him. "It takes time and energy that I should be giving to finding the antidote."

"You're exhausted," the other man said. "You should get some sleep."

"Who is the doctor here?" Kitzmiller asked with grim humor.

"I can tell by looking at you."

"It is only because you are not accustomed to seeing me

223

up close like this," Kitzmiller said. "Usually with us it has been through a glass darkly."

"The one-way mirror was a necessary device. It would have been awkward to explain my presence in the room."

"Yes, awkward to say the least."

"You really should try to sleep," the man said again.

"There is no time. Even when I do lie down, there is no rest. I cannot forget what I have done. Do you know what they have called me in the press? 'Father of the Brain Eaters.' How would you like to live with that?"

"You're getting too thin-skinned. The brain eaters were an accident."

Kitzmiller half rose from his chair. "Ah, were they? Were they indeed an accident?"

"You know they were."

"I know what we are telling the people. That the whole thing was the unfortunate result of an experimental pesticide that was unfortunately not properly disposed of. At best a half-truth. There is no comfort for me in it."

"Are you talking to me about conscience?"

Kitzmiller subsided. "It is somewhat late for that, isn't it. Nevertheless, it becomes more difficult every day for me to sustain the lie."

"You don't have to talk to anybody."

"I know. Young Corey Macklin does all the talking for me. Nevertheless, the reporters are here. I see them outside the fence. I read in their eyes that they do not believe all that we are telling them."

"It's not important whether they believe or not. You know how vital it is that no rumors get started."

"By *rumors* do you mean the true story of the brain eaters? Who the real father is?" Kitzmiller's mouth twisted in a wry smile.

"It is vital," the other man repeated.

"So you say." He let several seconds go by, then sighed. "Very well. I will say nothing . . . for now." He pushed

224

himself up out of the chair. "I must get back to the laboratories."

The other man stayed in his chair, frowning, and watched him go.

During the drive from Milwaukee back to the Biotron plant, Corey came to a decision. He saw the absurdity of charting a new direction for his future at a time when he had no assurance there would *be* a future. All the same, it was a decision, and he felt better having made it.

He flashed his identification at the gate and was waved through by the armed security man. Only half a dozen cars were parked now in the executives' lot. Corey wondered grimly how many of the names still painted on the unused spaces belonged to dead men.

He entered the building and walked into the office used by Lou Zachry. The government man was talking on the telephone. He held up a hand signaling Corey to wait while he concluded the conversation.

"You're sure of your facts?" Zachry said into the mouthpiece. Then, after a pause, he asked, "And what makes you think this Karloff is our man? . . . Description fits, eh? . . . And Raslov knows? . . . I see. I guess all we can do is try to head him off at this end."

Zachry hung up the phone wearily and exhaled between clenched teeth.

"Lou," Corey began, "I want to talk to you."

"Sit down. How was Milwaukee?"

Corey remained standing. "Milwaukee was depressing. Lou, I want out."

"Yeah, don't we all. The press conference was a little sticky this afternoon without you here. I tried to work up a handout for the pool people, but I don't have your knack. Better try to come up with a fresh angle for them next time."

"Lou, hear me. I want out of the job. Now."

Zachry looked at him. The square, all-American face

sagged with weariness. "You can't mean that. You're upset about something."

"I'm upset, all right, but I mean it like I never meant anything else. I quit. I'm through. I don't want to do this chicken-shit job anymore."

"Do you know what kind of a bind that leaves me in, Corey?"

"I'm sorry, but—"

"It's not like I can go out and hire somebody else. We all signed on here for the duration—however long or short a time that may be."

"I don't remember signing anything," Corey said.

"A figure of speech."

"I don't feel bound by a figure of speech."

Zachry pinched his eyes shut and massaged them with thumb and middle finger. "No, you're right. There's no contract. I've no right to keep you if you don't want to stay."

"Lou, don't do a Knute Rockne number on me. The important work here is being done in the laboratories. That will get done, or it won't, regardless of whether I'm here to hand-hold a bunch of reporters. I don't know how much time I've got left, but I don't want to spend it making up phony press releases."

Zachry gave him a shrewd look. "What happened in Milwaukee? Did you decide to take one of the book contracts?"

"Hell, no. I don't give a damn about writing the brain-eaters story anymore. Anyway, in a little while there might be nobody left to read it."

"What is it, then?" Zachry asked. "I know you're frustrated with your role here, but—"

"It's more than that, Lou. I'm not sure what happened to me. Maybe I got religion."

Zachry leaned back in the chair. "Okay. Whatever it is you feel you've got to do, I wish you luck. You were a big help to me here. I'll make some arrangements, but it won't be easy. Especially now." He inclined his head toward the telephone. "Do you know what that call was?"

Corey shook his head.

"Those Russians who came through here last month—the so-called agricultural delegation—it seems they lost one of them in San Francisco."

"What do you mean lost?"

"The FBI botched a routine surveillance. Thought they were supposed to detain the people. Everything got confused, and by the time it was straightened out, one of them, Anton Kuryakin, was missing."

"What of it?"

"Kuryakin is probably the Soviet Union's top man in biochemistry. They've traced him to a flight out of San Francisco for Chicago. To me that means he's coming here."

"Isn't that kind of a jump in logic?"

"Not really. The man is an Iron Curtain version of Kitzmiller. He tried to talk to Kitzmiller while they were here, but you know our Dr. K and his Commiephobia."

"It sounds like you've got a touch of that yourself."

"Maybe. But I'm as sure as I sit here that Kuryakin is on his way. Worse, Viktor Raslov and the two goons aren't far behind. Just one more thing for me to worry about"—he paused for a beat—"in addition to writing handouts to keep the media pool off my back." He looked up at Corey through knitted brows. "But none of this is your worry anymore, is it."

"I'll write the goddam handouts," Corey said.

"You're staying?"

"Gimme the ball, coach."

Zachry came around the desk and wrung Corey's hand. "I can't tell you how much this means to me." He glanced at his watch. "And just in time. I promised the pool an extra briefing this evening when you got back from Milwaukee. Told them you were checking out some important new leads."

"You son of a bitch," Corey said.

"It's a dirty job, but somebody's got to do it." He gave Corey the old all-American grin.

Corey found Dr. Kitzmiller in the laboratory, huddling with his associates. Dena cocked a questioning eyebrow at him. He gave her a tell-you-later look and managed to separate Kitzmiller from the others momentarily.

"I have a briefing scheduled with the reporters in a little while," he said, "and I need some help from you."

"I don't care what you tell those *dummkopfs*, Mr. Macklin. Just keep them out of my hair."

"Dr. Kitzmiller, I can't go on feeding them the same baloney. These people are not stupid. If they seem intrusive, that's their job. This is a terrible time for our country, but the people still have a right to know what's going on. And we have a duty to tell them something."

"What do you suggest?"

"I want to tell them about the blood test to detect presence of the parasite."

"I have already explained to you that we have only preliminary data. Any announcement would be premature."

"The old rules don't apply anymore, doctor," Corey said heatedly. "What might have been premature last year is damn near too late now. The people out there are waiting to hear what we're doing to try to save them. I want to tell them."

Kitzmiller took a step back as though to have a better look at Corey. "You sound different, young man."

"Maybe I'm thinking different."

"Very well. If you feel it is so important, tell the people about the blood test. Make it clear, however, that this is not a cure, nor will it necessarily lead to a cure."

"I'd like to have the specialists themselves tell the reporters about it. It was Dr. Pena and Dr. Knight who developed the test, wasn't it?"

"Yes, it was, but I could not possibly spare them for—"

"Half an hour," Corey said. "If we give the pool reporters half an hour of real news coming from somebody with real credentials, they'll be a lot easier to live with."

Dr. Kitzmiller sighed heavily. "Everywhere I turn today I meet with opposition. Very well, take my doctors, but not one minute more than your half hour, or I swear I will bar you from the laboratories, too."

"It's a deal."

Corey put out a hand, but Kitzmiller ignored it and hurried back to his teammates.

Drs. Pena and Knight proved to be an unqualified hit with the reporters. Marcus Pena was relaxed and friendly, with the unlined face of a teenager and a respect for the intelligence of his audience. Dorothea Knight said little, but she had a sensational chest, which was more than enough for the news-starved media. At last television had something to show pictures of.

After the briefing was over, Corey returned the two doctors to Kitzmiller's care and retired to his cramped little room. He turned the lamp to the wall, sat down on the bed, and pulled off his shoes. Then he lay back with his hands clasped behind his head and stared at the ceiling. A spider that had somehow gotten into the pesticide palace was optimistically spinning a web up in one corner. While Corey's eyes followed the progress of the little creature, his mind was many miles away.

A knock at the door.

"Enter."

The door opened, and Dena Falkner stood there. Her caramel-colored hair was down and was given a soft halo effect by the brighter light out in the hall.

"Hi," she said.

"Hi."

"Want to talk about it?"

He hesitated, then said, "Not really."

"Okay." She turned to leave.

"No, wait, Dena. I guess I do want to talk."

She came back in and closed the door.

"How did you know?" he asked.

"You're different somehow."

"Lou Zachry said almost the same thing to me. Even Kitzmiller. I must be easy to read."

"You're not so tough."

"In more ways than one," he said. "I wish I'd thought to pick up some bourbon while I was in Milwaukee."

Dena pulled a flask from her laboratory smock and held it up for his inspection. "Is Canadian all right?"

"What's that, a specimen bottle?"

"It's Canadian Club. But if you're squeamish—"

"No," he said quickly. "Canadian is terrific. And you must be clairvoyant."

*"Sympatico,"* she corrected.

Corey produced two tumblers. They poured the whiskey, sat down side by side on the bed, and toasted each other silently.

"Doc Ingersoll's dead," he said.

Dena touched his hand.

"He shot himself today when he knew the brain eaters were in him."

"Oh, Corey, I'm so sorry."

"I was with him this morning. I was right there in Doc's apartment when those little bastards were eating him up. The pain he felt must have been unspeakable. And I didn't even notice."

He paused for a swallow. Dena watched him silently.

"I was too wrapped up in my own miserable little complaints to notice that my best friend was in agony. How's that for sensitive?"

"We're all kind of unfocused these days," she said.

"I can't blame it on 'these troubled times,'" he said. "It's me. It's the way I've always been. I've spent the better part of my life looking for the Big Story. Not because I gave a damn for the story but because it was going to make Corey Macklin rich and famous. A celebrity. Doc told me I was going to be a celebrity. That's all the brain eaters meant to me. They were my Big Story. So a few people died. I couldn't help that. So then a lot of people died. I still didn't understand. Then Doc died. The one man in the world who was my friend. He damn near died in front of my eyes, and I didn't see it. Some friend."

Dena poured more whiskey into their tumblers. She said, "Okay, so you were a bastard. What are you going to do about it?"

"When I came back here, I was going to quit."

"That's no answer."

"I see that now. I guess I'll hang around and do whatever I can to be useful. Who knows? We might beat this thing yet."

"Who knows." She grinned at him.

"You sure don't allow a guy much time for self-pity."

"Not on my booze."

"What time do you have to be back?"

Dena's smile softened. "There's no bed check tonight."

He took the glass from her hand, set it down along with his on the night table, and drew her into his arms.

# Chapter 27

Anton Kuryakin looked around him with a deep sadness. A great country was being brought to its knees. The streets of the cities were clogged with debris and abandoned cars. Shops were closed and shuttered. Others had their windows smashed out and stood open and gutted like dead animals.

For the most part, people stayed off the dying streets. Those who had to be out hurried along, huddled in upon themselves, avoiding contact with any others they might meet. The eyes of many of the people were already dead.

Worst were the screamers. The wild, agonized victims of the brain eaters. They ran along the streets, hopelessly trying to rip the parasites from inside their heads. People recognized them now for what they were. They knew the terrible violence such victims were capable of, and they shunned them like the lepers of ancient times.

Kuryakin stood at the intersection of Michigan Avenue and Milwaukee and looked about him at the dying city without pleasure. He had always believed that the superiority of the Soviet system would one day bring down the Western democracies, but it gave him no enjoyment to see the old adversary beaten in this terrible way.

After his flight left San Francisco, there was the short period when they were airborne and everything might have been normal. Normal, that is, except for the grim tension on the faces of the passengers and the crew and the soft sobbing of an old woman in the seat behind him. At least they were isolated at sixteen thousand feet from the ugly reality on the ground. The fragile sense of normality collapsed when they landed.

After that, Kuryakin had seen the situation become rapidly more desperate. There was near chaos at O'Hare International Airport in Chicago. Flights to all points were being canceled, People fought for seats on airplanes that would never take off. There was no reliable information on what was coming in, and the anxiety in the faces of those who waited was awful to see.

While people dashed frantically and pointlessly from counter to counter, Kuryakin placed himself stolidly in line at the shuttle-flight boarding gate. Thus he managed to get a seat on one of the last flights to take off for Milwaukee.

The scene at Mitchell Field was a smaller version of O'Hare. Everybody was in a panic to leave the city, but nobody knew where he wanted to go. With other countries closing their borders to Americans, they were trapped with the brain eaters.

Getting from the airport to downtown Milwaukee had been the easiest part of Kuryakin's journey. Almost all the traffic was in the other direction, and the few taxis that were still operating were glad to take a fare back into the city. Getting from Milwaukee to his final destination was proving to be much more difficult.

"Can you drive me to the Biotron factory?" he asked the cabdriver who had brought him from Mitchell Field.

"Where's that?" the man asked, looking back at his passenger and running a critical eye over his too-short haircut and the unstylish drape of his suit.

"It is located in a village called Wheeler."

The cabbie looked blank.

"That is near a larger city called Appleton."

"Appleton? Are you crazy?"

"I am not crazy. That is the name of the city. Do you not know where it is?"

"Sure I know. This Biotron place—is that the one on TV

233

where those doctors are trying to come up with something to stop the brain eaters?''

''That is correct. You will take me there?''

''Do you know how far that is?''

''No.''

The driver cocked his head speculatively. ''How much money you got?''

''American money?''

''Hell, yes. What do you think, pesos?''

Kuryakin pulled out his worn leather wallet and carefully counted the bills inside. ''I have thirty-three dollars in American bills and some coins.''

''Shit. And you want me to drive you to Appleton for that?''

''Yes, please.''

''Mister, you already owe me twenty bucks for the trip from the airport. What you got left ain't going to get you out of town, never mind all the way to Appleton.''

Kuryakin paid the man his twenty dollars and accepted the scowl he got for not adding a tip. One day the Western workers would understand the insult of offering a man a gratuity on top of the wages he earned for merely doing his job.

There were no buses running out of Milwaukee. No trains. No public transportation of any kind. Kuryakin sat down on a deserted bus-stop bench to think. As best as he could remember, the drive from Milwaukee to the Biotron plant had taken two or three hours. While he rode as a passenger in the back seat of the car supplied by the American State Department, he had paid little attention to the route followed by the driver. However, as a product of the Russian school system, he was an excellent reader of maps. If he could obtain a map of the highway system, he was sure he could locate the town of Wheeler, and once he was there, it would not be difficult for him to find Biotron. His means of traveling there was another problem to be faced.

There were an unusual number of police and soldiers on the streets. They paid no attention to Kuryakin. He understood that they were too busy with the problem of the brain eaters to concern themselves with him. Under normal circumstances, he no doubt would have been arrested long ago and would now be in some secret police prison facing the harsh interrogation for which American police were noted. Even though he felt relatively safe, he did not wish to jeopardize his anonymity by approaching one of these men for help. He would simply have to rely on other means to get where he wanted to go.

As Kuryakin sat organizing his thoughts into a plan, a big American car jounced up over the curb and crunched its gleaming front end into a light standard. The door on the driver's side burst open, and a man tumbled out. He wore a T-shirt with the name of a popular beer on it. His eyes bulged, and his mouth gaped in a scream. On his face the red boils worked as though there were tiny mice under the skin trying to chew their way out. Kuryakin recognized the symptoms of the brain eaters.

The man took off in an erratic run down the sidewalk, hammering his fists against the unyielding plate-glass windows as he stumbled past.

Two men in army uniforms on the opposite side of the street shouted at him. He turned in their direction, roaring out his pain and madness. He started across the street toward the uniformed men.

"Halt!"

Kuryakin heard the shout clearly on the near-deserted street. Several people peered cautiously from doorways at the commotion. From around the corner came several more men in uniform.

The stricken man continued to run at the two soldiers. His hands were stretched out in front of him, the fingers bent into claws. One of the soldiers fired his automatic rifle into the air. The man continued to charge. Both soldiers dropped to a kneeling position and fired. His body jerked, and he stumbled backward as the bullets tore into him, but he righted himself and came doggedly on for another half-dozen steps before he fell.

Hesitantly, keeping their weapons at the ready, the soldiers approached the fallen man. The others, who had been attracted by the shouts and gunfire, joined them. A few civilians came out of the buildings. They formed a cautious circle around the unmoving man on the ground.

Kuryakin was ignored in the excitement. So was the automobile the man had been driving. It still sat with its front end mashed against the light standard, the door hanging open.

Kuryakin rose from the bench and walked to the automobile. One of the headlights was smashed, but there seemed to be no disabling damage. No fluids were leaking out underneath. He got in behind the steering wheel and pulled the door shut.

He knew that maps were usually stored in a compartment on the right-hand side of the dash panel. He released the catch, and the door popped open. Inside the compartment he found a wad of the crinkly receipts given to American drivers when they purchased gasoline on credit. There was an aspirin bottle with only a few tablets left inside, a pair of sunglasses, a box of facial tissues, a can opener, a woman's compact, a comb, a roll of breath mints, two ball-point pens, several loose keys, assorted screws, and three maps.

One of the maps detailed the streets of Milwaukee. The others were for the states of Wisconsin and Illinois. Kuryakin discarded the Illinois map and spread the other two out on the seat beside him. He found his present location by matching the street names on a sign at the intersection to the grid of the Milwaukee map. On the state map he located the village of Wheeler and plotted the route he would have to take to get there.

Out on the street none of the people gathered around the dead man paid any attention to Kuryakin or to the automobile. Damaged and abandoned cars were no longer a novelty. And no one had time to notice an oddly dressed man climbing into one.

As a scientist of some repute in his native country, Kuryakin was privileged to have access to an automobile. The solid, sensible Ilyushin he drove on the streets of Moscow was a much simpler and sturdier machine than the gaudy American vehicle, but the principle was the same.

As a driver himself, and rather proud of his ability, Kuryakin had taken every opportunity on this visit to discuss the differences between Russian and American machines with the drivers assigned to his delegation. He thought the American cars were overly padded and contained too many controls and gauges that had little to do with the machine's operation. However, he was too diplomatic to criticize an important product of the host country.

He tried now to remember the things he had learned. The engine, he recalled, was started by a twist of the key. The keys to this vehicle, in a shiny leather case, had been left dangling from the lock on the steering post by the doomed owner. Kuryakin gave the ignition key a twist as he had seen the American drivers do.

Nothing happened.

Kuryakin frowned at the controls. He must have forgotten something.

The gear lever; that was it. The pointer had to be in a specific location to allow the key to activate the ignition. Kuryakin experimented until he found that the *P* position freed the key switch. The engine came to life. He glanced out onto the street, but the only activity was around the body of the car's late owner. Very carefully he moved the lever to the *R* position and backed the big automobile back onto the street. He shifted to *D* and eased forward past the knot of people and around a corner heading toward Highway 45.

While Anton Kuryakin picked his way carefully through the cluttered streets of Milwaukee toward the highway, Eddie Gault lay curled into a tense fetal position between the damp, twisted sheets of the bed he shared with Roanne Tesla.

The inside of Eddie's head was on fire. It felt as if something were in there trying to push his eyeballs out. It seemed much longer than two days earlier that he was assuring Roanne that he felt just fine.

Eddie thought he knew all about pain. There was that impacted wisdom tooth a couple of years before. And the time he chopped off a toe splitting logs on his uncle's farm. Or when he was hit in the balls by a line drive while pitching in high school. None of those times had hurt like this. And it was getting worse.

From out in the living room he heard the murmur of the television set. Roanne must be watching. She deserved a little time to herself. She had been at his side almost constantly, both during the short flu thing and now since the headaches had started. That day, though, he had noticed that she was looking at him a little bit sideways. Eddie thought he knew why.

He freed himself from the tangled sheets and pushed his feet out of the bed. He sat there for a minute, then stood up. Every movement he made hammered at his skull. Biting down hard to keep from crying, he walked unsteadily to the doorway leading into the living room.

On the television screen two people in white doctor coats were talking to one of those pretty-boy television reporters. One of the doctors was a young Oriental, and the other was a woman with big tits. Eddie listened for a minute and figured out that they were part of the group working out at the Biotron labs to find a cure for the brain eaters.

Their words came to Eddie filtered through the throbbing pain, but he got the sense of what they were saying. They had come up with some kind of a test where you could tell for sure from a person's blood whether he had the brain eaters in him.

A small groan got away from him.

Roanne looked around and saw him standing there. She

238

quickly got out of the chair and snapped off the television set. She made no move to come closer.

"Why did you shut it off?" he said.

"I thought it was disturbing you."

"Those doctors said they've got a test for the brain eaters."

"You know how doctors are. They'll say anything to make it look like they're accomplishing something. Why don't you go back to bed, baby?"

"I think I got 'em, Roanne. I think I got the brain eaters."

She moved a hand as though to comfort him but came no nearer. "Don't say that, Eddie. It's just nerves."

He pressed both hands to his temples. "No. Something's in there. It hurts so bad, I can't tell you."

"Lie down, baby. I'll make a poultice for your head."

"It won't do any good. Nothing's going to do any good. I got 'em."

Roanne put a hand to her mouth and shook her head in denial.

"I want to go to the plant."

"No, Eddie."

"I want to see those doctors. Maybe they can do something for me."

"They aren't letting anybody in. They have guards at the gate."

"They'll let me in. They'll do it because I'm the one who set the brain eaters free."

"They think it was an accident."

"I'm going to tell them it wasn't."

"You can't do that," Roanne said.

"I've got to. Then they'll have to let me in. They'll have to help me."

"They'll lock you up."

"I'm going in," Eddie said stubbornly.

"They'll lock you up. Then they'll come and get me."

Eddie stared at her through pain-dimmed eyes. His tortured mind worked sluggishly. "That's what you're really scared of, isn't it—that they'll find out what you made me do. You don't care about me at all.''

"That's not true, Eddie. I love you.''

"Then why are you backing away from me?''

"I—I've never seen you acting like this before. You scare me.''

Eddie gripped his pounding head and rocked it from side to side as though it were something that didn't belong on his body. "I'm going to see the doctors,'' he said. "Don't try to stop me.''

He stumbled across the room past Roanne. She shrank back against the wall as he fumbled at the knob, finally opening the front door.

He staggered out onto the patch of dirt in front of the house where they parked the van. Roanne watched as he pulled himself in behind the wheel and started the engine. He knocked over the mailbox as he turned onto the road and weaved off in the direction of the Biotron plant.

Roanne watched him drive out of sight, then left the window and picked up a newspaper. It was three days old, the last she had been able to buy. She frowned at the picture on the front page and the boxed caption next to it. Then she picked up the telephone.

After several seconds she heard the familiar buzz of the dial tone. Good old automated telephone company. Still working. She dialed a number and spoke briefly to the voice that answered on the other end. Then she hung up and went back to the window.

Clouds were gathering. There was going to be a storm.

# Chapter 28

The alarm buzzed.

Corey reached across Dena and slapped the clock into silence before he was fully awake. He lay back for a moment, eyes closed, allowing the sleep to drain out of him. Dena lay on her side, facing away from him. She did not stir when the alarm went off. He shifted his body over closer to hers. The day was hot and muggy. Dena's skin was very warm and moist against his.

He lay against her for five minutes with one hand resting on the smooth swell of her hip. He felt himself getting aroused. Dena did not stir. She deserved the rest, he thought. She probably had not slept through a full night in weeks.

Still, he had to wake her up. They both had things to do that morning. And maybe, he thought with a lascivious grin, she would be in the mood for a little morning sex.

He moved his hand to her bare shoulder and rocked her gently. She gave him a little moan of protest but did not awaken.

"Dena," he said softly, "time to get up."

She moaned again, a little more loudly.

"C'mon, rise and shine."

Dena rolled over onto her stomach. She raised her head and looked at him blearily through a damp tangle of blond hair. Her eyes seemed unnaturally bright.

"Hi, there." She gave him a sleepy smile and started to

drift off again. Then, abruptly, she turned her head to peer at the glowing red numbers on the digital clock.

"Oh, God, look at the time. You should have woken me up."

"I just did," he said.

She turned back and smiled at him again, more alert now but not quite focused.

"Right," she said, and kissed him quickly on the nose.

So much for morning sex, Corey decided.

She peeled back the covers and sat up, swinging her long legs out on her side of the bed. She groaned. "What did you give me to drink last night?"

"You brought the C-C, remember?"

"Oh, yeah." She raked the hair out of her eyes with her fingers. "Where did you hide my clothes?"

"You left them over there on the chair."

Dena stood up, stretched her arms, and walked to the chair, where her clothes lay in a folded pile.

"Are you always so neat?" he asked.

"It's a compulsion. Can I take a shower?"

"Sure." He got up and found her a bath towel on a shelf in the closet.

When he came around to where she was sitting to hand her the towel, Dena hugged her arms and shivered.

"Is it cold in here?" she said.

He looked at her curiously. "No."

"I must have had a chill." She stood up and took the towel from him, fashioning it into a sarong.

He gave her a leer. "Are you in a big hurry?"

"Why, do you have something in mind?" She let her eyes range downward. "Oh, yes, I see you have. But I'd better get to work. Maybe we can do something about that later."

Corey watched with open admiration as Dena scooped up her clothes and walked into the bathroom. She was a woman who knew how to move. He heard the cough and hiss of the shower starting up, and he smiled. The comfortable domesticity of the scene made him feel good but at the same time a little bit nervous. He had the crazy feeling that if they got out of this brain-eaters business, he was going to marry this woman. If they got out.

He pulled on a pair of jeans and made a halfhearted pass at straightening the bed. He touched the pillow that still bore the indentation of Dena's head, and he smiled again.

The shower stopped, and in a few minutes Dena came out. She was dressed in the white pants and short-sleeved blouse she wore under her laboratory smock.

"It *is* cold in here," she said. "Do you have the heat on?"

"There isn't any heat," he said. "And it's probably eighty degrees outside." He stepped closer and took hold of her arm. "What's this?"

Dena looked down at the raw patch on her elbow. It was surrounded by reddened, slightly puffy flesh.

"I scraped my elbow the other day. It looks like there may be a low-grade infection. I'll put something on it in the lab."

The tone of her voice did not quite match the casual words. Corey kept hold of her arm and looked at her.

"Where did you get this, Dena?"

She let a beat go by before she answered. "When I went over to Carol Denker's house."

"On the day the brain eaters got to her?" Corey asked. He felt a clutch deep in his gut.

"Yes," Dena said levelly. "But that doesn't mean—"

"And you've got chills," Corey interrupted.

She nodded without speaking.

"Oh, Jesus." Corey blinked and turned away for a moment.

"Let's not be hasty," Dena said. "The odds are all in favor of its being just a simple chill or a touch of the flu. . . ."

Their eyes met, and she could not finish the sentence.

"Yeah, that's the odds," he said tonelessly.

"And if the worst is true, then I've got them, and it won't change anything to stand here worrying about it. At least I'm close to the people who're looking for a cure, so maybe I'd better get to work."

"Yeah, right," Corey said. He turned away quickly so she would not see what was in his eyes.

The black limousine slid up to the gate at Biotron, and the uniformed security men converged on it cautiously. The guards were no longer Biotron employees. Too many of them had been lost to make up an effective force. In their place were agents from the Department of Justice and the intelligence arm of the Defense Department. In spite of the oppressive weather, they were dressed in full uniforms with jackets and ties.

Two of them took up positions on either side of the car, their hands inconspicuously near their guns. A third approached the driver's window.

Since the arrival of Dr. Kitzmiller and the brain-eater task force, the guards had brusquely turned away all would-be visitors to the plant. This car, however, looked important. It was a hired limousine with a chauffeur in full livery. Considering the difficulty of getting any kind of transportation during the emergency, this would have to be a VIP. Behind the tinted glass, three men could be seen in the wide back seat. They wore dark, heavy suits and expressions to match.

The senior security man leaned down and touched his cap as the chauffeur made the side window whisper out of sight. The smallest of the three men in the back seat leaned forward.

"I am Viktor Raslov of the Soviet agricultural delegation. I wish to speak with whoever is in command here."

"I'm Lieutenant Purdue. How may I help you?"

"I don't mean in command of the guards," Raslov said testily. "I want the man who is in charge of the operation."

"That would be Dr. Frederich Kitzmiller," said the lieutenant. "Is he expecting you?"

"He is not. Open the gate, please."

"I'll have to check with Dr. Kitzmiller first."

Raslov worked his facial muscles. "Then do so," he said.

Lieutenant Purdue walked to the guard shack and dialed the extension of Lou Zachry's phone. Standing orders stated that no calls except class A emergencies were to be routed directly to the laboratories.

"Raslov, you say?" Zachry repeated into the phone. With an effort, he shifted his thoughts away from another urgent problem to concentrate on what the lieutenant out at the gate was saying.

"Yes, sir. There are two men with him besides the chauffeur. KGB, from the look of them."

That would be Raslov, all right, Zachry decided. Of all the things he did not need right now, the Russian was high on the list.

He said, "Stall him. I'll talk to Dr. K about letting him in, but it's doubtful."

"Yes, sir."

Zachry hung up the telephone and pushed himself wearily up from the desk. He buttoned his collar and pulled the knot of his necktie up, then headed for the laboratories.

"Absolutely not!" Kitzmiller stormed. "I have no time for some sneaking, spying, double-talking pig of a Russian now. For every minute that goes by, people are dying. Now a member of my staff is infected."

"If you would just talk to him—"

"No! I have no time for Raslov and no time for you! Now please leave me to my work."

Zachry started to make a last protest. "Doctor—"

"*Out!*"

Zachry glanced quickly around at the other doctors in the laboratory. Their attitude was one of intense, urgent effort, as well it might be. He wondered which of the team was infected by the brain eaters and how big a threat that presented to the rest of them. A look at Kitzmiller's face persuaded him against asking. He nodded and went out.

At the door to the laboratory he met Corey Macklin coming in. The reporter's face was set in grim lines. There was none of the usual mocking humor in his eyes.

"Corey," he began, "we've got a situation out in front that—"

Corey cut him off. "Not now, Lou."

Zachry turned and stared at the younger man. "Something wrong?"

"Plenty." Corey pushed past him and made for the still-glowering Dr. Kitzmiller.

Zachry watched him for a moment, then suddenly knew which of Kitzmiller's staff had been stricken. He shook his head and walked away.

Dr. Kitzmiller looked at Corey with the air of a weary lion on the point of attacking his keepers.

"Can I not have five uninterrupted minutes in which to do the work I am here for? What is it, Mr. Macklin?"

"Dena—Dr. Falkner—was going to take the blood test."

"Yes. The test was administered by Dr. Pena this morning."

"Do you have the results?"

"I do."

Corey waited for several seconds, then burst out, "Well?"

Kitzmiller sighed. "The results are positive. The parasites are in Dr. Falkner's bloodstream."

"Ooohh, shit."

"We are trying a new approach to the problem today," Kitzmiller said in a more gentle tone.

"What's the prognosis?"

"We may as well be optimistic, since the alternative is despair."

"Yeah. Sure."

246

"Now, if you will excuse me, the sooner I can get back to my work, the better chance we will have of finding the cure in time."

"Yeah," Corey said again. "Thanks."

He caught Dena's eye from a counter where she was working and gave her a grin. She toasted him with an Erlenmeyer flask of murky liquid and returned to her notebook. Corey walked out silently.

The three Russians were standing outside their car, sweating in their woolen suits, when Lou Zachry approached. Viktor Raslov, slight and balding, with steel-rimmed spectacles, stood in the middle. The two KGB men flanked him like twin turrets. Raslov's face was reddened with anger. Zachry put on a conciliatory smile.

"Mr. Raslov, it's a pleasure to—"

"Never mind that," the Russian snapped. "Am I allowed to enter, or am I not?"

"The fact is that Dr. Kitzmiller will admit no one. He can make no exceptions. You understand it is for the protection of both those inside and out here."

"I understand that this is a grave insult to my country."

Lou Zachry's expression hardened. "I think, Mr. Raslov, that diplomatic insults are low priority these days, to Dr. Kitzmiller and to everyone else. Perhaps if you told me your business—"

"What is your position here?"

"I represent the United States government."

Raslov considered for a moment, then said, "I have reason to believe that a countryman of mine may have come here and may be inside. His name is Anton Kuryakin."

"Why would he come here?"

"That is not of immediate importance. Is he here?"

"He is not."

"Am I to accept your word for that?"

"I'm afraid you don't have a choice."

"If he does come here, can I depend on you to see that I am informed?"

"I can't promise that."

Raslov gave him a long, icy stare. "And you will not allow us inside?"

"I don't have that authority," Zachry said.

"Then I must take steps to protect the welfare of my countryman. Furthermore, your government may expect this matter to be protested in the strongest possible terms."

Zachry nodded gravely and watched the Russians get back into their hired car. They drove a little way down the highway and stopped.

Go ahead and park there, he thought. Park there till Moscow votes Republican, for all I care. He nodded briskly to the guard and walked back inside. He turned to watch the security man relock the gate behind him.

Anton Kuryakin bounced on the stiff springs of the pickup truck as he drove along, gripping the wheel. The big, cushiony sedan had succumbed outside Hortonville to concealed damage to the radiator sustained in the collision with the light standard in Milwaukee.

Kuryakin had abandoned the sedan and walked a mile to the nearest farmhouse. When no one answered his knock there, he opened the door, to find a family of four sprawled in various grotesque attitudes. They had been dead at least two days. He shooed away the fat buzzing flies long enough to remove from the man's overall pocket the keys to the truck parked in front of the house. The pickup was a nononsense, serviceable machine, closer to the Russian automobiles than the spongy sedan he had driven from Milwaukee.

The clouds had lowered in the sky and darkened to a dull slate gray. The heat pressed down like a giant hand. Kuryakin rolled down the windows on both sides of the cab and removed his heavy suit coat. He rolled up the sleeves of his shirt.

On the seat next to him was a yellow-billed cap of the kind that adjusts to all head sizes. On the front of the cap was the name John Deere, which Kuryakin recalled was an American manufacturer of farm machinery. He tried the cap on and regarded himself in the rearview mirror. It looked rather well, he thought. He left it on.

He drove on along the highway he had carefully plotted on the map and slowed the pickup when he felt he must be nearing Biotron. He searched for familiar landmarks, but along that stretch of highway everything was the same— neatly kept farmhouses, with their cluster of outbuildings, separated by patches of dense forests.

Then, suddenly, there was a tall chain link fence on his right with posted warnings for trespassers. The truck passed a clump of maple trees, and Kuryakin saw up ahead the guard shack and gate of the Biotron plant.

Kuryakin's elation died abruptly when he saw the limousine parked outside the gate. A small knot of men stood beside the machine, talking. There was no mistaking the dark, poorly cut suits of Viktor Raslov and the KGB men. Kuryakin kept his eyes on the road, his hands on the wheel, and drove on past the gate, being careful to maintain the same moderate speed. He gave silent thanks for the yellow cap and the rolled-up sleeves. A pickup truck such as he was driving was a common sight on Wisconsin roads, but even had someone taken the trouble to look at the driver, he would pass for an American farmer.

The trouble was that now he would have to wait. And like Frederich Kitzmiller, Anton Kuryakin was keenly aware that for every minute that slipped by, more people would die.

# Chapter 29

The pain came and went in waves for Eddie Gault as he trundled the old van along the road toward Biotron. He had to keep slowing down as the fierce headache hammered at him and dimmed his vision. He kept up a constant muttered monologue in an attempt to focus his mind away from the pain.

No matter what image he tried to conjure up, Eddie's thoughts kept returning to Roanne Tesla. From the beginning he had questioned why anyone so beautiful and so much smarter than he would love him. It was a doubt he had kept tucked back out of sight while he enjoyed her attentions, but it never quite died. Now, in the moments when he was lucid, Eddie grew convinced he had been used. The thought made him angry, and the anger helped him stand the pain.

All of Roanne's talk about the purity of the natural environment and the greed of the big companies had been easy enough for him to accept. Eddie had not possessed any strong opinions of his own, and he was happy to adopt Roanne's in exchange for the sensual pleasures she delivered. Now he wished he had spent more time asking her about her motives and less time with his cock in her mouth.

As he neared the Biotron gate, Eddie ground his teeth in an effort to maintain control against the devils that wanted to come screaming out of him. He had things to tell Dr. Kitzmiller, and he had to hold on that long.

He saw the black limousine parked on the other side of the road, but he could not be bothered thinking about it. Faces were visible behind the smoked glass, but they were no more than white blobs to Eddie. He passed the limousine and turned in at the gate.

Two men in civilian clothes came out from the guard shack to meet him. Others in uniform watched warily.

"Eddie Gault?" one of the men said. He was taller than his companion and wore a neat moustache. Both men were about thirty and looked to be in good physical shape.

Eddie nodded, relieved that he would not have to make the effort of identifying himself. Dimly, he wondered how they came to be expecting him, but the thought did not take hold.

"Come with us, please," the man said in a voice of quiet authority.

He got out of the van, grunting with pain from the small jolt when his feet hit the asphalt.

"Over here, please." The second man, the clean-shaven one, took Eddie's arm and led him to a beige Plymouth that was parked next to the guard shack.

"Dr. Kitzmiller," Eddie got out with an effort. "I got to see Dr. Kitzmiller."

"We're going to take you to him," said the first man. "Get in the car, please."

Eddie got into the back seat of the Plymouth with the clean-shaven man. The one with the moustache got behind the wheel. They drove away, keeping the windows rolled up despite the fact that the car had no air conditioning. Eddie was sweating heavily before they had gone a quarter of a mile.

"Where . . . where we going?" Eddie said with difficulty. Each word he got out felt as if it pulled a little bit of his brain with it.

"We're taking you to see Dr. Kitzmiller," the driver said, not looking at him.

"He's . . . back at the plant," Eddie managed. "I saw him on TV."

The driver glanced back at the man sitting next to Eddie, who said, "He had to leave the plant for a little while. We're taking you to him."

The Plymouth turned off onto a dirt road that twisted off into one of the dense patches of forest. The sway of the car made Eddie's head hurt like an open nerve.

"Stop," he said. "I don't want to go in here."

"It's just a little farther," said the man sitting next to him.

"No. You're lying."

The man in the seat next to Eddie tensed. He leaned forward and whispered something to the driver.

"Lemme out," Eddie said. "No Kitzmiller here. My head hurts."

The Plymouth pulled to a stop where there was a small clearing on one side of the road.

"This is it," the driver said.

"Here we are, Eddie," said the man with him in the back seat. "You want to get out?"

Eddie wiped his eyes, trying to clear his pain-streaked vision. Outside was nothing but the dirt road, the small clearing, and the thick growth of trees—white ash, birch, and bigtooth aspen. No buildings, no trail, no people.

"There's nothing here," Eddie protested.

The man with the moustache had already got out of the car. He pulled open the door on Eddie's side.

"Get out, please."

Even in his pain and his doubt the lifetime habit of following orders made Eddie lever himself out of the car. His head was about to burst. Something was crawling under the skin of his face.

"Walk over there, please." The man with the moustache pointed toward the far edge of the clearing, where the encroaching trees formed a thick barrier.

"Why?"

The two men stood side by side, facing him grimly.

"Walk," said one of them. Eddie could not be sure which one spoke.

Eddie turned, shuffling his feet on the leaf-covered ground. He took a lumbering step toward the trees. Another. Then he stopped.

"Keep walking."

Eddie's body stiffened. The inside of his head churned and bubbled like molten lead. His face felt like one of those balloons with eyes, nose, and mouth painted on it. He turned back toward the men.

"Oh, shit, look at his face!" one of them said.

Then they had guns in their hands.

Eddie heard a voice howling in his ear and only dimly recognized it as his own. He charged at the two men. His movements were no longer clumsy and slow. The pain had become so terrible that he had somehow transcended it. His sensory system had taken all it could stand; then it blew out like an overloaded circuit.

The boom of the guns blended with a distant roll of thunder. The impact of the bullets was no more than a small tug at his flesh. Eddie's hands reached out and seized the nearest of the two men—the one who had sat beside him in the car. He found the man's throat and closed his fingers like metal claws around the bobbing Adam's apple and the windpipe. The man's scream was lost in a sudden rustle of wind through the leaves as Eddie ripped out his trachea.

The man with the moustache fired his pistol wildly. His mouth gaped; his eyes bulged in terror.

Eddie stepped over the body of the man with no throat. He could feel the freshly risen boils on his face begin to burst. He reached for the man with the gun and caught his arm. He yanked on it, and the gun thumped to the ground. Eddie heard the man's shoulder separate with a crackling sound.

The injured man cried out and pulled free. The pistol lay forgotten among the dead leaves. With one arm flopping uselessly, he dragged himself into the car. Eddie started after him. The engine ground to life, and the driver frantically wheeled around and headed back toward the highway, scraping the side of the Plymouth on a tree as he fought for control with his one working arm.

Eddie took a couple of steps after the fleeing car and stopped. The pain came in short terrible bursts. He felt the warm fluids oozing down his face where the pustules had broken. His mind veered along the edges of insanity. He was dying, and he knew it.

But before he surrendered to death, there was something he had to do. Someone he had to see. There was a debt to be paid, and Eddie Gault willed himself to stay alive long enough to pay it.

Thunder rumbled again, and Eddie started back along the dirt road.

The gloom of the lowering skies outside his window suited the mood of Lou Zachry. He sat slouched in the chair behind his desk in the Biotron plant, wondering if somewhere along the line he could have made a different decision and everything would have turned out right.

Fantasizing, he told himself. Wishful thinking. Not Lou Zachry's style. He had just slipped away from the afternoon media briefing being handled by Corey Macklin. It had been a string of tired clichés that Corey hadn't even tried to disguise as real news. The reporters were grumbling, and with justification. They had kept their bargain not to harass Dr. Kitzmiller and the task force. In return, they were supposed to be kept informed at the twice-daily briefings.

Zachry knew Corey had excuses for his spiritless delivery that day. Anybody with eyes could see what was happening between him and Dena Falkner. If Dena was now infested with the brain eaters, it was not so strange that Corey's enthusiasm for his job would flag.

But damn it, almost everybody had lost somebody. You had to do your job even when you were hurting. That had

254

been Lou Zachry's code as long as he could remember, and he expected the people around him to live up to it.

Then there were the damn Russians sitting across the road in their air-conditioned limo, eyeballing the gate. Couldn't those people read English? Didn't they watch television? If they knew what was happening, how could it matter a damn if one of their people defected or got married or turned queer or whatever they were afraid he was doing?

And there was Kitzmiller. He was no help with his rigid old-time anti-Russian stance when a couple of words from him might send Raslov and his goons on their way. Sure, he had his reasons, but they dated back to another war in another time. Everybody had reasons.

Underneath these major worries, like a fragment of half-remembered music that won't go away, was the phone call from the woman. She had gotten his number from the newspaper and was calling to warn that Eddie Gault was a victim of the brain eaters and was on his way to Biotron for some crazy purpose. She had refused to give her name, but some vaguely familiar note in the young voice troubled him.

Zachry was well aware of the potential danger if Eddie Gault talked. It was possible, of course, that the brain eaters would make the whole question academic, but Zachry could not wait for Armageddon. Eddie Gault had to die.

He was, in fact, a dead man the moment the brain eaters had entered his bloodstream. Zachry had talked to the task-force doctors enough to know what the little parasites could do to the human brain. He figured he'd been doing the man a favor by sending Quick and Vollney to help Eddie Gault out of this world.

The thought made Zachry wonder where the hell Quick and Vollney were. How long did it take to shoot a man?

Zachry reached for the telephone. He snatched his hand back reflexively as the thing rang just as he was about to touch it. Then he picked it up and cleared his throat.

"Zachry."

"Lieutenant Purdue at the gate, sir. Agent Vollney is out here."

"Vollney? What about Quick?"

"He's alone, sir, and he's . . . hurt."

"For Christ' sake, send him in."

Zachry slammed down the receiver and ran out the door, heading for the front entrance to the plant. As he burst out the door, he saw Agent Donald Vollney making his way across the asphalt of the parking area. His left arm hung limp at his side. He clutched the shoulder with his right hand.

Zachry met him at the edge of the walkway before the building and helped him up the low curb.

"I'm sorry, sir," Vollney said in a strained voice.

"What happened?"

"He went crazy. Killed Seth."

"Eddie Gault killed a trained agent?"

"Yes, sir. He was like nothing human."

Vollney's legs sagged, and his eyes started to roll up. Zachry grasped him around the waist and supported him into the building and into his office. Inside, the agent recovered and refused a chair.

"Tell me about it," Zachry said.

Vollney made an effort to get control of himself and in a voice purged of emotion related the events of the afternoon to Zachry. "Everything was going according to schedule. We intercepted the subject at the gate, transferred him to our car, and transported him to the location selected in advance for termination."

"What condition was Gault in when you took him?" Zachry asked.

"He was obviously suffering some distress, but he was coherent and ambulatory."

"All right, go on."

"When we reached the designated location, we exited the car, and I instructed the subject to walk toward a growth of

256

trees. He started to comply, then turned back. He began to . . . howl.''

"Howl?" Zachry repeated.

"Yes, sir. More like an animal than a man."

Here Agent Vollney's emotions welled up, and he dropped the awkward locutions of report language. "His face . . . the guy's face . . . I've never seen anything like it. It looked like he'd walked into a hornet's nest. There were bumps all over the skin, and right while we were watching, they broke open." Vollney had to pause and swallow something that had come up in his throat. "They made little popping sounds and squirted gunk out of them. Jesus, it was ugly."

Zachry gave the agent a minute to collect himself, then said, "What happened to Seth Quick?"

Vollney retreated back into the formalized, emotion-free jargon. "The subject became violent and charged Agent Quick and me. We both discharged our weapons. I observed several bullets strike the subject, but they seemed to have no effect. The subject seized Agent Quick by the throat and he—he killed him. When I tried to render assistance, the subject grasped my arm, knocking my weapon to the ground. I sustained an injury to my shoulder. I managed to reach the vehicle and returned here."

"Gault escaped," Zachry said, trying to keep his voice steady.

"Yes, sir. We—we just messed it up."

"Nothing to do about it now," Zachry said. "Go on back to the lab and get somebody to look at that arm."

"Yes, sir." Vollney lingered for a moment as though there were more he wanted to say but changed his mind and went out.

"Damn, damn, damn!" Zachry said to the empty office. Now he had a vengeful brain-eater victim thrashing through the woods out there. Fortunately, there was little chance he would get past the gate guards even if he did make it this far.

Where would he go? To the woman, of course! Circuits

closed in the brain of Lou Zachry with an almost audible click. The woman, Roanne Tesla, had to be the anonymous caller. In the old days he would have punched up her name on the computer for a full report of the investigation they had done on her when Eddie had first come under suspicion. Now he had to pull out bits from his memory. *Roanne Tesla: No Nukes; Greenpeace; Save the Whales.* Your basic eco freak with leanings toward free-this and stop-that trendy radical causes.

Zachry thumped himself on the forehead. She was the one! Whether out of madness or twisted idealism or plain old villainy, this woman was behind the brain eaters. He was suddenly as thoroughly sure of her guilt as he was of his own name.

Zachry fairly leaped for the file cabinet and snatched out the folder labeled *Edward Gault.* He flapped it open on his desk, memorized the location of the house where Eddie lived with his girlfriend, and sprinted through the door.

As he dashed out of the building, a wisp of cool breeze ruffled his crew cut. Lightning forked to earth on the horizon, followed by the grumble of thunder. Lou Zachry shivered and ran toward his car.

# Chapter 30

All the lights blazed in the Biotron laboratory complex. The small employees' lounge adjacent to the labs was bright with an ersatz high-tech cheeriness. It made the gray-black sky outside look even darker.

Corey Macklin sat at a formica table in the lounge with Dena Falkner. On the table before them were two Styrofoam coffee cups, which they toyed with while their attention was elsewhere. A cigarette smoldered, forgotten, in an ashtray at Dena's side. Their free hands rested on the table, touching.

"You look tired," Corey said.

"It's been a long day," Dena answered with a weary smile. "Going to be a long night, too. Dr. K doesn't sleep, so he thinks the troops shouldn't sleep."

"You guys ought to have a union."

"I'll bring it up at our next meeting."

They exchanged smiles that were clearly forced. The conversation sagged. Corey looked around for inspiration. Through the window he saw the dark trees at the forest line toss their branches and lean forward as though they wanted to advance on the buildings that had taken their space.

"Storm coming," he said.

"Feels like it." Dena took her hand away to rub the gooseflesh on her other arm. She conspicuously avoided the patch of bandage on her elbow.

A look of pain flashed across Corey's face.

"Hey, I feel okay," she said. "No worse than a bad cold. Anyway, at the worst I've got what—a week?"

"You're the doctor," he said in a husky voice.

"Yes. Well." She glanced at the efficient wristwatch she wore and checked it with the big wall clock. "I'd better get back."

"Sure."

They stood up at the same time, leaving their cups sitting on the table with the cooling coffee untasted.

"I'll check with you later," Corey said.

"Good."

Dena turned and took a couple of steps away from him, then stopped. She turned back. The uneasy smile she had kept in place through the coffee break was gone. Her eyes held a hint of desperation. She and Corey took a quick step toward each other, and she was in his arms, her face pressed against his chest.

"I'm scared, Corey," she said, her voice small and muffled against his sweater.

He held her tightly, one hand patting her shoulder. "Hey, why wouldn't you be? I'm scared, too."

"I don't want to die," she said. "Not like this."

Corey's throat closed on him, and he could not speak for several seconds.

"It doesn't have to happen," he got out finally. "Like you said, if you had to get the damn things, you couldn't be in a better place."

Dena took one very deep breath, then stepped back away from him. Her smile was in place again, her eyes a little feverish but steady. "That sounds like a good-news, bad-news joke. Maybe later we can send it to *Reader's Digest*.

"Right," he said. "Later."

She turned again and walked from the lounge through the swinging door into the laboratory. Her step was firm, and this time she did not turn back.

Corey looked down and saw that his fists were so tightly clenched the knuckles were white. He forced himself to relax and to give Dena time to reach her work station; then he followed her into the lab.

Dr. Kitzmiller was a touch less hostile when Corey approached him than he had been earlier in the day. For the forbidding biochemist, this was a huge concession to personal warmth. He even left the table where he was reading over notes made by the other members of the task force and took Corey back into his small, chilly office.

"Any news?" Corey asked, making an effort to keep it impersonal.

"I thought your briefing of the media was finished for today."

"I'm asking for myself," Corey said.

"We are making progress, of a sort."

Corey leaned forward.

"There has been no breakthrough," Kitzmiller continued quickly. "We are approaching the problem from two direc-

260

tions. We must find a means of protection for those not yet afflicted and a cure for those whose blood already carries the parasites but who are not yet too ill to be helped."

"How ill is too ill?" Corey asked.

"Dr. Everett, the brain specialist, feels that once the parasites have been carried by the bloodstream into the brain tissue and have begun their damage there, it is too late."

"And it takes about a week from the time they enter the body for them to get to the brain?"

"That is no longer a valid assumption. Our reports show that as the cases have spread, the length of time for the parasites to reach the brain has decreased."

"How long?" Corey's mouth had dried up.

"Three, perhaps four, days."

"Jesus. But you say there is some progress toward finding a cure?"

"I said we were making progress of a sort. The preventive approach must take precedence to preserve the health of those who are not yet infested."

"That's not fair to the people who have the brain eaters in their blood. They could still be saved."

"Life, Mr. Macklin, is not fair. Now you must excuse me."

Corey sat alone for several minutes in the cold office, then pulled himself out of the chair and went in search of Lou Zachry. He badly needed somebody to talk to.

Zachry's office was empty. Corey walked to the entrance and looked out into the parking area. Zachry's car was gone. Lightning sparked down through the slate-colored sky, and thunder crashed like cymbals.

Corey sat down heavily on an ornamental concrete bench in front of the Biotron entrance. The wind made him shiver, but he paid it no attention. He stared unseeing out toward the gate, his mood darker than the skies. A first, fat drop of rain hit the bench beside him.

Anton Kuryakin sat in the pickup truck in a farmer's roadway where he had pulled off after his second pass by the gate to Biotron. Raslov and the KGB men were still there, parked across the road, waiting for him. Kuryakin knew they would park there indefinitely, watching the road, waiting to take him. Time was on their side.

Kuryakin made a decision. There could be no more delay. He shifted the pickup into reverse and backed out onto the highway, taking a small pleasure in his growing skill in operating the American vehicles. He pointed the machine back toward Biotron and hit the gas.

When he came to the end of the chain link fence, he began to pick up speed. There could be no stopping for explanations to the guards at the gate. Raslov and the others would be there too quickly, and one way or another they would surely prevent him from entering.

When he could see the gate and guard shack ahead on his right, Kuryakin pushed the accelerator pedal to the floor. He swung the truck to the far side of the road to allow himself a better angle for approaching the gate. There was no need for him to worry about oncoming cars; traffic along that road had dwindled to nothing.

Rain began to smack the windshield in fat, heavy drops. Kuryakin had no time to search for the wiper control; he needed all his concentration for the driving.

From the corner of his eye he saw movement behind the smoked glass of the parked limousine as the pickup roared past the spot where it was parked. Up ahead, the door of the guard shack opened, and a uniformed man stood looking out as Kuryakin yanked the wheel and swerved into a tire-screaming turn off the road and toward the gate.

He hit the heavy steel mesh of the gate with a jarring crash that threw him forward against the steering wheel. The breath was blasted from his lungs as the gate sagged inward and the truck came to a stop.

Kuryakin's chest heaved as he struggled to pull in air. I've failed, he thought as the men surged out of the guard shack. In the rearview mirror he could see the limousine across the road start to move toward him.

He kept his foot on the accelerator. The rear wheels spun;

the heavy air was acrid with burning rubber. The face of one of the guards appeared at the window. He was shouting something Kuryakin could not hear.

Simultaneously, with a blinding flash of lightning overhead, the gate gave way with a metallic *crack*. The spinning tires of the pickup bit suddenly into the wet asphalt, and the truck went skidding across the parking area, turning one complete revolution before Kuryakin could bring it to a stop.

Corey Macklin was the first to reach him as he climbed unsteadily down from the cab.

"I am Anton Kuryakin," he gasped. "I must speak to Dr. Kitzmiller."

Three men from the security force, weapons at the ready, ran through the rain toward the truck. The others were blocking the path of the limousine, which was trying to follow Kuryakin through the shattered gate.

Corey caught the Russian as he stumbled and helped him upright as Lieutenant Purdue, followed by two of his men, pounded up.

"We'll take over now, Mr. Macklin," said the security chief.

Corey stood his ground. "This is Anton Kuryakin. He's here on official business."

"I'll see that he's placed in protective custody," said Purdue.

"Please, I must talk to Dr. Kitzmiller," said the Russian. "For the sake of your country and its people, do not detain me."

Viktor Raslov, escorted by two of the gate guards, hurried up. The KGB men were being kept in the limousine where it had stopped at the shattered gate.

"This man is a Soviet citizen," Raslov said. "He is traveling on a diplomatic passport. You cannot hold him."

"Wait a minute," Corey said. "Nobody is holding anybody here." He turned to Kuryakin. "What is your business with Dr. Kitzmiller?"

"It is confidential."

Corey looked at Lieutenant Purdue, the security guards, and Viktor Raslov. He turned back to Kuryakin. "I think you'd better give us some idea of why you're here, or you will never get inside."

"This is a grave insult," Raslov complained. "This man belongs with my party."

Lieutenant Purdue turned on Raslov. "Sir, you are both guilty of trespassing on a government reservation. You," he said to Kuryakin, "have destroyed government property and forced your way into a highly sensitive facility. I am going to have to place you both under—"

"Wait a minute," Corey broke in. "Let's hear what he has to say."

Kuryakin looked from one of the men to the next and chose finally to speak to Corey. "In your American press Dr. Kitzmiller has been called the 'Father of the Brain Eaters,' has he not?"

Corey nodded. "I suppose that in a way I'm responsible for that."

"It does not matter, you see, because it is not true," Kuryakin said. "Your Dr. Kitzmiller is not the father."

The other men stared at him. Corey said, "What do you mean?"

"He cannot be the father," Kuryakin said evenly, "because I am."

Frederich Kitzmiller's lean face was darker than the storm outside. He glared at Corey Macklin as the two men stood in his office just off the laboratory.

"Absolutely not!" Kitzmiller thundered. "I have given you more time today than I should have because I let my sympathy overcome my judgment. But this is too much. I will not waste any more of my time with some double-dealing, lying pig of a communist!"

"The man is a scientist," Corey protested.

"So was Dr. Mengele."

"Won't you at least talk to him, doctor?" Corey said. "He's right outside with Lieutenant Purdue."

"Give me one reason why I should see this Bolshevik."

"He says he has critical information about the brain eaters," Corey said. "He claims that he developed the same parasites in Russia a year ago."

"Hah! Of all the discoveries and inventions the Russians have claimed over the years, this is one I would like to give them. But it is not true. I, Frederich Kitzmiller, brought what are now called the brain eaters into existence in this very laboratory."

"I know the story," Corey said impatiently. "You were experimenting with a new pesticide—"

"Bullshit pesticide!"

It was the first time Corey had heard the icy Dr. Kitzmiller use coarse language, and he stared at him.

"There is no point in keeping up the pretense any longer, regardless of what Mr. Zachry thinks. The brain eaters were developed to be exactly what they are, for possible use as a weapon."

"A weapon?" Corey felt as though he had been slugged over the head.

"Yes, of course. With the Russians' lead in chemical- and biological-warfare preparations, we felt it critical to have a response. It was done under a specific, highly secret contract from the Department of Defense. Did you really believe that such a horrendous result could come from innocent research on a pesticide?"

"A lot of people did," Corey said.

"Well, that was the intent." Kitzmiller's voice grew calmer, but the fire stayed in the flashing blue eyes. "It became an obsession with Zachry that the public should not know of the government's part in it. It would have destroyed the power of the Pentagon, he said, and with it the current administration." His thin lips stretched in a mirthless smile. "A lot that matters now."

"Lou Zachry is with the Defense Department?"

"Yes, of course. When the 'accident' occurred, he was sent here immediately to oversee the investigation. Which one of his made-up identities did he use on you? No, don't

265

bother to tell me. There isn't time, and it does not matter, anyway."

Corey was shaking his head. "I can't believe that anything so appalling could even have been considered as a weapon."

"Ah, but you see, we did not anticipate the terrible virulence of our little parasites. How could we? When experiments on animals gave an indication of what we really had, the project was immediately canceled and the single test canister marked for disposal. Had it not been for the unspeakable carelessness of one employee, the brain eaters might have been stopped then and there."

"But Kuryakin says—"

"The devil take Kuryakin and all Russians! Let Purdue deal with him."

*"No!"*

Kitzmiller looked up, surprised at the sudden snap in Corey's tone.

"I don't give a damn about your personal feud with the Russians. This man has taken a considerable risk in coming here. It's possible that he can help. If he has nothing to offer, we've lost only a few minutes."

Kitzmiller's mouth was a grim line. "Very well, I will see him. Alone. And only long enough for him to prove to me that he is a liar."

"I'll send him in," said Corey, and hurried out the door before Kitzmiller could change his mind.

The stocky Russian and the lean German scientist faced each other in the sterile office behind the Biotron laboratory. The air crackled with hostility.

"The agricultural expert, I presume," said Kitzmiller with heavy sarcasm.

"And I salute the maker of fertilizer," Kuryakin answered, speaking German.

They acknowledged each other with careful nods.

"I have heard of your work," Kuryakin said. "Your real work."

266

"And I yours. But apparently not all of it. Or so I am told."

"We do have our secrets despite your spy satellites and CIA."

"I have no time to compare espionage systems."

"I will make my point. These brain eaters of yours were discovered by me in a Moscow facility thirteen months ago. We called it Project Romanov. A bit of socialist humor."

"Why should I believe you?"

Kuryakin gestured toward a chalkboard along one of the office walls. "May I?"

Kitzmiller nodded brusquely.

The chalk clattered over the board as the Russian scribbled a series of formulas, talking as he wrote. "It was our thought that these parasites could be used in controlled circumstances as a biological weapon. Defensive, of course, to be employed only if we were attacked."

"Of course," Kitzmiller said. One corner of his mouth quirked in an ironic smile.

"We discovered, as you have, the full horror of these creatures, and the project was abandoned."

Kitzmiller studied the chalkboard notations when the Russian stepped aside. He said, "Very well, I can see that you might have achieved the same result as we did. What is it you want, my congratulations?"

"I want you to listen to me, you stubborn sausage head!"

Kitzmiller's eyes snapped wide.

"My colleague now waiting in front of your factory would have us flying back to Moscow, leaving your capitalist country to be consumed by your damned parasites."

"Why should you feel differently from Raslov?"

"Why should I not? Our personal codes of honor are not issued by the Politburo, regardless of what you may read in the American press."

"I was exposed to your Russian code of honor in 1945."

Kuryakin leaned down and glared, his face close to Kitzmiller's. "I have no more love for Germans than you have for my people. However, I do not waste emotion on atrocities of a long-dead war. I have come to share with you the second stage of my work. If you choose not to accept it, the tragedy will be on your head.''

''Second stage?'' Kitzmiller was stunned by the Russian's sudden vehemence.

''After I had brought the brain eaters to life, I did not stop my experiments. I also discovered how to kill them.''

# Chapter 31

The wind-driven rain slashed against the windshield, leaving greasy streaks where the wipers failed to clear it away. Lou Zachry sat hunched forward in the driver's seat, gripping the steering wheel, peering into the storm.

He almost drove past the weed-grown dirt road that angled off into the trees. The hand-lettered sign *Park Place* was obscured by blowing brush, and Zachry saw it only as he came abreast. He hit the brakes and skidded several yards beyond the road before he could get the car under control.

He drove carefully, avoiding the tree roots that reached up like crooked fingers from the road. Overhead, the trees thrashed in the wind.

As he rounded a sharp bend, he came suddenly upon the house. It was almost too cute, with its overhanging roof, rounded edges, gaily painted shutters, and lacy curtains. A warm light shone from inside. Pale smoke curled out into the wet night from a stone fireplace chimney. Zachry was reminded of the gingerbread house from Hansel and Gretel.

He brought the car to a stop on a muddy patch of grass in front of the house. From the glove compartment he took a short-barreled .38 Chiefs Special. He left the car and walked cautiously across the mud toward the front door with its little shingled portico.

In his haste Zachry had not bothered with a coat. His shoes squished with every sodden step. The oxford cloth shirt was soaked through and plastered to his skin. The short blond hair was flattened wet against his skull.

When he reached the front door, he pressed his ear to the panel, listening. The rising wind and slash of the rain outside damped any sounds that might come from within. He released the latch and pushed the door open.

Inside he crouched for a moment, tense, pistol ready. When nothing moved, he gradually relaxed.

The living room had a warm, cozy look. The furniture was mismatched, but somehow it all went together. Everything was comfortably cushioned and done in soothing earth tones. Birch logs crackled in the fireplace. A cold portable television set in the corner looked out of place in the homespun room.

Placing his feet cautiously and soundlessly, Zachry passed the kitchen, which was empty and smelled of herbs, and moved on to an open door to the lighted bedroom. From beyond it he could hear rustling sounds and a soft, feminine humming. He stepped into the doorway, gun in hand, and for a moment he just stood there watching.

The girl had milky blonde hair and a supple figure that was not concealed by the bulky sweater and faded jeans. She moved with unconscious grace as she transferred clothing from the drawers of the room's single bureau to the double bed. Open on the bed was a hiker's backpack that looked as though it had been well used.

Although Zachry made no sound, some instinct of the girl's made her straighten up and turn toward him. She gasped when she saw him standing there with the gun. Her face was clear and beautifully boned. Her eyes were a shade of blue that could not be bought.

"Roanne Tesla?" he said, embarrassed at the hoarseness in his voice. He had not expected her to be so beautiful. But

269

there was more . . . something in the vulnerability of her that caused a tightness in his throat.

The girl recovered quickly. The pale pink lips curved into a smile that held no warmth.

"I might have known you'd find me."

Zachry made his voice hard. "You'd better come with me. Eddie Gault is loose, and I expect he'll be looking for you."

"You people didn't kill him?"

The casual way she tossed off the question chilled the government man. He said, "No, we didn't. Now let's go."

"Am I under arrest or something?"

"Not officially, but if you don't come willingly, I'll take you." He stopped and looked closely at the girl. "Do I know you?"

The blue eyes narrowed. "No, but I know you. Your type. Mr. Macho. John Wayne. Win the war, salute the flag, take care of the rich, and to hell with the people. Build bigger weapons; kill more babies."

He knew now who the girl reminded him of. Jenny, the daughter he'd lost. The words that came from Roanne's soft pink mouth were the same Jenny had used to damn him the last time he'd tried to see her. They hurt him almost as much now.

For a moment, as the pain showed in his eyes, Roanne's expression softened. She almost moved toward him, then caught herself.

"Let's go." Zachry bit the words off. "Eddie got away from us not far from here. He killed one man and badly injured another. He was not in a good mood."

"No, I suppose he wasn't."

Roanne continued to fold the clothes on the bed and fit them efficiently into the backpack.

"Damn it, there isn't time for that."

"I'll be ready in a minute." She frowned at the gun, which was still in his hand. "Why don't you put that somewhere?"

"I might need it."

"What for, to make you feel like a real man?"

His face burned. He felt foolishly ashamed to show any weakness in front of the girl.

"Please," she said in a gentler tone. "Guns make me very nervous."

He laid the pistol on a low bookcase, keeping it within easy reach.

"All right?"

Roanne gave him a smile that seemed almost real. Zachry fought off memories of the laughing little girl named Jenny.

She packed the last of her things. Jeans, T-shirts, rough-woven sweaters, sneakers, a worn old panda bear. She shrugged into a red quilted jacket, hefted the backpack, and looked up at him.

"Okay, I'm—"

Her eyes widened suddenly.

A strong gust of wind rattled the windows. Zachry sensed a movement behind him an instant too late.

It felt like a baseball bat slammed across his shoulder blades. The breath was driven from his lungs, and Zachry stumbled all the way across the room and into the wall next to the window. There he slid to the floor, numb. For the next few moments Zachry saw the scene in the bedroom as though it were happening underwater.

The figure in the door was recognizably human and probably male, but beyond that nothing was certain. The face was a mass of oozing sores. The clothes were soaked from the rain and torn in a hundred places. Irregular dark splotches on the chest and upper abdomen looked like gunshot wounds.

Roanne recovered her composure quickly. She faced the monstrous figure in the doorway without flinching.

"Hello, Eddie."

A half growl, half moan spilled out of the ravaged mouth.

"Nobody's going to hurt you, Eddie. Not anymore."

The bloody thing raised a hand toward her.

Roanne extended her own hand and walked forward.

271

Still on the floor, fighting to regain control of his limbs, Zachry found his voice. *"No!"*

The girl ignored him. She took another step toward the thing that had been Eddie Gault. Zachry could hear its ragged breathing, smell the stink of blood and body waste. He saw the pistol lying on the low bookcase. It might as well have been in Milwaukee.

"Get away from him!" he cried.

Too late. As Roanne came close to him, Eddie drew back the hand he had extended and put all his maniacal strength into a backhand blow that knocked her onto the bed and across it to the floor.

Eddie took a step toward the bed. Roanne unsteadily tried to rise, holding her jaw where the skin had been laid open by the blow. For the first time her eyes showed real fear.

With an effort of will, Zachry got his legs under him and, gripping the windowsill, pulled himself upright. Eddie swiveled the ghastly head so that he was looking at him. He stood maddeningly between Zachry and the gun.

With a gurgling sound in his throat, Eddie returned his attention to Roanne, who was standing against the wall, her hands up in a useless pantomime of defense.

Lou Zachry pushed off from the windowsill and lumbered toward the bloody figure advancing on Roanne. He lowered his shoulder and hit Eddie in the chest with a sodden smack. The force of his rush backed Eddie up but did not knock him off-balance.

Zachry stayed close to him. He turned his head to shout back at the girl, "Get out!" When she did not move, he shouted roughly, "Go, damn it! Move!"

Without warning, Eddie's arms wrapped around Zachry and locked onto his body like steel clamps.

"Get out, Jenny!" The words were squeezed out of him as Eddie applied pressure.

Roanne snatched up the backpack and stepped past the struggling men to the doorway. There she lingered just for a moment and looked into the pain-filled eyes of Lou Zachry. Then she was gone.

Zachry concentrated all his strength on trying to break the punishing bear hug Eddie held him in. He could see the gun, tantalizingly close, yet not quite within reach. Eddie's rank breath stung his nostrils. The leaking sores dripped down the front of both men.

He could not get air into his constricted lungs. His visior clouded. Zachry fancied he could feel the microscopic eggs of the brain eaters filtering in through his pores, entering his bloodstream and hatching like malignant tadpoles, then swimming, swimming to his brain, there to chew away his sanity and his life.

A rib snapped. The white-hot pain momentarily restored Zachry's consciousness. Struggling was useless. The crazy strength of the ruined man holding him was more than any normal being could overcome.

Zachry rolled his eyes back up into his head so the whites showed. He forced his straining muscles to relax and went limp in the terrible embrace. Darkness closed in as real oblivion threatened to overtake the sham.

Another rib broke with a muffled *crack*. And a third. Zachry had no breath left to cry out with. Red flashes pinwheeled through the thickening black before his eyes. Would this crazy bastard never let go?

Something soft burst inside of Lou Zachry. He felt it go with a sickening sense of doom. His abdominal cavity began to fill.

Abruptly, Eddie Gault released his hold. Zachry folded to the floor like a half-filled bag of laundry. After ten seconds that seemed an eternity, he managed to pull in a tiny breath. The broken ribs stabbed him like flaming arrows. The soft thing that had burst inside him was loose.

Eddie turned slowly one way, then the other. His leaking eyes searched the room.

Zachry bit into and through his lower lip to keep from screaming as he dragged himself six inches at a time across the bare floor toward the bookcase. Six inches. Six more. Six more. Now he almost had it.

Eddie saw him.

273

With mucus and blood dribbling from his mouth, Eddie stumbled toward the fallen man. Zachry made an agonized lunge for the gun. Eddie dropped to his knees and grabbed his arm just above the wrist.

While Zachry writhed in wordless agony, Eddie squeezed the arm. The radius bone snapped under the madman's grip, then the ulna. Zachry's hand flopped on his wrist like a dying fish.

With an effort that blinded him for a second, Zachry twisted his body around. While Eddie still squeezed the useless right arm, he lunged with his left hand for the gun. The tips of his fingers grazed the gnurled grip, his nails dug in, the pistol clattered to the hardwood floor.

With Eddie intent on mashing his shattered bones, Zachry scooped up the pistol with his left hand. He jammed the muzzle into the oozing face and pulled the trigger. The explosion was muffled by the bloated flesh. Zachry continued to pull the trigger until all five bullets carried by the Chief's Special had blasted into the sick man's brain.

Incredibly, it took several more seconds for Eddie's grip to loosen. Finally, he let go and toppled sideways, slowly, as though lying down for sleep. And at last he was still.

Lou Zachry sat panting in shallow breaths, each one bringing a crunch from his shattered ribs. He tossed the empty gun at Eddie. It thumped to the floor and lay there, dead as the man. Zachry folded his one working arm across his stomach, trying to hold himself together. He felt his insides coming up, and there was nothing he could do about it. The bloody vomit spewed out of him, and he fell forward into blackness alongside Eddie Gault.

# Chapter 32

The sunlight flowed in through the window of Dena Falkner's room in the Appleton Physicians Hospital. She stretched luxuriously, then suddenly sat up in bed and blinked at Corey Macklin, who sat in a chair by the bed eating an apple.

"About time you woke up," he said.

"How long have I been asleep?"

Corey looked at his watch. "Three days. Ever since they gave you the brain-eater antidote."

"Of course, the antidote. Then it . . . worked?"

"You don't have a headache, do you?"

"No. God, I never want to *hear* headache again."

"While you were out, they took a sample of your blood. Pure as a mountain spring. The only reason you're in bed is because you worked yourself into exhaustion at Biotron."

"We almost had it, you know. The antidote. The formula turned out to be ridiculously simple. In a few more days . . ." She smiled ruefully. "But then that would have been too late for some of us, wouldn't it."

"It's great stuff," Corey said. "Cures anybody who's got the things in his bloodstream and gives everybody permanent immunity. It works orally, the way you took it, and it's effective sprayed from the air. That's how they immunized Russia when the government dumped the project over there."

"Sprayed," Dena repeated.

"Uh-huh. Helicopters have been up for two days over all

populated areas. They'll keep it up until there isn't a square foot of the country where the brain eaters can live. Kind of ironic, considering that's the way they got loose in the first place.''

Dena reached out, and Corey took her hand. In a near whisper she said, ''How many people . . . ?'' and could not finish.

''A lot,'' Corey said. ''The estimate is four million. It was bad, but in just a few more days it could have been so much worse.''

''What about the rest of the world?''

''Believe it or not, the U.S. and Russia are working together to make the antidote available to everybody.''

''Wouldn't it be strange if the brain eaters were responsible for finally bringing world peace.''

''It would,'' Corey agreed, ''but I'll lay odds we find something else to fight about soon.''

''Still the same old cynic,'' Dena said.

He squeezed her hand. ''Not quite the same one. I have, as they say, reordered my priorities.''

''That so? Am I included in any of them?''

''All of them.''

A nurse, rosy-cheeked and plump, peeked into the room. ''You're awake,'' she observed. ''I have a couple more visitors for you.''

Through the door came Frederich Kitzmiller and Anton Kuryakin. Kitzmiller's expression was set in its usual stern lines. Kuryakin's eyes betrayed a twinkle.

''So you are feeling all right,'' said Kitzmiller.

''Good as new.''

''And why would it be otherwise?'' said Kuryakin. ''The antidote is a hundred percent effective when the brain tissue has not been damaged.''

''Go ahead and take your bows,'' Kitzmiller said. ''My people almost had it.''

Kuryakin rolled his eyes. ''As we say in Russia, 'Almost butters no potatoes.' ''

Kitzmiller looked pained, but he could not quite keep the

trace of a smile from showing. "I suggested that our friend stay here where he could work in an atmosphere of freedom. There are many institutions that would reward him handsomely."

"Why would I stay here among strange capitalists?" Kuryakin said. "Russia is my country. She may have her faults, but I love her. I am most anxious to return."

"I suppose now that you're an international hero, it would be too embarrassing to send you to Siberia."

Kuryakin beamed. "What can one do with a hard-line cold warrior like this?" He pulled a worn pocket watch from his vest and peered at it. "Now I must say good-bye. My countrymen will be waiting for me at the airport."

"Do we have time for a farewell drink?" Kitzmiller said, not quite meeting the Russian's eye.

"I am sure we do," said Kuryakin.

"Then it's on me," said Kitzmiller. "Bourbon."

"Fine," said Kuryakin. "And on me is vodka."

Dena and Corey exchanged a smile as the two scientists walked out of the room together.

Outside, a helicopter hammered overhead. Dena looked up toward the sound.

"I know they're doing all they can," she said, "but I can't help but worry about the people who they'll miss."

"There are bound to be some," Corey said. "But not many. Every operating newspaper and all TV and radio stations are repeating the message that the copters are carrying the antidote. You'd have to be somewhere pretty remote not to know."

Roanne Tesla huddled under the shelter she had built by leaning branches against a boulder. She was safe now. The second day after she had left the house and headed into the forest, she had heard the helicopters far behind her. She could only guess what kind of poison they were spraying into the air this time. Whatever it was, it was not going to get her. She would stay there in the forest and live off the land as long as she had to.

Roanne hugged herself and shivered. Up until that day she had felt pretty good except for the cut on her face where Eddie had hit her. Now she seemed to be coming down with the flu.

# About the Author

Gary Brandner is the author of the highly-praised novels, *The Howling*, *Howling II*, *Walkers*, *Hellborn*, and *Quintana Roo*, all available from Fawcett. He was born in Saulte Ste. Marie, Michigan, educated at the University of Washington, and now lives in Huntington Beach, California.